For Barb
Your humor and creative spark helped create Spencer, Colorado
and inspired this story.

Your memory lives on in our hearts.

CALL ME MANDY

DEBRA HINES

Dear Christian,

Hope you enjoy
Mandy's story!

Debra

CALL ME MANDY

Debra Hines

Cover & interior design by Cat & Doxie Author Services

❦ Created with Vellum

The last man Miranda loved took everything from her...

The last man Miranda Buffet loved took everything from her. She throws herself into the preservation of Spencer's historic schoolhouse only to be drawn into the orbit of a handsome, infuriating architect.

On his first independent project, Declan Elliott's reputation and future hang in the balance. He's unprepared for his attraction to the spirited granddaughter of Spencer's wealthy patriarch, but when they end up in bed together, their passion is as deep and fathomless as Colorado's Twin Owl Lake.

Will Miranda risk her wounded heart to this self-made building designer? Can Declan overcome his habitual disdain for the heiress and her entitled family?

CHAPTER 1

*M*iranda Buffet shivered in her florescent hoodie and rubbed her arms. Though it was late August, mornings in the Colorado high country were chilly. She smoothed the paper number pinned just above her waist and drank in the magnificent vista of the Rocky Mountains, backlit by the rising sun.

Other runners, milling in place around her, also sported bright, body-hugging attire, their collective energy as unmistakable as their puffs of vaporous breath in the thin air.

A chorus of birdsong competed with the hubbub of the gathering crowd. Miranda shifted, doing alternate knee lifts and rising on her toes to warm up. Her body hummed with banked adrenaline. Running empowered her, healed her.

This half marathon was her fresh start since moving back to Spencer six weeks ago. One, small, positive step toward reclaiming her life after Nikki's death—after losing little Jeremy.

She'd been in the process of adopting Scott's four-year-old son from his first marriage, when her ex had packed up and left.

The last time she'd seen Jeremy, the small blue-eyed boy had been squirming, clutching his ragged teddy bear as Scott struggled to buckle him into his car seat. Jeremy's tearful howling still reverberated in Miranda's memory and pierced her heart.

She closed her eyes and drew the chilled air deep into her lungs. Exhaling through barely parted lips, she recalled the advice of her wellness coach. *Instead of dwelling on the past, remain in the present and focus on what is immediately around you.*

She opened her eyes. Directly in front of her, a tall slim man rose to his feet. Orange-framed sunglasses dangled from a cord around his neck and his black windbreaker gaped open, revealing number one seventy-seven. He lifted the faded Red Sox cap off his head and raked a hand through his dark hair. The rugged shadow defining his unshaven jaw suited his sculpted features. Features she found both appealing and familiar.

He tugged the hat back on and stretched his neck, moving his head from side to side, before consulting the chunky running watch on his wrist.

Miranda sucked air and ducked behind a noisy animated cluster of women all dressed in purple.

Declan Elliot.

There was no mistaking him. The architect's name was branded into her mind, as vivid as his intense blue eyes.

He'd glanced at his watch exactly the same way when she'd walked up to the microphone at last week's public hearing to read her argument opposing Snow Peak Properties' Resort and Casino.

A volunteer holding a bullhorn strode by. "Runners, line up!"

The crowd's anticipation ratcheted up a notch. The purple group tittered and shifted, revealing Elliot, who stood so close she could smell the clean scent of soap radiating from his lean body.

His remarkable eyes widened beneath the bill of his cap, and a slow dimpled smile lifted the corners of his mouth. "Ms. Buffet."

Before she had time to respond or ponder how he'd remembered her name, the crowd launched into a spirited countdown, followed by the loud crack of a starter's pistol. With a collective cheer, the massive press of participants slowly surged forward.

Elliot disappeared from view and Miranda forced her attention from the distracting architect back to the event. The pace picked up as runners gradually separated, stringing out like irregular beads in a fluid necklace.

Miranda transitioned from a brisk walk to a slow jog. She had thirteen high-altitude miles ahead of her and conserving her energy was critical.

She glimpsed Elliot, ahead and off to her right. He maintained an easy, springy jog, his long legs eating up twice the distance of most of the people he passed.

Judging by the muscular contours of his bare calves and thighs, the man was a seasoned competitor. His chances to win his division looked excellent.

Winning a race was one thing. Winning a legal battle with Spencer's Historical Society was another.

❧

Declan Elliot led a pack of runners through the visitor center's parking lot. An outraged stellar jay squawked from its perch on a nearby trash container. The course opened up onto a mountain lake, its glassy surface reflecting the surrounding trees. Puffy white clouds drifted across an orange-and-pink-streaked sky.

The cold air was so much cleaner and more energizing than Boston's heavy fuel-laden atmosphere. Leaving corporate America and relocating here to pursue his dream had been the right decision.

Smiling, he slipped on his shades and tugged the bill of his lucky cap, settling it firmly on his head. Not only was he going to get a finisher's medal, he'd take home the division trophy while he was at it.

Mile two continued along the lake and remained somewhat flat. Declan slowed his pace and dropped back behind the leaders. He wanted to keep an eye on the intriguing woman wearing number one thirteen.

What a pleasant surprise to discover Miranda Buffet standing beside him seconds before the start. A rosy flush had suffused her pretty face, creating that same fascinating contrast with her alabaster skin that had captured his attention last Thursday night.

Opposition to the development was not surprising. Before the planning commission meeting, Tom had briefed him about the concerned citizens group bent on keeping Spencer, Colorado mired in the twentieth century.

Most people didn't realize it was possible to design and build a resort in keeping with its surroundings, which, if done properly, posed a minimal threat to the environment.

Declan had been prepared to face the ringleader, known as Aunt Cora, the town's historian and self-appointed guardian.

Instead of the aging hippie, however, he'd been confronted by the much younger and far more interesting Miranda Buffet, the same Ms. Buffet, now wearing number one thirteen and running behind him.

A quick glance over his shoulder confirmed that she was still there, her copper ponytail swinging beneath her pink cap. Not only was she keeping up, she'd pulled within spitting distance.

Though she now wore mirrored shades, Declan remembered her stunning green eyes shooting daggers at him as she'd stood behind the podium. Besides being gorgeous, she'd presented her opposition to the project in a credible, passionate manner.

Doodling on his legal pad, he'd kept his expression neutral. Controlling his wayward mind was another story. He couldn't resist speculating as to what she'd look like without the black-rimmed glasses, her long copper hair loose over her shoulders and a whole lot more of her fair skin showing.

The trail climbed steeply, forcing Declan's attention back to the first real challenge of the run. He dug in, thighs straining, and blew the carbon dioxide out of his lungs.

By mile four, he was dragging. He couldn't get enough air and he had nine more miles to go. Must be the altitude.

Ms. Buffet was still running with the group directly behind him, apparently content to stay where she was. He couldn't risk more than an occasional glimpse. He needed every ounce of energy to breathe and concentrate on the ground beneath his feet.

Declan licked his parched lips, slowing to a clumsy jog. Uncapping his water bottle, he took a couple of quick gulps and wiped his mouth with the back of his hand.

Pounding feet approached from the rear.

He spotted Ms. Buffet's pink cap as the group thundered past. She glanced in his direction. Bright sun reflected off the mirrored lenses of her shades. She flashed him a smile and a thumbs-up, before striding ahead with the others. All he was left with was the tantalizing vision of her long shapely legs and her equally tantalizing ass.

Declan swore. Replacing his bottle, he shoved off after

them, picking up his pace. He'd push through this. He was a seasoned runner, and he'd be damned if he'd be beaten by the passionate, self-righteous Ms. Buffet.

The run up Dry Gulch road wiped out all thoughts of victory and taking home the division trophy. His lungs burned and pain tightened like a vise around his head. Six grueling miles left. He wasn't sure he could finish and failure gnawed at his gut.

Those two beers he'd had with dinner last night at the Wild Card hadn't helped, but Tom had talked him into it.

Tom Nagle, the king of bullshit, prided himself on making lucrative deals, often boasting that talking rich people out of their money was his specialty.

Great as a business partner, not so hot as a friend.

Declan stumbled, pitched forward and hit the rocky path hard.

Scrambling to his feet, he gritted his teeth against the pain in his throbbing knee and broke into a stiff jog. Thank God Ms. Buffet and the pack were long gone.

❦

Training the last two weeks in the high altitude had paid off. The first five miles had been easy, but the agonizing trail up Dry Gulch Road had been the most challenging Miranda had ever run.

She shook her hands and exhaled. Craving oxygen, she inhaled once, exhaled twice and repeated the process until her breathing steadied and she established a reasonable pace on the rutted forest access road.

Miranda glanced at the other runners around her. Declan wasn't among them. She'd passed him before Dry Gulch and hadn't seen him since. Guilt stabbed her as she remembered the gloating thumbs up she'd given him. The poor man had licked his lips, his faded shirt dark with sweat.

Despite his tortured expression and his ragged breathing, she'd accelerated, leaving Declan behind. Her behavior had been appalling and she regretted it, even if he was *the enemy*, according to Aunt Cora.

Minutes later, Miranda turned left on Devil's Gulch and checked her pace. All thoughts of Declan evaporated at the breathtaking panorama of snow-capped peaks towering around her. Several runners slowed to snap quick photos on their phones.

She shortened her stride to control her speed down the steep winding slope.

The morning breeze dried the sweat off her body, cooling her down and boosting her spirits. Miranda smiled. She was home, running beneath the bright blue canopy of the Colorado sky, amid groves of pine and aspen. She belonged here, embraced by the mountains and fast-flowing sunlit streams she remembered from her childhood.

Arms and legs pumping, she shifted into the zone overtaking other runners. She might as well run to win, as Grandpa Jake would say.

She frowned at the sudden memory of his gruff, emphatic voice when scolding her or while intent on driving home his point. That was the side of Grandpa she dreaded and the reason she still hadn't responded to his repeated invitations to join him for breakfast.

Though she'd been in Spencer over a month, Miranda had dodged all family texts and phone calls. Life without Scott and Jeremy was hard enough. Pile the complication of her dysfunctional family on top of that and she'd be back to popping Xanax in no time.

Running had been her cure, a healthier choice for coping and a better fix than her mother's or Nikki's.

Nikki. Her cousin had called her, reached out for help. She couldn't think about that now.

Miranda lengthened her stride.

Put aside what you have no control over. Focus on the immediate future—in this instance, crossing the finish line.

She paused at the next water station to top off her bottle. Swallowing a mouthful of the cool liquid, she cast a backward glance, relieved to see Declan jogging behind the group in purple. She couldn't help a triumphant grin. Even the purple ladies were beating him.

Five minutes later, mile ten flashed by. She passed two runners sporting Bronco jerseys. Three more miles and she'd be done.

The purple ladies still ran strong, but Declan had stopped. He was bent over, hands braced on his knees.

She continued a few yards further. *Dammit!* The last water station was half a mile behind them and there wasn't a volunteer in sight. Someone else would help him, she reasoned. *Sure, Miranda, keep telling yourself that.*

Although most running injuries were minor, she'd seen serious, even life-threatening situations when she'd lived in Wisconsin.

The purple ladies were no help. They rumbled past, oblivious to his distress.

Why did she always have to be the good Samaritan?

❦

Bent double, Declan couldn't endure the cramping pain in his gut any longer. He staggered to the side of the path and into the sheltering screen of trees.

Swamped by a wave of nausea, he steadied himself against a boulder and surrendered to the spasms that racked his body.

He knew better. This wasn't his first race. Hell, he'd run two marathons this past summer at twice the distance and placed in both. *Yeah, but you've never run at ten- thousand feet above sea level before, idiot.*

The course description had even cautioned participants in bold print about the perils of high-altitude running. This was a hell of a payback for his smug attitude.

Continuing to lean against the boulder for support, he closed his eyes and shivered in spite of the sun. He should've quit at the last water station. He'd had to push himself every inch of the way up that gulch from hell, or whatever its name was.

Another gut-wrenching cramp hit him and Declan groaned. His head throbbed, his scraped knee stung, and his entire body ached like the mother of all hangovers. The last thing he wanted to do was put anything in his unruly stomach, but he needed to hydrate himself.

Through the foggy haze of his misery, he also realized he was out of sight of the course or any other runners who might help him. Miranda Buffet flashed through his mind, but she was long gone. Dehydration and altitude sickness was serious. He had to get back to the road and flag down help.

Pushing off the boulder, he swayed. The ground tilted, merging with the blinding sky. His feet slid out from under him and he collapsed on his back, legs splayed, arms stretched out. He closed his eyes in a fruitless attempt to stop the nauseating vertigo.

Someone squeezed his arm hard. Declan blinked and stared up into Miranda Buffet's rosy face, her brow creased with concern. The mirrored shades had disappeared. Beneath the brim of her cap, the vivid emerald color of her eyes reminded him of the grass on the Boston Common in spring.

He hadn't been touched by a beautiful woman in months. He managed a weak grin and hoped she'd keep her hand resting on his chest.

She smiled. "That's better. You had me worried." She removed her hand to grip his wrist, her cool fingers firm, her expression thoughtful.

Declan remained quiet, content to study her delicate, heart-shaped face framed by fine, untamed tendrils of auburn hair that had escaped her ponytail and clung to her temples. A faint sprinkling of freckles dusted her pert nose, and he longed to trace the lush, pink curve of her mouth.

Before his exhausted mind could register her actions, she'd deftly untied the windbreaker from around his waist and stripped him of his shirt.

"What are you doing?" he croaked.

"We need to cool you off and have you drink some water."

She slipped an arm beneath his neck and lifted his head, drawing him closer. His skin tingled pleasantly in all the places where her bare flesh touched his. An intoxicating combination of coconut and citrus mingled with the arousing heat of her body. His eyelids drifted shut, and he imagined tasting the salty texture of her skin.

Beneath her smooth shirt, the yielding pressure of her breast nudged his cheek as she angled the spout of a water bottle between his lips.

"Take small sips."

The tepid liquid eased his parched throat. Declan took another swallow. His head still hurt like hell, but at least the cramps were fading.

❦

Miranda adjusted the water bottle and gazed down at the exhausted man. Her arms trembled from supporting his limp weight. She shifted her position to relieve her aching back. Precious minutes ticked away with every slow, agonizing sip he took. Once the event was over, the staff and volunteers would be gone before they could get help. Winning a medal of any kind would soon be out of the question.

The seductive friction of Declan's heated skin against hers was impossible to ignore. She couldn't keep her truant gaze from his broad, muscled chest and flat abdomen, liberally dusted with dark hair. Her traitorous imagination wandered beneath the waistband of his running shorts.

As though sensing her wayward mind, Declan lifted his hand and gently chucked her under the chin. Tilting his mouth in a slow, perceptive smile, his dark blue eyes, ringed with sweat-dried grime, probed hers.

He took another pull on the bottle and tapped his watch. "Tell you what…"

Heaving a profound sigh, he rolled out of her arms onto his hands and knees, before struggling to sit up on the rocky ground beside her. Panting, he hung his head between his legs. "Shit."

He cleared his throat. "You get me up to the course, then take off so you can finish. The clean-up crew can bring me down."

"You're sure? You still look a little pasty. I don't want to rush you, but we should go if we want to get any help."

Nodding, he sucked in a deep breath. With her assistance, he scrambled to his feet, leaning the bulk of his weight against her.

Even though she'd braced herself, Miranda's feet skidded and she stumbled before regaining her balance.

"Sorry." He groaned and exhaled as though he'd been sucker punched. Swaying, he clutched her shoulders. His hands slipped down her arms, his long fingers grazing her hip. Goosebumps pebbled her skin.

Lips clamped together, she kept an arm anchored around his bare chest as they hobbled in the direction of the course. Her cheek was pressed against his heaving ribcage.

Declan gave a hoarse chuckle. "We'd make a great team in a three-legged race, wouldn't we?"

"You're not funny. Help me out here."

She'd done all she could. Declan needed immediate medical attention, and she needed to put as much distance as possible between them and get on with her life. Hopefully, she could flag someone down.

CHAPTER 2

*W*ednesday afternoon, Declan hauled himself off the couch and went back to work. He needed to concentrate on Standing Bear Casino instead of Miranda Buffet. Not only was she the spokesperson for the historical society, but research on the internet revealed she was also the granddaughter of the Aspen Gold's legendary owner, Jakob Spencer.

The last thing Declan needed right now was an emotional entanglement with Ms. Buffet—or anyone else. Better to focus on his designs and the creative end of his business partnership with Tom. It wouldn't hurt to get Snow Peak's name out there and drum up future clients either. Promotion of the fledgling development company was primarily Tom's territory, but Declan wanted to protect his financial investment and his future.

Declan mounted the stone steps to Tom's house and the company office. He winced, not only at the pain of his aching muscles, but because of his humiliating performance in Saturday's run.

Regardless of her social status, Miranda had been willing

to sacrifice her own finish to double back and help him. There had to be some way to thank her without getting involved. A note seemed too impersonal and flowers too extreme.

Declan draped his sheepskin coat opposite Tom's sleek leather jacket on the antique wood rack that stood in the tiled entryway. The double doors leading to the office stood open. A mountain of mail littered their administrative assistant's vacant desk. The smell of scorched coffee hung in the air.

Tom looked up from his laptop and raised his brows. "You look like shit." He turned back to his computer and scowled. "I thought you were taking the week off."

"I changed my mind." Declan laid his briefcase on top of his drafting table. "Where's Heidi?"

Tapping a series of key-strokes, Tom glanced back up at Declan. "Heidi's gone. Breezed in this morning and told me she'd been offered a full-time job in Longmont. Would you believe they wanted her to start immediately?"

Tenting his fingers in front of his pursed lips, he stared at his screen.

"You look serious." Declan skirted the stool at his work station and crossed to peer over Tom's shoulder. There was nothing to see except Snow Peak Properties' elaborate business logo superimposed over their new website.

Tom vaulted out of his chair and clapped Declan on the back. "Me, serious? Nah, just a temporary snag, but I've got the perfect solution." He paused, his long face expectant, his small dark eyes bright.

Declan nodded and folded his arms. Knowing Tom's past history with women, a temporary snag meant his classmate would soon find another semi-qualified, hot babe to replace Heidi and assume the clerical position.

Shrugging, Tom retreated back behind his desk. He

peered at his platinum Rolex and flashed Declan an uneasy smile. "Like I said, I've got a way out, that is, if you agree. Take a seat and let me get you a cup of coffee. We'll talk and then you really should get your sorry ass home. I wasn't kidding when I said you look like shit."

Declan tensed his jaw and examined his partner's veiled features. This was about more than Heidi's leaving. "What the hell do you mean by, 'a way out'? A way out of what?"

"Now, who's serious?" Tom's half-hearted grin warred with his furtive expression.

Lowering his aching body into the chair opposite his partner, Declan closed his eyes and dragged a hand down his face. "Screw the coffee. Just give me your solution."

Tom's gaze drifted above Declan's head. "What do you think about selling that schoolhouse left on the property?"

Selling the schoolhouse? What the hell was he talking about? Seized by a white-hot impulse to grab his partner by the throat, Declan gripped the arms of the chair until his knuckles whitened. "That's your solution? A solution to what?"

"Wait, hear me out. Before you came on board, that wacko, Aunt Cora, had contacted me. The historical society wanted to turn the place into some kind of museum, only they didn't have the money to buy it. Would you believe she had the balls to ask me to donate it?" He swiveled in his chair, clasping his hands behind his head. "So, I'm thinking, now that we know Miranda Buffet's got a rich grandpa like Jakob Spencer, there could be some serious money available."

He tapped his temple with a smug smirk. "It's a *win-win* Declan. They'd get their schoolhouse, and we'd get a good chunk of cash, which we can use, believe me."

Declan's eyes burned and his head throbbed. He fought to keep his tone level. "Where did the fifty thousand I invested go?"

Tom frowned, preening his tie with his fingers. "We had a cash flow problem before you signed on. Your money went for permits and the damn environmental tests." He waved his arm. "The list goes on and on, but I'll tell you one thing, our investors are stoked about your plans. Believe me, it's important to keep those guys happy."

Tom's phone vibrated and he popped up out of his chair. "Time to go." Powering off his laptop, he closed the lid and slipped the computer in his briefcase. "I've got a meeting in Boulder with a couple of environmental investors that should make you happy.

"Truthfully, they're not that crazy about the casino in Spencer idea, but they like your sustainable design concept and can't wait to hear more about it. Which reminds me, send me your residential portfolio. The more I have to show them the better. Here, catch."

Declan reflexively caught a pair of small keys. "What are these for?"

"The padlock. Tell Aunt Cora or whoever at the historical society they're welcome to check out the building."

Snagging his briefcase off the desk, Tom slanted Declan a cocky grin. "This meeting could lead to a sweet deal. That means more work for you. Gotta go, bro."

"Wait, I haven't agreed to do anything regarding the schoolhouse, *bro*." Declan raised the fisted keys and enunciated the last word.

Tom paused mid-stride and addressed the toes of his tasseled loafers. "I suppose if our Boulder investors come on board, we don't have to sell. At least not right away."

He rubbed his chin. "Think of it this way. Whether we tear it down or sell it, the schoolhouse has to go. You're the one who's big on preserving historical buildings. Why don't you contact Ms. Buffet and suggest meeting with her over dinner?" He flashed Declan a sly wink. "Now, I really do have to go."

Declan hoisted himself out of the chair. The idea appealed to him, but he'd never admit that to Tom. "So, what's our asking price, if I should decide to run the sale by her?"

"Shit, you can check comps, but I'd start at ten to fifteen grand. That builds in wiggle room for negotiation. And tell them if they want an appraisal, they can pay for it. We'll talk tomorrow."

"That's a hell of a lot more than a chunk of change to a small-town historical society," Declan called after him.

Tom reappeared in the doorway. Tilting his head, he tapped his temple. "It's a drop in the bucket for your hot little running buddy. Go home. I'll catch you later about the meeting."

His partner's roguish chuckle echoed in Declan's ears. It was a damn good thing Tom left. A tight, sick knot twisted in the pit of his stomach. Something was off about the financial side of this project.

Tom was the MBA, in charge of the money end of their partnership, and Snow Peak was his baby.

Declan frowned and chewed on his lower lip. Checking up on Tom behind his back was not his job. All he wanted to do was focus on his designs and the creative end of the business.

The established, diverse firm he'd worked for in Boston had definitely had its advantages. A startup company like Snow Peak couldn't support an accounting department, much less a legal staff.

Tom's advice to go home was tempting. Declan scowled at Heidi's neglected desk. With a weary sigh, he brewed a fresh pot of Sumatra in the small kitchen area.

Setting his steaming mug down amid the clutter

surrounding his aging, but reliable desktop, he hovered over
a fresh legal pad and rapidly scrawled a list of contractors, as
well as city and county agencies to call.

It was too damn cold and he was too damn tired to tramp
all over Spencer, checking up on the financial status of Snow
Peak and Standing Bear Casino.

Sipping the hot energizing brew, Declan recalled Tom's
rambling explanation regarding where the money had gone.
He crumpled a piece of scratch paper into a ball and pitched
it at Tom's expensive leather chair. "Creative partner, my
ass."

Maybe fifty thousand dollars wasn't much of an investment from Tom's perspective, but Declan had worked hard
and saved every dollar of that money, and he wanted all of it
accounted for.

He spent the rest of the afternoon working down his list,
leaving a series of voicemails. He wouldn't count on hearing
back from anyone until sometime next week.

Outside the small circle of light cast from his desk lamp,
the office was dark. His caffeine kick was long gone. Rolling
his aching shoulders, he clasped his hands over his head and
stretched. *Time to quit.*

Declan stood, clutching the stool until his throbbing head
cleared. Maybe he should've stayed home the rest of the
week. He was still feeling puny, and hypothesizing where his
money had disappeared to wasn't helping.

Was he being paranoid?

No, dammit. As an investing partner, he was entitled to a
complete financial accounting. He should have asked for a
report in the first place.

Declan slipped the tablet into his briefcase. Everything
had happened so fast. Tom had called offering him the partnership. The timing had been perfect. He'd given the firm his
notice the next morning. They weren't happy about losing

him, but understood this was a career move he'd been working toward and wished him well.

Mom and Dad had been thrilled. Spencer was only a couple hours drive from their house in south Denver. Within two weeks Declan had headed west, his rental truck loaded to the max, one-step closer to his dream. A financial report had been the last thing on his mind.

Until today.

After a brief stop in the restroom, he shut off the coffeemaker and picked up his briefcase.

His phone lit up.

Green people backed out. Have more to call. One HUGE. Could be spectacular for us!

Tom's text eased his suspicions and his headache. He'd give his partner the benefit of the doubt until proven otherwise.

Which reminded him.

Miranda's name, printed in red capital letters, had remained the only unchecked item on his list. While he'd been laid up at home and bored out of his mind, he'd called the historical society, on the off-chance Miranda would answer. Instead, his call had gone directly to voicemail. On the fly, he'd manufactured a quick request to speak with Ms. Buffet to clarify a couple of items she'd referred to at the last public hearing.

Close to the truth.

What he'd really like to do was debate integrated architecture with her over drinks and dinner at the Golden Grill. The upscale restaurant was smaller and preferable to dining at her grandfather's lodge.

Later that same day, Aunt Cora had called back and given

him Miranda's number. Miranda was the public face of the historical society and the person he should deal with regarding all matters connected to the casino.

Declan grinned. Swiping his phone's glowing screen, he waited for his connection. Taking Miranda out to dinner at the Golden Grill would be perfect. Discussing the schoolhouse would take care of business and his obligation to thank her with little risk of involvement.

❦

Miranda dragged the heavy rectangular carton into her living room. She carefully lowered the box to the floor and slit the packing tape at both ends. Kneeling, hands on hips, she stared down at the cardboard container, dread filling her throat. She'd avoided unpacking the framed photographs long enough.

Putting the box cutter on the coffee table, she cupped her fingers beneath the crystal bowl of a large wine glass and took a generous swallow of her favorite red. She'd brought the bottle with her from the kitchen. There was enough left for one more serving.

Helping Aunt Cora and the historical society was rewarding, but she still had too much time to think about all the scattered pieces of her life.

The gunmetal gray box on the top shelf in her bedroom closet contained her divorce papers, the letter from the university granting her leave and the contract on the sale of her house.

Miranda took another bracing swallow. Her first house, bought before she'd married Scott but divided up as community property.

Other pieces of her life, like Nikki's death and losing little

Jeremy, were less tangible, but carried more pain and similar crushing side effects.

Being cooped up inside all day hadn't helped. She'd caved and skipped her daily run with the lame excuse of freezing temperatures this morning. All she'd needed was a half hour to take the edge off. She'd run tomorrow, no matter how cold it was and check into a membership at the Flatiron Health Club this weekend.

A couple more sips of wine and the warm, reassuring glow she craved kicked in. Lightly smacking her lips together, she smiled. "Okay, Miranda Jane, let's get this over with."

Miranda Jane.

She recalled a distant, sun-drenched afternoon ages ago and Nikki's high, reedy voice. That summer, bright yellow dandelions blanketed the grassy meadow behind Grandpa's stables.

She and Nikki had sat cross-legged, holding hands. Nikki's solemn green eyes locked on hers, her fingers squeezing so hard it hurt. "Miranda Lorraine, from now on you'll be Miranda Jane."

Miranda licked her lips, her ten-year-old brain desperate to respond with an equally acceptable new middle name for Nikki.

A horse had whinnied in the distance, breaking the silence, and she'd blurted, "Louise! Nicole Suzanne, you will be Nikki Louise."

Nikki had made a face and pushed Miranda over on her back. "Is that all you can come up with? Louise is an old lady's name. Miranda Jane, Miranda Jane, sometimes you are such a pain." Nikki's whispery chant echoed in her mind.

Her cousin had grown into a beautiful woman, passionate about life, devoted to her boys, but obsessed with her appearance and the constant need to feel loved.

Miranda closed her eyes and swallowed another mouthful. No amount of wine would make her forget Nikki's last voicemail.

If only...

Life was too full of if onlys.

Like her therapist had been so fond of reminding her, fixating on what has already happened won't change anything and solves nothing.

Miranda stared at the carton. She hadn't known what to do with the stack of framed photographs when she'd moved, so she packed them while the movers loaded the truck and told herself she'd figure out what to do with them once she got here. She still didn't know what to do with them, but it was time she decided.

She drained her glass. The liquid's tart, peppery flavor had taken on a bitter aftertaste. Dwelling on family memories or those she'd loved and lost was not productive. She'd get this last box unpacked and accomplish at least one thing today.

Heaving a deep sigh, Miranda set the wine glass on the table. Grasping the first bubble-wrapped object, she peeled off the tape and opened it.

College graduation. *With honors.* Grandpa, Heath and Hunter had attended, but her mother had been conspicuously absent. Deirdre had been in rehab for the umpteenth time.

Unshed tears pricked her eyes. She bit her lip and inhaled through her nose. Deirdre had missed every one of her significant events, beginning with kindergarten. Miranda lightly touched the older man's image. Grandpa had been the one to walk her to her classroom for the first time.

Her throat tightened. Going back down that road was pointless. She'd learned a long time ago she couldn't control what her mother did or didn't do. Laying the photo aside,

Miranda seized the next picture and jimmied the large customized oval frame out of the carton onto her lap.

She yanked off the sticky tape, balled it up and pitched it at the fireplace. Her wedding had been the exception. Deirdre had been between husbands and managed to grace with her presence the one momentous occasion Miranda would rather forget.

Peeling the plastic wrap aside, Miranda gasped and ran her finger over the cracked glass covering the expensive bridal portrait. Scott had said both the photograph and the eight by ten leather-bound album were a ridiculous waste of money. He'd been right, the bastard.

She wound a lock of hair around her finger and tried to ignore the crawling sensation marching across her skin. She should've taken a Xanax, but she'd opted for wine instead.

Nikki's death had unexpectedly triggered panic attacks. Sometimes a simple word or a random association was all it took.

Scott had accused her of behaving like her loony mother. As ridiculous as it seemed now, at the time Miranda had believed him. She'd gone to a psychiatrist, who'd prescribed a small dose of Xanax.

After Scott left her taking Jeremy, Miranda's dependence on the little blue pills mushroomed.

She'd power through this. She wasn't about to quit now. Shoving the damaged article behind her, Miranda took a deep steadying breath and cautiously un-wrapped the next bundled photo. The glass was intact. Relieved there was no damage, she tenderly cradled the candid shot of sweet, little Jeremy against her chest and bowed her head. A tear oozed from the corner of her eye.

She missed his joyful, chubby-cheeked face, his shrieks of laughter and his tender, watery kisses. He'd almost been hers.

Still clutching Jeremy's picture, Miranda awkwardly rose

from her cramped position on the floor and surveyed the devastating wreckage of her past. Time for a refill. She bent over the low table, setting Jeremy's picture down beside her empty glass.

Desperate to numb her aching heart, she uncorked the bottle with trembling hands and hastily poured what was left of the wine. Most of the dark red liquid missed the goblet, splashing all over the table and Jeremy's picture. Tears stung her eyes, and her voice choked on a curse.

Miranda snatched the portrait off the table and sprinted into the kitchen. She frantically wiped the surface clean. She looked down at her splotched pink shirt, her first, last and only Mother's Day present from her precious little boy.

Yanking the garment over her head, she tossed it into the sink, snatched her phone and frantically googled how to remove wine stains.

Clad only in her sweatpants and athletic bra, Miranda followed the online instructions and loaded the treated garment into the washer.

Squaring her shoulders, she marched into the living room, flipped the gilded frame over and removed the wedding portrait. Proclaiming Scott a heartless, selfish bastard, Miranda set her jaw and ripped the photo in two. She deposited the torn remnants in the trash on top of the wine bottle.

She was on her hands and knees scrubbing the floor when her phone buzzed. The number was local and she was the designated contact for the historical society. Standing, she wiped her hands on her pants and swiped the screen. "This is Miranda."

"Hello, Miranda. This is Declan Elliot, the poor idiot you rescued at the run last weekend."

Gasping, she hunched over, crossing an arm across her nearly bare breasts as though he could see her. She almost laughed aloud at herself. Declan's rich, warm voice was the perfect topper to the day.

"I called for a couple of reasons," he said.

Miranda chewed on her lower lip and twisted a lock of hair around her finger. She still felt guilty about leaving him behind, even though a volunteer in the area had radioed for a cart. Declan had urged her to continue the run, and thanks to him, she'd placed in her division and earned her finisher's medal. "How are you feeling?"

"I walk like a dead zombie, and I'm told I look just as bad."

A smile tugged at the corner of her mouth. "Zombies are dead, Mr. Elliot. Have you been drinking enough water?"

He chuckled. "Now you sound like my mother."

"And you're calling now, because…"

Declan cleared his throat. "I want to thank you again for helping me out and to proposition you, I mean, offer you and your group a business proposition. Over dinner."

Miranda gaped down at her phone as though it was possessed. "Dinner. When? No. No," she repeated, toning her refusal down a notch.

She paced across the room, stopped and eyed the ceiling, as though seeking inspiration. "Call Aunt Cora and discuss your business proposition over dinner with her."

"I did and she told me to call you. Honest."

Miranda narrowed her eyes. "Are you laughing?"

"No. Hell, no." He sighed. "Okay, I'm smiling. It's ironic, okay? Are you going to hold it against me? I swear, I talked to Aunt Cora, and she told me to discuss the proposal with you first. By the way, is she really your aunt?"

"No." Miranda resumed pacing, twisting her hair tighter. Technically, meeting with interested parties fell under her job description. She padded over to the table, picked up a pen and printed Declan in large red caps on the back of an envelope. "She's not my aunt. Dinner is out. Where's your office? I'll be happy to meet with you there."

"Our office is out of town and much less convenient. Dinner is my way of thanking you and taking care of business at the same time."

Damn, the man was persistent. She underlined his name. "I appreciate your gratitude, Mr. Elliot, but I'm more comfortable meeting you at your office."

"Please, call me Declan. All right, I hear you, but our office is located in my partner's private residence, which is about a fifteen-minute drive from the center of town."

Miranda frowned. That didn't feel right either.

"Look, would you be more comfortable if we met for lunch? Just name the time and place."

She rolled her eyes. What part of no did he not understand?

"I'll meet you for coffee. This Saturday at the Rocky Mountain Bookstore. Do you know where that is?"

A whoosh of pent-up breath blasted in her ear. "I'll find it. What time?"

Miranda jerked the phone away and put him on speaker. "The bookstore opens at nine. Is that too early?"

"Hardly, see you Saturday at nine."

Miranda jabbed 'end call' and glared at her phone.

Dammit, he'd been smiling again.

What had possessed her to suggest meeting Declan for coffee at the bookstore? She might as well have taken out a full-page ad in *The Herald*. The locals would have the two of them engaged by noon. Certain members of the historical society would probably misconstrue the meeting as some kind of collusion.

She collapsed on the couch and closed her eyes.

Small-town gossip never changed. Growing up in Spencer, as Deirdre Spencer-Buffet-Lawe's daughter,

Miranda had often been the object of speculation, forced to bear the sting of criticism directed at her mother, obligated to defend Deirdre's honor, along with hers and that of her younger twin brothers, Heath and Hunter.

Even more galling at the moment was how she'd just managed to sabotage her own resolve, giving another man a victory at her expense.

Miranda curled her legs beneath her and finger-combed her tangled locks. Declan was an alarming complication she hadn't anticipated. Not only did he threaten everything she and the historical society were trying to accomplish, but he posed a beguiling obstacle to her goal of reclaiming her life. A complication she didn't need, she didn't want and she couldn't afford.

CHAPTER 3

*M*iranda arrived at the Rocky Mountain Bookstore fifteen minutes before she'd agreed to meet Declan. She needed the advantage of being there first, seated and in control.

She'd tucked her hair into a knot at the base of her neck and dressed in charcoal gray slacks, jacket and low heels. She didn't want Declan to think this was anything other than a business meeting.

Even though she'd run earlier to tamp down her anxiety, her pounding heart threatened to leap out of her chest.

Miranda pushed open the door, and the bell tinkled overhead. The interior of the bookstore was just as she remembered. The cozy shop embraced her with its shelves of books, paper and the alluring fragrance of strong, pungent Arabica.

The owner, Kate Michaels, stood beside the vintage cash register conversing with an older woman. Miranda averted her gaze but out of the corner of her eye caught Kate's fleeting glance confirming her presence.

As much as she liked Kate, the last thing Miranda wanted

to do was engage in conversation. Until today she'd avoided contact with any of her friends and family. She had a feeling avoidance was no longer an option. Tightening her grip on the handle of her briefcase, she continued down the main aisle to the back of the shop.

A fire crackled in the stone fireplace. The same burgundy wingback chairs, grouped around low tables, were still there —and so was Declan.

Her breath caught in her throat, and her swinging briefcase banged against her thigh.

His blue eyes widened. He stood, and a warm smile creased his handsome face. He shot a rueful glance down at his red crew neck sweater and faded jeans. Even his ruddy flush was charming.

"Sorry about the clothes, Miranda." He enveloped her hand in a firm grip. "I take this meeting seriously, regardless."

Miranda fisted her tingling fingers and raised her chin, struggling to ignore her heated response. She flashed him a professional smile. "I appreciate your honesty, Mr.--" she cleared her throat, "Declan."

Full of goodness. She'd looked up his name online. Declan was a nice name and a perfect fit. His candid expression and natural manner inspired trust. Even sick and exhausted, he'd convinced her to go on and finish the race.

She strolled over to the coffee bar and stared at the pastries in the glass case. He followed and stood so close his heady scent of citrus and sandalwood teased her nostrils.

"See anything you like?" His warm breath tickled her ear.

Miranda inched away. She couldn't seem to draw enough oxygen into her lungs. "Too many carbs," she said, flashing him a quick glance.

Too much man and too much testosterone was more like it.

She caught the attention of the teenage girl behind the counter. "I'll have a large skinny mocha with no whip."

The girl nodded, her blushing smile directed at Declan.

"I'll have a black coffee and one of those." He pointed to the stacked display of chocolate croissants.

Miranda unclasped her briefcase to retrieve her wallet, but Declan handed his card over. "I've got it. Business deduction, remember?" His dazzling smile included the barista, who giggled and batted her thick black lashes.

"Thank you." Miranda cradled her briefcase and looked to the front of the store. She should never have agreed to this. He made her feel like she was back in high school talking to the hot quarterback of the football team.

Then there was Kate, who could be counted on to wander over to make conversation, which was bound to lead to uncomfortable, prying questions. The impulse to bolt back up the aisle and escape consumed her.

"Miranda." Declan touched her shoulder. "Why don't you sit down. I'll bring everything over."

His kind smile and hushed tone eased the panic that gripped her. Scott would've told her to suck it up and left her at the counter to wait on him.

After serving Miranda, Declan retrieved his own order and sat across from her. "I'm glad you suggested meeting here. This is a great place." He raised his mug to his lips and grinned. "Books and good coffee. Not to mention my favorite croissants." He cut a piece of the flakey pastry. "Sure you don't want some of this?"

Miranda bit the inside of her lip and shook her head. He'd already seized control of this meeting, but she still reserved the right to dictate what she put in her mouth. She sipped her mocha, the bookstore's signature Aspen leaf swirled in the pale, milky foam. "No thanks."

"Are you training for another run?"

Her distracted gaze lingered on his long fingers and neatly clipped nails. "Not really. I haven't had a chance to check out any events coming up, but I run almost every day."

He nodded and forked another bite into his mouth. His very nicely shaped mouth. An unruly wave of heat scorched her cheeks.

He wiped his lips with a napkin and dusted crumbs from his jeans. "Me, too. Not much since I've moved here." He shot her an apologetic smile. "Which was obvious last weekend. I'd run on the Common every morning before work when I lived in Boston."

His expression grew pensive and he carefully set his fork on his plate. "I had a high stress job and running helped. It got rid of all the extra junk that gummed up my brain." He shrugged. "I also like to push myself, sometimes too much. So, why do you run?"

She tilted her head and studied the *Foodie* display over his shoulder. Her wellness coach had suggested running as therapy.

"Stress." She glanced at him. "Like you. It helps me manage my anxiety issues."

She sipped from her large cup. *Better than getting stoned on Xanax.*

Licking a fleck of foam off her lip, Miranda smiled. "I love running here. I can't wait until the Aspen turn. Fall's always been my favorite season."

"Yeah, fall in the Colorado high country is hard to beat." Declan set his empty plate on the table. "I grew up in Denver. When I was a kid I liked winter because I could build snow forts." Sinking back in his chair, he extended his long legs. "I'd design different ones and build a whole town. My mom wasn't quite as devoted as Frank Lloyd Wright's, but she'd be outside in the snow with me as much as she could."

Declan tugged his ear and shot Miranda a crooked grin. "She used to call herself my foreman."

For a fleeting moment, Miranda glimpsed the boy that still lived inside the man, his face pink from the cold, his blue eyes bright with excitement. Declan and his mother all bundled up, playing together in the snow.

He laughed. "Dad thought the two of us were nuts. He still says he'll take summer over winter any day.

"We'd spend every summer camping up in the mountains. Dad still likes to take off before daylight to fish one of his favorite lakes. I've got a feeling I'll be making a lot of those trips again, now that I live closer."

He took a healthy swallow from his mug. "So, did you have a crazy mother who played outside in the snow with you?"

Miranda stared into the foamy dregs of her cup. She had a crazy mother all right. The only times her mother had paid attention to Miranda were the brief intervals between husbands or boyfriends.

Miranda's father lived in London and sent her ornate, impersonal cards with generous checks enclosed on her birthday and Christmas. According to Deirdre, Gordon Buffet had abandoned them both upon Miranda's birth.

This conversation had turned way too personal. Straightening her posture, she swiped imaginary crumbs off her lap. "Frank Lloyd Wright is one of my favorite architects. I've always admired how he integrated his designs with the surrounding landscape."

Declan gave her an enthusiastic nod. "Exactly. I think Falling Water is his best example. Have you seen it?"

Miranda shook her head, setting her cup on the table. "I'd like to. I've seen the Guggenheim and a couple of his prairie-style homes in Illinois and Wisconsin."

"You need to go." Declan raised his mug. "I'm getting a refill. Would you like one?"

"No, thanks." Miranda checked her phone. "I have to leave soon. I'm working on a grant for the schoolhouse."

"Right. I'll fill this and we'll get down to business."

Declan strode over to the coffee bar, his jeans just tight enough to emphasize his lean hips. She recalled his sculpted muscles the day of the race. Sexy and incredibly nice.

Kate sauntered over with a teasing grin and whispered, "Aren't you going to introduce me to your friend?"

"He's not my friend." Miranda lowered her voice. "We're discussing business. It's to do with—"

Declan returned, his expression curious.

Kate thrust her hand out. "Hi, I'm Kate. I own the bookstore. Mandy and I have known each other forever."

Declan flashed his heart-melting grin. Setting down his coffee, he grasped Kate's hand. "Declan. I'm new to Spencer, and I'm happy I've discovered your bookstore, thanks to Miranda."

The color in Kate's face deepened. "Well, Declan, welcome to Spencer. Drop by the Rocky Mountain Bookstore anytime. If the two of you will excuse me, I'd better go find my daughter and see what she's up to. Nice meeting you."

She gave Miranda a quick hug. "Give me a call sometime, Mandy."

Miranda nodded. "Sure."

Kate had hugged her like that at Nikki's service last summer. She and her daughter, Madison, had sat with them at the luncheon afterward.

Madison had been so sweet. She'd grasped Jeremy's hand and asked Miranda if she could take him to the church's playroom and show him all the toys.

"I know you have to get back to your grant." Declan resumed his seat and cracked open his battered briefcase.

He withdrew two printed pages from a file folder and absently tugged on his ear as he looked them over.

"It appears that Cora Fleming, on behalf of the Spencer Historical Society, contacted Snow Peak in March of this year, with the explicit request that the schoolhouse be donated, including relocation to a specified lot in Olde Town."

Declan glanced up. Apprehension flickered in his eyes. He rubbed the back of his neck and blew out a gust of air. "Apparently, Snow Peak rejected the request at that time and informed Ms. Fleming that the structure might come up for sale at a later date."

Miranda stiffened. She'd already read the company's curt rejection letter at her initial interview.

Aunt Cora's defeated expression had softened Miranda's heart, and she'd immediately signed on as the historical society's public advocate, in addition to raising funds and writing grants.

To be fair, she'd listen to what Declan had to say and bring it back to the committee for discussion. It was up to her to negotiate the best possible outcome on behalf of the historical society, and that was precisely what she'd do, regardless of the man's disarming magnetism.

Declan tossed the folder on the table. Clasping his hands, he leaned toward her, his gaze earnest. "Snow Peak Properties is now prepared to sell the schoolhouse to the historical society." A muscle twitched in his jaw. "The asking price is ten thousand dollars."

"Ten thousand dollars?" She dropped her voice. "That's ridiculous. I haven't looked at the building, but I've seen photos. Several members, including Ms. Fleming, have told me that the schoolhouse has been neglected for years. How do we know if it's structurally sound?"

She cast Declan a withering stare. "You're the architect. Can you honestly tell me that it's worth ten thousand in its present state?"

He blinked and opened his mouth as though to protest. Instead, he sank back in his chair and steepled his fingers, his blue eyes watchful.

Miranda lurched to her feet and seized her briefcase. "I'm out of here."

She barely missed colliding with a small boy, who darted in front of her. Giggling, he skirted the table and ducked behind Declan's chair.

An exasperated young woman, toting an infant strapped to her chest, half-trotted in the toddler's wake. "Carson, it's time to go."

The little boy peeked around the arm of the chair, his brown eyes bright. His trill of merry laughter and chubby cheeks reminded Miranda of Jeremy.

Her throat constricted and unexpected tears pricked behind her eyes.

The toddler's mother stopped beside Declan, who'd also risen. "Sorry about that." She glanced at Miranda and recognition dawned on her face. "Miranda Buffet. My mom said she'd seen your picture in the *Herald*."

Miranda's stomach clenched. Nikki's catty friend from high school. Meeting here had been a horrible idea. Running into Kate was one thing, but colliding with Lauren, the witch with a capital B, spelled catastrophe.

The boy crept from behind the chair and clung to his mother's leg. The woman coyly tucked a wayward strand of hair behind her ear, giving Declan the same rapt smile that Kate and the barista had earlier.

Shrugging, he shot Miranda a helpless look and introduced himself. "Miranda and I are working on a project for Spencer's historical society."

Miranda and I? Oh God. What nerve, and of all people to say it to. Lauren would tweet her spin on it and news of their torrid affair would be the local hot topic of the hour.

The woman wrapped her fingers around Declan's. "Nice to meet you."

She turned to Miranda, rearranging her features into a somber expression. "I still can't get over Nikki's death. It was shocking, losing an old friend like that. Given the circumstances, it must be even harder for you and your family. And poor Matt, left alone with those two little boys. My daughter, Chelsea, is in Zach's class."

Lauren rested her hand on her son's shoulder. "I haven't seen Matt since Nikki's funeral. How's he doing?"

Miranda swallowed and plucked at the neckline of her sweater. Declan stood next to her, his intent expression taking it all in.

"I've been so busy unpacking from the move and working on grants that I haven't had a chance to do anything else."

Lauren looked pointedly at Declan. "That's surprising. You know how people talk in a small town. Rumor has it that you came back to Spencer to help Matt raise Zach and Stevie. Zach, especially. He seems to be acting out. Chelsea says he's in trouble all the time."

She gazed down at the top of her little boy's head and sighed. "I suppose it's to be expected, considering…"

Miranda resisted the powerful urge to slap the woman. Lauren was still a bitch.

Declan cleared his throat and gave Lauren an impersonal smile, then returned his gaze to her. "Miranda, before you leave, I have one more option I'd like to discuss."

Carson yanked on his mother's arm and said, "I wanna go to the park."

Lauren ruffled his hair. "Okay, buddy." She looked from Declan to Miranda. "Nice talking to you."

Miranda tightened her lips, combating her rising panic. She should never have moved back to Spencer. She wasn't ready. She'd lost Nikki. She'd lost little Jeremy after Scott had traded her in for his younger grad assistant. Her uncertain future was too overwhelming.

She flinched at the firm, circular pressure of Declan's warm hand between her shoulder-blades. "Screw her," he said and guided Miranda back to her chair. "I was serious. Please, hear me out."

Her rapid pulse throbbed in her ears. Declan was too nice, too likeable. One more complication in her already too-complicated life.

Miranda clenched her fists in her lap, struggled to breathe deep and failed. She scanned the cozy sitting area, seeking something to focus on, *anything*—.

Her gaze rested on the gleaming handle of her briefcase, the briefcase Scott and Jeremy had given her last Christmas.

"Excuse me." She stumbled off in the direction of the restroom, desperate to get somewhere private.

Locking the paneled door, Miranda sagged against the wood, pressing her fists against her closed eyes. The Xanax tablets she carried for insurance were tucked away in the zippered pocket of her briefcase.

She'd thought if she came back to Spencer to help Aunt Cora and be with Grandpa—. Instead, everything had just gotten more convoluted.

Nothing had changed. People knew her here. She should have gone somewhere else, anywhere else. A peaceful place, where she wouldn't get caught up in everyone else's drama and expectations.

Drawing a deep, shaky breath, she held it for four seconds and exhaled, repeating the process until her spinning mind hushed. She could do this. She'd worked through her panic before and she could do it now.

Declan was outside waiting for her. She'd finish listening to what he had to say, because she represented the historical society and that was her job.

As soon as possible, she'd inform Aunt Cora that she'd be happy to work on writing grants and advocate behind the scenes, but someone else would have to be its public face. That's the only way she could remain in Spencer.

Minutes later Miranda emerged and returned to the sitting area. Declan was hunched over a yellow pad balanced on his lap, studying a column of scribbled figures. He tapped a silver pen against his lips.

"You have something you wanted to run by me?"

Declan looked up, his expression concerned. "Are you okay?"

Miranda took her seat and folded her hands in her lap.

Breathe. "I'm fine. I'm hoping you've come up with a better alternative to your previous offer."

His eyes probed hers, asking questions that he mercifully kept to himself.

She leveled her gaze to his, gaining confidence in the decision she'd made in the restroom.

Declan set the pad on the table, adroitly catching the pen before it rolled off onto the floor. He planted the instrument above the tablet's binding and clasping his hands, leaned toward her.

"First, I apologize for calling this meeting and trying to bluff my way through the proposal. Not only did I waste your time, but my intention in meeting with you today was more personal than business."

He hesitated, as though waiting for her to say something.

Pleasurable warmth flooded her veins. He was attracted to her, too. The scrawled figures on the yellow pad were difficult to read upside down, but preferable to drowning in his deep blue gaze.

Declan sighed, running a hand through his hair. "You're right. Given the structure's age and its long-term vacancy, it probably isn't worth ten thousand. My partner's going to disagree."

He was willing to negotiate. Elated, Miranda reached over and gripped his forearm.

His muscles tensed beneath the sweater's textured material, and a wry smile tugged at the corners of his mouth.

Releasing him, she perched on the edge of her chair and dialed her enthusiasm back a notch. "Look, can you give me a reasonable asking price? One I can take back to the society for consideration?"

Declan's smile faded. He scrubbed a hand down his face and stared down at the legal pad. "I'll have to hash this out with Tom first. To be fair to both parties, I'd want an outside appraisal. Do you think your people can wait until the middle of next week?"

"That shouldn't be a problem," she replied. Waiting a few more days before talking to the committee would be perfect. Aunt Cora or the designated spokesperson could negotiate with him from that point on.

Declan reached for his pen and the tablet, peering at his figures. "Something else you and your people need to consider. Whatever happens, I wouldn't advise moving the schoolhouse without an inspection. If it's recommended that the building be dismantled and reconstructed at its final location, I'd be happy to supervise on both ends of the operation." He glanced up. "If my partner and your group are agreeable to that, of course."

Miranda's pulse quickened at the possibility of protracted negotiations. She reminded herself that even if the committee agreed to work with him on the project, she would no longer be involved. Disappointing, but better for her recovery in the long run.

In spite of her reluctance to prolong this meeting any longer, she couldn't help herself. "From what I've heard about Tom Nagle, you don't seem the type to be partners with that kind of a person."

Declan scrubbed his hand down his face and gave her a wary smile. "What are you talking about?"

It was on the tip of her tongue to tell him about the suspicions raised by Aunt Cora and other committee members. He should know the buzz they'd heard around town.

Glancing down, Declan pulled his cell phone out of his pocket and checked the screen. The corners of his mouth tightened and his brow furrowed.

"It's my partner. I have to go." Tucking the yellow tablet and folder back inside his briefcase, Declan slipped a hooded Red Sox sweatshirt over his head, tousling his dark hair.

"I'll talk to Tom about what we discussed and get back to you. Oh, I almost forgot…" He dug in the front pocket of his snug-fitting jeans and produced a pair of small, tarnished keys strung together with fishing line. "There's a padlock on the door. In case you or any committee members want to check out the schoolhouse for yourselves."

Instead of dropping them in her outstretched hand, he pressed the flat keys into the sensitized flesh of her palm. His warm fingers lingered. "Sorry to cut this short. I'll call you."

Miranda fisted the keys and shoved them deep in the pocket of her slacks. Her nerves triggered to an exquisite tension, she stacked their used dishes. Anything to keep from looking at him. "I'll inform the committee."

By the time she'd cleared the table, Declan had left the shop. Exhaling through pursed lips, she picked up her briefcase and marched up the aisle. Passing the cash register, she sketched a wave to Kate.

Miranda wanted out of the shop before Kate or anyone else could stop her and grill her with unwanted questions.

The keys Declan had given her branded her hip. Filling out forms and writing grants paled in comparison to future meetings with Snow Peak's charming architect, but those mundane tasks were the safer and wiser choice.

CHAPTER 4

*D*eclan pulled his truck up beside Tom's SUV and jumped out, his feet hitting the dirt. Thankfully he'd caught Tom before he'd left.

Mom in hospital. Emergency surgery. Will call.

As soon as he'd read Tom's text, Declan had terminated his meeting with Miranda. He'd driven to Tom's as fast as he'd dared.

A pang of guilt stabbed him. He'd been pissed at his partner for the past three days, but he was sorry to hear about Tom's mom. Without an admin there might be things he needed to do in the office while his partner was away.

Glancing at the SUV's tinted windows, he frowned. A closer look at the front seat revealed the company's server, belted in and securely cushioned with a bath towel. What the hell?

Declan's gut tightened. Why was Tom taking the tower? It

contained everything to do with Snow Peak, including his specs for *Standing Bear Casino*. He couldn't do business without that info and all the rest.

All his earlier suspicions came rushing back. His mind raced as he tore up the steps to the building.

Declan had confronted him last Wednesday and Tom had spent every day away from the office since. He'd assured Declan that he was meeting with more prospective investors and had hinted broadly that he might even have to travel to win them over. Now, out of the blue, his mother had to have emergency surgery? It could be a rotten coincidence. Declan wanted to believe the guy, but Heidi's abrupt departure and Tom's shifty behavior wasn't building any trust.

Declan jogged into the house and halted at the open French doors to the office, sucking air into his starved lungs. His heart thudded painfully against his ribcage. Was it the high altitude or the bad vibe gnawing at his gut?

The low hum of the shredder and its glowing blue light snagged his attention. The stacks of mail on Heidi's cluttered work space had vanished. He didn't like this at all.

Tom stood over his own desk, stuffing a handful of papers into his bulging briefcase, his tailored suit and silk tie replaced with faded jeans and a t-shirt that looked like he'd slept in it.

Not like Tom at all.

He snapped up his head. A wary expression flickered across his narrow, unshaven face. "You got my text? I hate running out on you like this, bro, but I'm needed back home." His gaze dropped to the platinum watch on his wrist. "Such a shock. My mother's always been so incredibly healthy."

"What the hell?" Declan's breathless voice barely carried across the room.

Tom pulled open the center drawer of his desk, gave it a quick once-over and closed it again. "I don't have time to explain, but I'll call you once I get to the hospital and find out how she's doing."

He was saying all the right words, but they rang hollow. Tom wasn't that worried about his mom. He'd worn the same shifty-eyed expression last week, when Declan had asked him where his fifty thousand dollars had gone.

Declan clenched his jaw until his teeth ached and slowly advanced into the room, hands fisted in his pockets. "What's going on?" He spat the question, cautioning himself to control his rising fury. "You're obviously cleaning out your desk, and why the hell is our server packed in your car?"

He glared at his partner, willing the man to look him in the eye and give him a straight answer. Was the bastard even capable of the truth?

Tom snapped his briefcase shut, flashing Declan the winning smile he reserved for 'closing the deal,' as he called it —sincere on the surface, but above all, convincing.

He pulled up the handle of his carry-on and set the brief-case on top, tapping it emphatically. "I'm working on a couple of sweet deals, both out of state. Would you believe one's actually out of the country?" He tilted his head and sucked in a deep breath. "Anyway, I figure I can work on them in between." He shrugged. "You know how much down time there is in hospitals. My dad will need a break, and my mother will be sleeping a lot."

Declan dropped his jaw and ran his hand over the back of his head. Why hadn't he seen it before? He couldn't wrap his mind around what was happening, yet it was patently obvious. "Okay, I get it now. You're trying to sell me on this story, aren't you? You're conning me like you've conned your other investors. Declan shook his head and gave a mirthless laugh. "I've been screwed."

Tom stiffened. Narrowing his gaze, he stared Declan directly in the face. "Decs, chill, dude. You're my partner.

There's no one I trust more. I know you'll take good care of us while I'm gone." He gestured at the door with his thumb. "I'm dropping the server off at the shop on my way out of town. I think the mother board is fried. The piece of shit blew up on me when I booted up this morning. I'll have them call you when it's ready."

Declan's adrenaline level spiked and his voice shook. "Cut the bullshit, 'dude.' How stupid do you think I am? The only time I remember you calling me Decs was back at Princeton, when you wanted something."

Declan's stomach cramped, and he swallowed the sour taste in his mouth. "Yeah, 'buddy,' something like writing a term paper, borrowing my car or loaning you twenty bucks." He lowered his head and inhaled as deeply as he could, measuring his words. "I'm asking you one more time. What the hell is going on?"

Tom flung his arms wide, palms out. "Jesus, Declan. I'm sorry. All I'm asking for is some time off for my family. My dad's a mess. He could hardly talk on the phone."

Leaning across Tom's desk, Declan pressed the knuckles of both fists hard against the wood. Tom not only looked like a bum, he smelled like one. "You're lying."

Declan straightened and gestured around the room. "Your sports prints are gone, and so is your swimsuit calendar." Striding over to the wheeled coffee cart, Declan hoisted his chipped Red Sox cup. "Sure you don't want to take my mug? You've taken everything else of mine."

Tom rocked back on his heels and pursed his lips. He slid his phone out of his pocket and glanced briefly at the screen. "That's my second reminder. It's getting late. I'd better hustle if I want to make my flight."

Declan slammed his mug down on the cart. The ceramic cup shattered against the hardwood surface. "Screw your flight, asshole. You're not going anywhere."

Blood pulsed in his face and spots floated in his vision. He leaned heavily against the cart and swallowed. "We're going to sit down, and you're going to tell me the truth."

"Declan, seriously. Calm down or you're going to stroke out." Tom raised a hand to his neck, blinking rapidly.

Declan licked his lips. He needed a drink of water. The jerk actually looked cowed, but it didn't last long.

Tom blew out a breath and shifted his stance. He stepped away from his desk, wheeling the carry-on ahead of him. "I'm going to need you here to handle the day-to-day operations. We need to hire a part-time administrative assistant. Check with the temp agency in town first, and then go wider if you have to."

He tilted his head. "Which brings us back to you. How was your meeting with Spencer's granddaughter?"

Unbelievable. The bastard was doubling down. Declan straightened, looking Tom square in his lying face. "Her name is Miranda, and we're not talking about her. We're talking about you and—"

Tom's small eyes widened. He folded his arms and snorted. "Sonofabitch. You're falling for your hot, little running buddy, aren't you?"

Declan fisted his hands and opened his mouth to object, but Tom held up a finger, his arrogant attitude fixed back in place. "Making friends with your competition is not a good idea. We'll talk more when I get back."

He glanced at his watch again and grasped the handle of his carry-on. "Shit, I really have to go." Reaching in his pocket, he pulled out a ring of keys. "I won't need these until I get back. The key to our safe deposit box is on there. Any files you might need are in Heidi's desk. I got through most of the mail last night."

Declan lifted the receiver off the phone on his desk. He'd had enough. His stomach burned like hell. He closed his eyes and thought he might puke. "I'm calling the sheriff."

"Dammit, Declan. We're friends. I offered you this partnership, an excellent opportunity by the way, and this is how you thank me? I've got a flight to catch. My mom's in the hospital and--"

Tom broke off in mid-sentence. Outside, there was the sound of an engine. Tires crunched on gravel. Rushing to the window, he yanked up the blinds. "I can't see who it is."

A second surge of adrenaline hit Declan. His partner acted as though the FBI was about to raid the place. Declan dragged his hand down his face and struggled to regain some semblance of composure.

Heavy footfalls rang on the porch, followed by a sharp rap on the unlocked door. The sound of boots thudded in the entry. "Nagle? You in there?"

"We're in the office, Roger. Come on in."

A tall, lanky man wearing jeans and western boots walked through the open doorway, ducking his head. He did not look happy. He halted when he saw Declan.

His gaze flickered to Tom. "Where're you going?"

Who the hell was Roger? Declan replaced the receiver and crossed his arms. He'd managed to calm down, but the acid churning in his belly burned. Still, he couldn't help speculating how Tom was going to squirm out of this one.

Tom sighed and assumed a solemn expression. "My mom's in the hospital. I was just briefing my partner here, before I take off."

Bastard. Declan forced a smile. Walking over to Roger, he stuck out his hand. "Declan Elliott, Snow Peak's architect."

The man narrowed his eyes, but shook hands, his work-roughened grip firm. "Roger Jensen. I own this house, so I guess what I have to say concerns both of you."

"Rog, I'm sorry. I really have to book." Tom sprang into

motion, the carry-on's wheels rolling over the planked floor.
He lifted the briefcase in his other hand, indicating Declan.
"Declan will write you a check for the full amount." Tom
paused in the doorway, directing his gaze somewhere
between Declan and Roger. "Company checkbook is in
Heidi's desk. Locked middle drawer. I already gave you the
keys."

He flashed a phony grin at Declan. "Thanks, buddy. I
appreciate this. I'll call you from the hospital. Rog, again I
apologize."

Tom disappeared into the hall.

And he was gone. Declan's fifty thousand dollars was
gone, and soon Snow Peak would be gone.

Thank God he hadn't called the sheriff. He needed time to
look into Snow Peak's financials and time to unravel the
legal mess in which Tom had mired him. He'd need to find a
good lawyer.

His mouth tasted rank. Declan walked over to the cooler
and filled a paper cup. Maybe the water would help his stomach. Automatically, he turned to the man standing at the
front desk. "Roger, can I get you some water, a cup of
coffee?"

Roger shook his head with a grim smile. "Just the check
will be fine."

Declan nodded. He sipped the cold liquid and winced.
Not helping. Dizzy and hot, he swallowed hard, certain that
if he told Roger he was going to be sick, Roger would still
insist he write the check first.

Write the check. Get Roger out of the office. Would he
even find the checkbook in Heidi's desk? He had to put Tom
and Snow Peak out of his mind or he'd never get through
this ordeal.

Write the damn check. Hands shaking, Declan unlocked the
drawer. He exhaled and flipped the large spiral book open.

Plenty of checks with the company's logo. As to how much money there was in the account—he couldn't go there right now.

Locating a pen in the center drawer, Declan scrawled the date and Roger's name. Jensen with an e. "How much do we owe you?"

Roger pulled three folded invoices out of his back pocket. He opened and smoothed each one down on the desk in front of Declan, the last slip with the total overdue amount, circled in red.

Holy shit. Declan clenched his jaw and swallowed. Thank God the landlord was standing and couldn't see his face. No way in hell was there enough money in the account to cover three months back rent.

A wave of hopelessness crashed over him.

He rose to his feet, looked Roger in the eye and handed him the check. "On behalf of Snow Peak and my partner, I apologize."

Roger nodded, his shrewd eyes assessing. "Are you all right? You look white as a sheet." He held the narrow piece of paper at arm's length and squinted at the writing. "This check good?"

White hot pain twisted his gut. Declan clamped his lips together to keep from bending over and throwing up. He extended his hand with a shaky smile. "I need to get something to eat is all and yes, I'll personally guarantee the check."

And he would. He might be stupid and naïve, but he was honest. He'd find the money somewhere, even if he had to borrow from his parents.

Roger shook his hand. He folded the payment and stuck it in his wallet. "Then I'll be going." He hesitated and rubbed the back of his neck. "I don't like to talk bad about anyone, but your partner rubs me the wrong way. He talks big, but he can't always look me in the eye. To me, that's a liar, and over the years I've learned not to trust that kind of people."

He clapped Declan on the shoulder. "I was going to tell Tom I was taking him to court, but I'll hold off—at least until his mother's out of the woods. Tell him I want to talk to him as soon as he gets back, will you?"

Declan nodded and somehow managed a smile. "I will. Thank you."

Roger patted his bulging back pocket, where he'd slid his wallet. "Thank you."

Once the sound of the landlord's vehicle faded away, panic consumed him. Roger would be back. Tom would not.

Monday was less than forty-eight hours away. Roger would walk into his bank with that check, and by then it had better be covered. How was he going to scrape up enough money and deposit it by then?

The bathroom was across the room. He'd never make it. Declan grabbed the nearby wastebasket and vomited.

CHAPTER 5

*A*nother giant gust of wind slammed into the car. Miranda tightened her fingers around the wheel. The keys Declan had pressed into her palm at the bookstore yesterday scorched a hole in her coat pocket, not to mention her memory.

She'd picked up Aunt Cora right after breakfast. Miranda couldn't wait to get this over with. They'd check off the schoolhouse today, she'd return the keys and finish the grant. No more distracting phone calls or business meetings.

Miranda glanced over at Aunt Cora, who stared out the window. With the gloved fingers of her right hand, she fiddled beneath the wool scarf around her neck. Her depressing silence matched the sullen gray sky.

A cold front had moved in last night, bringing high winds and rain, which would possibly turn to snow in the evening.

When Aunt Cora had gotten into the car, she'd broached the subject of picking a nicer day, but the woman had sagged back in her seat and closed her eyes. "Just drive."

She hadn't said a word since, which was not like Cora. Usually, she positively glowed with energy and could always be counted on to generate a constant stream of conversation. Everyone was entitled to have a bad day. Miranda had suffered her share of them the past year, but this behavior was just plain weird.

Miranda banked the car around a curve. Stealing another quick look at the older woman, she plastered an optimistic smile on her face. "Not the greatest weather for trudging around in the mud looking at an abandoned schoolhouse. I was thinking we could stop at Pearl's for lunch after. My treat."

Cora sighed heavily, reached over and patted Miranda's arm. "Honey, it sounds nice, but I didn't sleep at all last night. The damn wind was banging that loose shutter against the house. I'm afraid I wouldn't be much company. I'm tired, cranky, and I need a nap."

So much for lifting the mood. Miranda swallowed her irritation. If Aunt Cora was that frickin' tired, she should've stayed home. They both should've stayed home.

A fine drizzle coated the windshield. Miranda turned on the wipers. At least it wasn't icy. Yet. Okay, since Cora didn't want to talk, she'd listen to some cheerful music.

She activated her playlist, tempted to blast some heavy metal. That would stir the shit. Instead, she relieved the dense silence with a lilting selection from her favorite Irish CD.

Much better. She rhythmically tapped her fingers on the wheel, relaxing her tense shoulders.

Declan was an Irish name. With his dark hair and blue eyes, Declan fit the profile.

Miranda pictured him standing in the middle of an emerald green field, clad in a cloak and belted tunic, arms folded, legs spread, surveying his kingdom as leader of his clan. Her fantasy sharpened. Irish chieftains had beards and long hair.

He'd look hot. Long hair would make his eyes look bluer, but his dimples would be lost under his thick beard.

The scrape of the wipers on the windshield and strains of a melancholy oboe interrupted her musing.

Aunt Cora's head tipped forward, eyes closed. Miranda's heart softened. Poor thing. This project was wearing her out.

The large white sign advertising *Snow Peak Properties* suddenly emerged out of the mist. Miranda hung a quick left, bouncing down a rutted dirt road leading to the site where the schoolhouse stood.

Cora lurched forward against her restraint and gripped the overhead handle. "Good grief, Mandy. That's one way to wake me up. What did you just say?"

Miranda gritted her teeth, intent on avoiding the deep potholes in her path. "This road sucks. I was reading their sign. 'Snow Peak Properties, A Slice of the Rockies at Affordable Prices.' What a load of bull."

Cora licked her lips, peering out her window. "I must have dozed off. Give me a minute to get my bearings."

The building sat in the midst of several orange-taped stakes. A rusted-out mobile home squatted nearby. Miranda parked next to the trailer and cut the engine. The music stopped. Outside, the wind howled, whipping anything that wasn't nailed down in its wake.

Pulling her hood up, she looked over at her silent passenger. "Are you going to be warm enough?"

Cora tugged a knitted cap down over her ears. She fixed her long braid beneath the muffler and turned up the collar of her quilted jacket. "Let's get this over with. It's not going to get any warmer by waiting."

Clutching her hood, Miranda ducked her head and followed Cora over the rocky ground.

The older woman walked erect, impervious to the icy

wind whipping her long skirt. She gripped the camping
lantern she'd insisted on bringing with her.

Miranda surveyed the ring of granite peaks, the wide
expanse of open meadow merging with the dense cover of
spruce blanketing the side of the mountain. She shuddered at
the idea of this magnificent piece of land disappearing
beneath earth-gouging bulldozers, and being transformed
into a paved Mecca, attracting more cars, more tourists and
more shops peddling tacky souvenirs.

It was hard to connect Declan with this development,
especially after talking to him yesterday. If his partner's text
hadn't interrupted their conversation, maybe Declan
would've told her "the long story" about his relationship with
Tom Nagle.

Cora halted. Miranda nearly ran into her. The older
woman dropped the lantern and raised her gloved hands to
her mouth. She stalked over to a fallen tree, neatly sawed in
sections. "Son of a bitch. They chopped down our tree. Take
a picture of that."

Miranda obliged. Slipping her phone back inside her
pocket, she snagged the abandoned lamp, jogging to
catch up.

Passing more "No Trespassing" signs like those along the
road, she grinned. "Hey, Aunt Cora!" She pitched her voice
above the wind. "Someone used the signs for target practice
and shot them full of holes. I love it."

Oblivious, Cora marched on.

Up close, the schoolhouse's weathered walls were bare of
paint. The window glass was long gone, replaced with
plywood sheets.

Miranda paused to peel off her glove again and take more
pictures. A sudden burst of freezing wet air whipped her
hood off, stealing her breath.

Shit. Shifting her feet to keep warm she captured several

images from different angles, before plunging her numb hand, along with her phone, back inside her pocket.

She sprinted over to Cora, who stood at the base of the uneven steps, and passed her the lantern. "Take this thing. It's heavy and I'm tired of keeping track of it."

"I wondered where I'd left it". Cora climbed the steps. "You have the keys?"

"Yes, of course." Stung at the older woman's dismissive tone, Miranda stepped in front of her and grasped the rusted padlock.

At first the warped door refused to budge. Finally, using their combined weight, Miranda and Cora were able to shove open the door wide enough to squeeze inside.

"Let's hope we can get it closed again." Miranda switched on the LED flashlight she'd brought from her car.

The gloomy interior smelled musty. At least it was dry. Miranda directed a narrow beam around the small, outer room and sneezed. Trailing Cora into what had once been the classroom, she sneezed again.

She set her flashlight down on a waist-high stack of old newspapers. Retrieving her phone, she scrolled through the photos she'd taken. "I don't know, Aunt Cora. The exterior of the building looks in pretty bad shape. Lifting this off its foundation to move it terrifies me. What if the whole structure collapses? There could be other issues.

"Forget buying it. Even if Declan could talk his partner into donating the schoolhouse, I don't see how we can come up with enough funds to cover a complete restoration."

Cora didn't comment. It was as though Miranda wasn't there. The woman loosened her scarf, running her fingers along the filigreed chain around her neck.

Miranda was done with diplomacy. "Aunt Cora, are you okay? I don't mean to be so pessimistic. I want to save the schoolhouse and see it restored as much as you do." She gazed into the older woman's face. "We can apply for more grants. There are foundations."

Cora switched on the lantern and a swinging arc of light flashed around the room. "Let's shine more light in here and see what we've got."

Miranda trained her flashlight in Cora's wake. Instead of desks and bookshelves, rusty shovels and rakes were propped against a precariously leaning tower of boxes. Boards and shingles littered the silt-covered floor.

In spite of what she'd just said to Cora, facts were facts. The schoolhouse was in ruins, and the historical society had only so much money. Maybe that's what Aunt Cora had already determined. That would explain her strange, depressing behavior.

There was one other solution, one Miranda had already considered, but hoped to avoid. It involved swallowing her pride and asking. After all, she argued with herself, it was on behalf of Spencer.

"The situation isn't hopeless." Even to herself, the tone of her voice lacked conviction. "Besides the grants, there's always Grandpa."

She sighed and lowered her gaze to the tops of her boots.

There was no love lost between Cora Fleming and Jakob Spencer. Miranda and Nikki had never been able to unearth that mystery.

Cora set the lantern atop a nearby crate and brushed off the shoulders and sleeves of her coat. She clicked her tongue. "What a damned shame this is. Your grandpa and I spent a lot of hours in this place."

Miranda didn't know what she'd expected. At least Cora was talking, which was an improvement. "Really?"

Illuminated by the beam of her flashlight, Miranda examined the chipped and pitted surface of the blackboard, imagining how it must have looked over sixty years ago.

She tried to picture Aunt Cora and Grandpa as young, wide-eyed students. "What was Grandpa like?"

Cora snorted and moved to stand next to Miranda. "He was a green-eyed, tow-headed devil, always leading with his chin. Jakob Spencer spent more time on the stool in the corner than Murphy Webster and I put together. Getting his knuckles smacked with a ruler didn't faze your grandfather one bit.

"We used to butt heads even back then." Cora planted her hands on her hips and shook her head. "Your Great Aunt Naomi and I used to play jacks at recess. She was his sister, yet she was as good-natured as Jakob was aggravating."

Once again, Cora stole her hand to the necklace at her throat and curved her lips in a secret smile. The pensive expression on her face reflected something closer to her heart than girlish friendship.

Miranda recalled the framed portrait of David Spencer in Jakob's office. David was Grandpa's younger brother, and had died years ago. That was all she and Nikki had been told.

Once, as curious teens, she asked Grandpa what had happened. He'd gotten tears in his eyes and looked so sad neither of them had mentioned his brother again. David Spencer became the mysterious, handsome hero they'd woven romantic stories about.

Cora's wistful look connected the link in Miranda's mind. If Aunt Cora had gone to school with Grandpa and Great Aunt Naomi, she had to have known David too.

In the yellow light of the lantern, Miranda caught a fleeting glimpse of a tall, slim girl with long russet braids and large, liquid brown eyes.

Miranda had a hunch Cora had known David Spencer quite well.

"We were one of the last classes to graduate from here before the new high school was built." Cora flashed Miranda an appreciative smile. "I can't tell you how grateful I am that you've taken an interest in defending Spencer's history. I couldn't pass the torch on to anyone better. It sure eases my mind." The older woman heaved a sigh. "I just don't have the same energy as I once did."

"That's why you insisted that Declan meet with me instead of you."

She smiled and patted Miranda's arm. "Yup. So, tell me. What are you thinking?"

Miranda targeted the beam of her flashlight around the perimeter of the room. "I'm going to take more photos. Hopefully, our lights and the flash on my phone will be enough. Now that we've actually seen the building's dismal condition, the price they're asking is a joke."

Cora rubbed her chin. "Funny, I figured Mr. Elliot to be the more reasonable man in the partnership."

"He is." Miranda took a picture of the plywood sheet covering the nearest window. "I could tell he thought the asking price was as ridiculous as I did. He actually apologized and offered to negotiate. He has to talk to his partner first."

She took photos of the walls, the floor, the ceiling and the piles of junk. "As soon as I hear back from him, I'll present a report to the committee."

Cora nodded. "Sounds good."

Miranda scuffed the toe of her boot in the dust and the words spilled out of her. "Like I told you on the phone, I know communicating with all parties involved is part of my job description, but we need to find someone else, especially regarding Declan and *Snow Peak*."

"And why is that?"

"Because, he has undue influence on me."

Cora snorted. "Undue influence? What do you mean, Mandy?"

Miranda crossed her arms and expelled an exasperated breath. "Look. I'd have no problem taking on Tom Nagle. He's a turd, but Declan is nice." She threw her arms up in the air. "I find myself attracted to him, and it's too soon after Scott. I don't need another hopeless relationship with a man right now."

She chewed on her lip. "Who on the committee would be good? Ask Denise. No, not a woman. Ask Gary. Yes, Gary would be perfect. Nobody could charm Gary."

Cora's soft chuckle exploded into a cascade of delighted laughter. "Well, you're right about Gary."

Miranda's mood lightened. Aunt Cora was acting more like herself. "What's so funny?"

"Your remark about Gary was priceless, and I've never seen you let the lid slip off." In the circle of light cast by the lantern, Cora's features wore a tender expression.

Miranda smoothed the loose strands of hair at her temple. "What's that mean?"

"Since that first day you and Nikki walked into my shop looking for the perfect Halloween costumes, you've always been the quiet one. Miss Cool, Calm and Collected. Nothing like Nikki or your mother."

Cora cupped Miranda's cheek. "I'm excited for you, honey. You're finally stepping out and living your own life. I'm no fancy wellness coach, as you call it, but I've lived on this earth a few years. Your life might be terrifying for you right now, but moving on and making a fresh start is a good thing."

Miranda covered the woman's hand with her own and closed her eyes. Aunt Cora had always been there for her. "Terrifying doesn't begin to cover it," she whispered, a hitch in her breath. "Every time I've tried to live my own life, I've been crushed under someone's boot heel.

"When I took the position you offered me, I didn't expect

to become so invested in what happens to Spencer, and especially not this one-room schoolhouse. Yet, here I am." She laughed. "My wellness coach said I have a compulsive need to rescue the lost." Miranda's mind drifted to Nikki.

Her cousin was now beyond rescuing.

"If Nicole is who you're thinking about, you already know how I feel."

Cora trained wise brown eyes on Miranda. "As much as I still love that girl and feel for Matt and those two little boys, it's time you build a life of your own and let Matthew build his."

Cora gently chucked Miranda under the chin. "The way I see it, you stand at a fork in the road and your road-less-traveled leads to Mr. Elliot."

Heat flooded Miranda's face. She folded her arms and narrowed her eyes at the older woman. "How well do you know Declan?"

Cora shrugged and toyed with the delicate chain around her neck. "Not well at all, but my instincts about people are pretty reliable."

"Declan has offered to consult with us if the schoolhouse has to be dismantled and reconstructed." At the prospect, another crushing wave of doubt enveloped her. "This project is going to cost a lot more than we expected. Grandpa may consider this a bad investment. He could say no."

Wind rattled the plywood nailed over the missing windows, and an eerie moan echoed through the building, amplifying the deep shadows lurking in the corners.

Cora slipped a comforting arm around Miranda's shoulders. "Don't second guess yourself, girl. Declan didn't say it was a hopeless cause, did he? If we have to take this place apart board by board and rebuild it again, then by God, we'll do it. "The windows may be gone and the paint worn off, but this old schoolhouse is solid and was built to last."

She pulled Miranda close in a quick hug. "Where's that tough determination and can-do attitude of yours? Let's take this project one step at a time and wait to hear back from Mr. Elliot before jumping ahead to the next step. Shall we?" Releasing her, Cora grabbed the lantern off the crate. A wild bright arc flashed around the room. "I'm feeling better. Is lunch at Pearl's still on the table?

Encouraged by Aunt Cora's enthusiasm, Miranda squeezed out of the building after the woman and together they managed to shove the door closed and secure the corroded padlock.

Miranda fell into step beside Cora as they trudged back to the car against an icy headwind. Over hot coffee and burgers at the diner, she'd remind Cora about talking to Gary.

Mentally, she ticked off her list of to-dos by the end of the week: breakfast with Grandpa, finishing the grant, and returning the keys to Declan—in that order.

Recalling the firm pressure of Declan's warm fingers when he'd given her the keys at the bookstore, her pulse quickened.

What if she handed them back to him in the same manner? She bit down on her lip, and her face flamed in spite of the biting cold.

CHAPTER 6

*T*he sprawling white walls and red roof of the Aspen Gold Lodge dominated the mountain slope. Its structure was scarcely harmonious with the surrounding environment, yet Miranda's heart swelled with pride. The lodge and much of the town nestled in the valley below was Jakob Spencer's legacy.

Miranda would always be a Spencer. The family's heritage was in her blood, even though she'd married and had spent the last fourteen years thousands of miles away from Colorado and Grandpa's loving, iron-fisted control.

Although private access to the lodge was provided for the family and deliveries, she'd always preferred entering the hotel through the front entrance to soak up the nostalgic ambiance of the spacious lobby, with its crystal chandeliers and polished grand piano.

The security officer activated the scrolled gate to open and waved her through.

Security was Grandpa's top priority. The lodge was a popular retreat for wealthy, high profile personalities. They brought their families here and vacationed in privacy.

She pulled beneath the portico. A young man, clad in a navy blue polo shirt and khaki slacks, approached her car. "Good morning. Welcome to the Aspen Gold."

Miranda smiled. "Thanks."

Climbing into her white CR-V, he drove off, leaving her standing on the pavement below the wide veranda. Her stomach rumbled. She'd barely managed to choke down a banana after her morning run.

Miranda checked her phone as she mounted the steps and strode through the double doors into the brightly lit lobby. Three minutes early. Grandpa was a stickler about punctuality.

Crossing the gleaming wood floor, she took the wide elaborate staircase leading to her grandfather's office on the mezzanine. She paused at the top and took a couple of deep breaths.

It had been almost a month since she'd moved back to Spencer. Putting off this visit certainly hadn't made it any easier. She wanted to assure Grandpa that despite her divorce from Scott, she was capable of taking care of herself.

Photos of Jakob with past presidents and celebrities hung on the walls. Andi's office was still in the same place. Jakob's longtime secretary rose from her desk with a broad smile and embraced her.

"Mandy. It's so good to have you back." Andi's dark eyes brimmed with compassion. "We all miss Nikki, but it must be doubly hard for you. The two of you were inseparable."

A lump rose in her throat and Miranda nodded.

The woman gently grasped Miranda's arm. "Well, let's not keep Jakob waiting. He's been on pins and needles all morning."

Andi rapped on the intricately carved door and ushered Miranda into the room. "Mr. Spencer, your granddaughter is here."

Solid green paint above wood-paneled wainscoting had replaced the wallpaper she remembered. The heavy drapes were gone. Immense windows framed a breathtaking panorama of the lodge's artfully landscaped grounds, highlighted by Twin Owl Lake and groves of spruce, pine and aspen. A roaring fire crackled in the river-rock fireplace.

"There she is." Jakob Spencer walked toward her, arms outstretched.

Miranda's heart lifted. His wide smile and the warmth in his familiar deep voice was all the welcome she needed.

"Grandpa." She rushed to greet her silver-haired grandfather. He looked as dynamic as ever in his blue wool jacket and gray slacks.

Hugging him tightly, she closed her eyes, inhaling the long-remembered scent of spicy cologne and cigars. He'd always been there for her and he always would be. "I've missed you."

Max, her grandfather's large, energetic Borzoi squirmed between them, whining and licking her hand.

"Sit, dog." Max immediately responded and Jakob slipped the canine a treat from his pocket.

A robust chuckle rumbled from Jakob's chest and he stroked her cheek. "Well, it's about damn time, Mandy girl. I'm not getting any younger." Grinning, he looked her over. "But you're sure getting prettier."

Grandpa still sported a full head of white hair that was impeccably trimmed. Though his craggy features were deeply lined, his green eyes, the hallmark of the Spencer family, were as bright and shrewd as ever. "Just because I haven't seen you since you've moved back to Spencer doesn't mean I don't know what you've been up to." His mild tone belied his piercing stare.

Nikki had likened Grandpa's look to an alien mind probe,

sweeping over the terrain of their brains to ferret out their secrets.

Miranda sank into the nearest burgundy wingback chair and sighed. "That's exactly why I've put off seeing you."

She clenched her hands in her lap. "Why do you still have to be so overprotective?" She shook her head. "I'm an adult now. I just wish you'd trust me and give me some space."

Jakob sat down heavily in the vacant chair next to hers, absently rubbing his arm. "I saw you on television at the public hearing." He chuckled and grinned at her. "Cora and the historical society are damn lucky to have you working on their side."

Grandpa employed his customary diversion tactic to ignore her attempt at honesty. She couldn't help flushing with pleasure at his compliment. Squaring her shoulders, she said, "I'm sure you already know this, but my divorce is final. All my bills are paid and I've rented a small house in town."

She stared out the window at the grove of aspen. Soon they'd turn and their delicate gold leaves would shimmer in the sunlight.

Struggling to contain her conflicting emotions, Miranda stared down at the massive bear skin at her feet. The rug was another reminder wedged among her childhood recollections.

She and Nikki had named the rug Edgar. Miranda could still hear her cousin's conspiratorial whisper.

After midnight, Edgar comes alive and roams the upper halls of the Aspen Gold Lodge.

Jakob's voice, the gruff gentleness in his tone and the firm pressure of his hand patting her leg startled Miranda back to the present.

"I'm sorry, Mandy. I've been told I can be a hard-headed meddling old fool."

He smiled, but his green eyes clouded with emotion.

She studied Jakob's bushy white brows and the aristocratic bridge of his nose. This was her Grandpa, the man who'd cuddled and loved her from her earliest memories.

Her fondest recollections were his reassuring hugs, the time spent with her and Nikki, teaching them both to drive a stick shift in his ancient Range Rover. That was the soft, tender side of Jakob Spencer that she treasured. Miranda reached for his hand. Blinking rapidly, she swallowed before she spoke. "I came home to be with you. To be with my family."

"You've always been my courageous one, Mandy girl." He shook his head sadly. "Always loving and dependable, so unlike your mother."

He thumped the arms of his chair. "You've been more of a mother to Heath and Hunter than she ever was."

The room was silent, save the ticking of the rosewood clock, still stationed on the mantel.

Deirdre and Grandpa were like oil and water. Her twin brothers had what could only be termed as a jaundiced relationship with their grandfather.

Miranda had always been close to Jakob, but Hunter still refused to even talk about Grandpa, while Heath swore that the old man had always favored Miranda and Nikki over the boys.

A soft rap on the door interrupted the silence. Miranda immediately recognized the petite, attractive woman, dressed in a long, multicolored skirt. She wheeled a linen-draped cart laden with covered dishes over the threshold. Salivating smells of fresh brewed coffee and bacon accompanied her appearance.

Miranda scrambled to her feet. "Willa."

Willa Samuels smiled. Crossing the room, she gave Miranda a quick hug, enveloping her in a fragrant cloud of vanilla and lavender. "I didn't mean to interrupt the two of you, but breakfast is ready."

Several rings adorned the older woman's slender, slightly gnarled fingers, but Miranda didn't spot a wedding ring.

Deirdre still insisted that Jakob and Willa were secretly married, in spite of Great-Aunt Olivia's trust.

Miranda disagreed. Grandpa could be stubborn, critical and dictatorial, but secretive he was not. However, it was impossible to miss the affectionate glance that Grandpa shot Willa along with her blushing response.

"I hope the two of you don't mind, but I thought we'd have breakfast here." Willa included Miranda in her statement, but the woman's soft violet gaze remained fixed on Grandpa.

He grinned. "Fine with me. Mandy, do you remember those old metal TV trays you and Nikki used to play office with when you girls were little? Well, they're still around, and now Willa and I use them."

He approached the cart, where Willa was busy uncovering plates. "Here, sweetheart, let me help you."

Willa shot a pointed glance at Max, who responded by lifting his head from his front paws and licking his chops. "You can help by putting Max in his crate. Otherwise, he'll be begging from poor Miranda."

Jakob snapped his fingers and dug into the pocket of his trousers with his other hand. "Max. Come."

The hound dutifully trailed his master out of the room.

Miranda set up three trays along with the napkins and silverware Willa handed her.

After he'd returned and taken his seat, Willa set a plate of poached eggs on toast, asparagus and two sausage links on Jakob's tray. "Coffee, Miranda?"

"Yes please." Miranda joined Willa at the cart and

accepted a steaming china cup. "This smells heavenly. Thanks."

She sipped her coffee and observed another tender glance between the couple as Willa poured for Jakob. They might not be married, but the two of them were obviously in love.

Jakob caught Willa's free hand and tugged her closer. "Mandy, this woman brings out the best in me."

A fleeting expression of alarm crossed Willa's features. She slipped out of Jakob's grasp and turned to inspect the covered dishes. "Hush. Drink your coffee before it gets cold."

Grandpa winked at Miranda and dutifully raised his cup.

He'd never shown such affection with Grandmother Marguerite. She'd never forget the time Grandmother had slapped Grandpa's face and called him, "a cheating, hard-hearted bastard."

She and Nikki had been in this office, playing Old Maid. Grandpa's face had gone pale, except for the red mark where Grandmother had hit him. A muscle had twitched in his jaw, and his green eyes had looked dangerous. She and Nikki had burst into tears.

Grabbing Grandmother by the arm, he'd steered her across the room and out the door, slamming it behind her.

Grandpa had immediately knelt, gathering both Miranda and Nikki into his embrace. "Sometimes adults say things that aren't meant for little girls to hear."

He'd gently pinched her cheek, then Nikki's. "Tell you what. Let's walk down to the barn and give the horses a carrot or two, and then we'll have ourselves some ice cream."

"Mandy, are you going to drink that coffee or stand there holding it?"

Miranda blinked. Both Grandpa and Willa were looking at her with puzzled expressions.

She smiled. "Sorry, I was just thinking about the grant I'm working on."

Willa warmly returned the smile and picked up a plate. "Let's eat before everything gets cold. Mandy, you first, please."

Miranda served herself eggs, bacon, toast and fresh fruit. She sat across from Jakob and glanced at his breakfast. "Grandpa, are you on a diet? You used to eat twice that much."

Jakob patted his stomach and chuckled. "I wouldn't call it a diet. I'm eating healthy."

"So, Mandy, have you gotten settled in?" Willa sat down on the leather sofa against the wall.

"I've finished unpacking what I brought." Miranda dabbed her mouth with her napkin. "The rest is in storage back in Wisconsin."

Grandpa scowled at her from beneath his craggy brows, his fork poised in midair. "What's that mean?"

"I'm sure you already know that I've taken a year's leave from the university."

Laying his fork on his plate, the older man absently wiped his mouth with his napkin. "Yes, yes, but why leave anything behind?" He leaned forward, his half-eaten breakfast forgotten.

Miranda sighed. "Grandpa, technically, I'm still tenured and on staff. I took some time to decide what I want to do now that I'm single again."

Jakob half rose from his chair, bumping the tray askew. He jabbed his index finger at her, his color high. "Now see here, Miranda, I've already lost one of my girls. I don't aim to lose both of you."

Miranda stared over at Edgar, lying in front of the fireplace. Unshed tears stung her eyes as she recalled all the times she and Nikki had played here as kids. Her grief, guilt and Grandpa's expectations threatened to crush her hopes for a fresh start. She lifted her chin, swiping at the tear tracking down her cheek.

"Grandpa, I'm sorry. I'm sorry Nikki is dead. I'm sorry that —" she bit back her confession, blurting her seething emotions at the older man, "I can't live my life for you, or for anybody else."

Rubbing his arm, Jakob sank back in his chair, looking every one of his seventy-plus years.

Willa's posture was rigid, her anxious gaze focused on him.

Miranda fisted her hands, nails digging into her palms. "I'm sorry, Grandpa. Nikki's death was horrible. I'm furious with her for selfishly taking her life without thinking about anyone else. She left behind a good man who loved her and two precious little boys, who need their mother."

Edgar's glassy black eyes mirrored the flickering glow of the fire. Miranda recalled Saturday's run-in with Lauren at the bookstore.

She sighed and gave Willa and her grandfather a helpless shrug. "Sorry, I didn't mean to rant like that. How's Matt doing? I haven't been to see him or the boys."

Jakob cleared his throat and extracted a cigar from his breast pocket. "Matt's keeping his head above water. His folks have been helping out with the boys." Jakob shook his head. "That Zach is high-strung, a lot like his mother."

Miranda closed her eyes and rubbed her temples. She needed to call Matt this week, along with finishing the grant and returning the keys to Declan.

"Grandpa, I need to talk to you about Standing Bear Casino. I'm sure you already know this too, but the historical society wants the old schoolhouse that's sitting on the construction site. We want to move it into Olde Town and restore it. I met with one of Snow Peak's partners yesterday."

Declan's dimpled grin came to mind. Heat blazed a trail

from her chest and flooded her face. She forked scrambled eggs into her mouth and studiously spread jam on a corner of her toast. "They've offered to sell us the schoolhouse."

Jakob rolled the cigar beneath his nose. "I'm not surprised. I've heard they've been having cash flow problems. Their creditors want to be paid. What's their asking price?"

"Ten-thousand, which we won't even consider and there's been no appraisal yet. Aunt Cora and I went out and looked at the building. The entire project is going to cost more than we estimated. I'm hoping to get most of the labor and materials donated."

Jakob laid the cigar next to the half-eaten breakfast on his plate and moved the tray aside. He leaned forward, resting his hands on his thighs. "Forget the appraisal for now. Keep working on the donations, but I don't think you need to worry too much. I've done some digging into Snow Peak Properties, Tom Nagle in particular. They're behind on tests and permits." His candid green eyes met hers. "I hate to say this, but bringing on Mr. Elliot as an investing partner was about as effective as putting a bandage on a hemorrhage."

Jakob sighed and tightened his lips. "Elliot's background checks out, but based on Nagle's past history, I'm afraid he's in for a rude awakening."

So the rumors were true. Miranda swallowed her lukewarm coffee to wash down the toast stuck in her throat. All she could think about was Declan's gentle concern after Lauren had blindsided her, and she recalled his offer to negotiate a fair price for the schoolhouse.

Willa quietly rose and collected their plates. She refilled their cups before sitting down with a copy of the *Herald*.

Jakob clipped off the end of his cigar. "I figure I'll wait for the company to go belly up, and then I'll get the property at a good price." He slipped the cutter back in its place. "I'm looking at putting up some nice affordable cabins for young families." He shot Miranda a charitable smile. "Your architect's going to need a job and I'd like to see what he can come up with."

Miranda rolled her eyes. "Grandpa, he's not *my* architect."

Standing, Jakob shot her a teasing grin. "Sure he is. Now you can try to tell me it's strictly business, but your pretty little face pinks up every time we talk about him. Isn't that right, sweetheart?"

Willa folded her arms. "Honestly, Jakob, you can be quite merciless at times." She turned to Miranda. "Isn't that right, Mandy?"

Miranda met the woman's sparkling violet eyes and gave her a thumb's up. Grandpa had finally met his match.

Jakob shrugged. Plucking up the cigar, he stuck it in his mouth. "Time for me and Max to go for a walk."

"Grandpa, I need to update Aunt Cora on what you've just told me. We'll apply for the grant I've been working on, along with an application to the David Spencer Memorial Foundation, but I'd like to tell her on the quiet that you'll be willing to eventually donate the schoolhouse to the historical society."

He slipped the cigar out of his mouth and arched his bushy gray brows. "How's the old girl doing?"

Miranda snorted. "Like you don't know?"

Jakob frowned. "I'd like to talk to her myself. Our little feud's lasted long enough. I want to rent our costumes and personally invite her to my Halloween ball." He grinned and slanted a glance at Willa, who was absorbed in the newspaper. "Cora's probably going to tell me to go to hell, but I'm going to ask her anyway."

He winked and gently pinched Miranda on the cheek. "You'll get your schoolhouse, Mandy, and I've got a hunch down the road you'll get your architect."

Grandpa exited with a hearty laugh, leaving a faint whiff of tobacco and spicy fragrance in his wake.

Miranda thoughtfully sipped her coffee. She was relieved that the schoolhouse project would move forward, but Grandpa's lighthearted prediction was unsettling.

CHAPTER 7

*T*uesday dawned, the air crisp, the autumn foliage a riot of russet, orange and gold. Miranda submitted the grant online and planned to work on the Spencer Foundation application tomorrow. Tonight, she'd celebrate with a nice long run around the lake and a juicy steak dinner at the Wild Card.

No obsessing about Standing Bear Casino or other things in her life she had no control over. Enlisting Grandpa's support was a small victory in itself. She and Aunt Cora had rescued the one-room schoolhouse after all.

The project would take time and a lot of work, but someday the dilapidated building would stand in Olde Town, wearing a fresh coat of white paint, and be an enduring tribute to education and Spencer's history.

Thoughts of Declan had plagued her all weekend. She should return the keys the hot architect had given her ASAP and move on. She'd envisioned several unnerving scenarios, beginning with professional, advancing to platonic and rapidly accelerating to sexual.

Miranda tightly knotted the laces of her running shoes.

She'd hand Declan the keys, safely enclosed in an envelope to prevent any more skin-to-skin contact than necessary and inform him that he'd be working with a different committee member from now on.

But not today. Today was hers to celebrate.

She left the house heading toward the lake at a brisk walk. Declan needed to know what Grandpa had found out about Tom Nagle. Telling him was only fair, but she hated to be the one to deliver the news. Doubtless he'd despise her afterward, but maybe that was best.

Jumping into another emotional entanglement so soon after Scott would be insane. She'd watched her own mother repeatedly trade one man out for another over the years, a detestable habit Deirdre excelled at and one Miranda swore she'd never adopt.

She was supposed to be celebrating today, dammit. Miranda sucked a deep breath and broke into a ground-eating jog. The last thing she wanted to think about was Deirdre and her endless string of boy toys.

After her run, Miranda lathered up with her favorite lemon soap and stood under the shower until the hot water gave out. She donned a comfortable pair of soft, denim jeans and her new teal sweater.

Fifteen minutes later, she walked through the doors into the Wild Card. A healthy mix of tourists and locals packed the vestibule, clutching black pagers with glowing lights. A table would take forever.

Spotting one lone seat down at the far end of the bar, Miranda threaded her way into the restaurant. The tantalizing aroma of char-broiled meat drifted from the kitchen. Steak, a loaded baked potato and a glass or two of robust red wine sounded perfect.

Her breath stalled in her throat and her stomach dipped. Declan, rugged and handsome in jeans and a faded plaid shirt, sleeves rolled up to the elbows, occupied the adjacent stool.

Miranda bit her lip. Not tonight. She wanted to be up front with Declan about Tom, but not tonight. Tonight was supposed to be her celebration.

Declan shot her a sour look as she approached and raised his glass. "Cheers."

Miranda gripped her wallet tighter and exhaled through pursed lips. Something was wrong, terribly, terribly wrong, but she couldn't turn around and walk away. Well, she could, but she wouldn't. She sat on the stool, a weight settling on her chest.

Declan arched a brow. "News travels fast. Come to gloat?"

His normally open face was tight, his blue eyes dulled by alcohol.

Gloat about what? Grown man or not, the urge to wrap him in her arms was overwhelming.

But it wasn't up to her to comfort Declan. Miranda reached for a laminated menu and slid it toward her. She'd be nice, but keep her distance. She had enough drama in her life without adding his.

Declan drained the amber liquid from his glass. "Forget I said that. I'm lousy company tonight."

Miranda forced an exaggerated sigh. "This is the only available seat, so I guess I'm stuck with you."

Rubbing her temple, she studied the menu, acutely aware of Declan's broad shoulders, his muscled arms and denim-clad thigh inches from hers.

The bartender approached.

"I'll have a glass of Cab and a rib-eye, medium well," she said.

With another disquieting smile Declan pointed two fingers down over his empty glass. "Hit me again, Jimmy."

Jimmy hesitated before replying smoothly. "Let me get the lady's order in. I'll be right back."

Minutes later, the bartender returned with Miranda's wine and a bottle of Irish whiskey. "This is your last drink. Gotta cut you off, dude. Ace's rules."

"Yeah, you gotta do what you gotta do." Declan's voice oozed sarcasm. He tilted precariously in Miranda's direction. "We all gotta do what we gotta do. Isn't that right, Ms. Buffet?"

Reflexively, Miranda stuck her arm out, bracing her hand flat against his warm chest. He was inches away from taking a header and plunging face first into her lap. She caught a pungent whiff of whiskey on his breath, thrusting her back to another time.

More than once she'd helped Deirdre stumble into the bedroom, and struggled to drag her mother as far as the canopied bed and leave her to sleep it off.

Those childhood memories were better left buried.

Righting himself, Declan blinked hard and dragged a hand down his face. Hunching his shoulders, he lowered his head and swigged his drink. "Sorry."

An untouched bowl of popcorn sat on the bar between them. She snagged it and started nibbling, something to do besides gawk. He was a completely different person tonight.

She'd seen firsthand what alcohol did to people, but Declan didn't seem like the type. What had happened?

Miranda thought back to Saturday. Declan had received the text from Tom and had immediately cut their meeting short. *Shit.*

She sipped her wine, not wanting to ask, but asking anyway. "You want to talk about it?"

Declan trailed his index finger around the rim of his glass and sighed heavily. "Nope."

Reaching over, she rubbed his bare forearm. "I'm sorry."

Declan's focus momentarily snapped from his drink to her, his gaze intense. He gulped the whiskey and gritted his teeth. "Not as sorry as I am."

Miranda withdrew her hand, sliding her tingling palm across the bar's cool, wet surface. The heat of his hair-roughened skin seared into her brain. She hadn't been able to help herself.

Her steak arrived. Slicing into the tender cut of beef, she forked a bite into her mouth, savoring the meat's juicy flavor with a tinge of regret. She missed Declan's engaging grin, the way it deepened his dimples…

Her sideways glance connected with his. Heat flamed her face. Miranda shot him an awkward smile and polished off the last of her wine.

On his next pass, the bartender indicated her empty glass. "Want a refill?"

Not even a whole bottle would salvage this evening. As tempted as she was, one glass was more than enough tonight. She needed her wits about her. "I'll have a club soda, please." Miranda inclined her head in Declan's direction. "And whatever my friend would like to eat."

Crossing her arms, she fixed Declan with an obstinate look she was far from feeling. "I hate eating alone, and you need to soak up all that booze with something."

He snorted softly and shook his head. "I'll have what she's eating, except make mine rare." He tossed back his remaining whiskey and snickered. "Add it to my tab."

The man looked from Declan to Miranda, shrugged, and ambled away in the direction of another customer.

Declan rattled the ice in his glass and cleared his throat. "Thanks."

Miranda studied his chiseled profile. Drunk or sober, Declan was too damned appealing. She drew a shallow breath. "For what?"

He sighed and shot her a quick glance. A wry tinge of humor lifted the corner of his mouth. "For looking out for me."

Miranda directed her attention back to her plate. Apparently, looking out for people was her strong point. Wasn't that always what she did best? Nikki came to mind.

Not always.

Her appetite had gone the way of her festive mood. When she got her drink, she'd ask for a box and the check.

She'd let Jimmy and Ace take care of Declan. She was done looking out for people tonight. She'd hang around until he'd eaten, and then she was out of here.

In the meantime, even though Declan had already told her he didn't want to talk, witnessing his misery was wearing on her and she had to know if what she suspected was true.

Miranda shifted closer and took the plunge. "What's going on?"

Declan stiffened. A muscle in his jaw contracted.

His bleak expression sent a shiver of remorse shooting through her. "I'm sorry. It's none of my business."

"Oh, but it is." His jarring laugh contained a bitter edge. "You can report back to your comrades at the historical society that Snow Peak Properties is a total rip-off. There will be no Standing Bear Resort."

He exhaled, gripping the glass so hard his fingertips whitened. "I lost my job, my savings." He shook his head. "I thought he was my friend, but that asshole threw me under the bus."

Tom Nagle. Guilt pricked her conscience. She'd known.

Leaning his elbow on the bar, Declan propped his chin on his unsteady hand and wagged a finger at her. "Don't ever trust anybody."

The bartender brought her soda and slid a sizzling steak

in front of Declan. Nodding at Miranda's request for a box and the check, he left.

Declan stabbed his fork into the steak and fumbled for the serrated knife.

Her throat tightened. She ached to close the gap between them, lay her hand on his arm again and tell him she cared. Instead, she fisted her hand in her lap, sipped her drink and tried not to watch him as he ate.

His fork clattered on his plate. Declan slipped off the stool and swayed. "Where's the restroom?"

"Let me help you." Miranda wrapped both arms around his upper body, absorbing his heat and a trace of his woodsy scent beneath the liquor.

Pulling free, he licked his lips and swallowed, a desperate look crossing his face. "I can walk. Just tell me. Fast."

She edged a few steps toward the back of the restaurant and waved her arm.

Hugging his midriff, Declan staggered a zig-zag course in the direction she'd indicated.

Once he'd disappeared into the alcove where the restrooms were located, Miranda released her pent-up breath and retrieved her debit card from her wallet. She couldn't leave him now.

The wiry, bronzed owner of the Wild Card walked over. "Hey, Ace."

"Everything okay? My bartender said Declan's in the bathroom. Is he a friend of yours?"

Miranda nodded and met the older man's perceptive gaze. "He definitely can't drive. Could someone help me get him out to my car? He can pick up his vehicle tomorrow if that's okay with you."

"Sure. I know Declan. Big Red Sox fan. Comes here to watch the games. He's usually a two-pint guy. I've never known him to get pissed."

"Well, he outdid himself tonight." Her voice faltered.

Ace laid his gnarled hand on her shoulder and gave a little squeeze. "I'll go check on him for you."

Miranda shot him a grateful smile. "Thanks."

Within half an hour, her semi-conscious passenger was securely buckled in the front seat next to her, a plastic trash bag gaping open on his lap.

Miranda navigated the parking lot, teeming with people and moving vehicles. Since Declan was in no condition to tell her where he lived, she'd reluctantly decided to take him to her place. "We'll be at my house in a few minutes. The bag's right there, in case."

Declan slumped forward, clutching his head. "I feel like shit."

"Wait until tomorrow." She silently prayed that he'd hang on until she got him home.

Ace had reported he'd found Declan draped over the men's toilet. "A waste of good whiskey and a great steak," the owner had commented dryly.

Miranda tightened her fingers around the steering wheel and cast another quick look his way. "Declan? Declan, you've got to stay awake."

She punched him lightly on the arm. "I can't haul you out of my car and into the house by myself."

"Ow! God, stop the spinning. I hate the spinning."

"Use the bag. We're almost there."

Please, use the bag.

Declan rubbed his forehead. "Don't worry. There's nothing left."

Minutes later, Miranda turned into her driveway. So far, so good. She pried the empty bag out of his grasp and tossed it onto the back seat.

Declan was curled up against the passenger door, his face pressed up against the glass.

Hopefully, the cold air would wake the man up enough so that she could get him inside. She cautiously opened Declan's door. Releasing his seatbelt, she shook his shoulder. "Declan. Wake up."

He groaned and kept his eyes closed.

Miranda nudged him harder. "Declan, now."

Linking both arms around his chest, she half-dragged him out of the car, adjusting her stance to accommodate his limp body. Her knees buckled, so, clutching his coat, she slowly went down, pulling his dead weight over on top of her.

She lay flattened against the cold hard cement, staring up at the light spilling from the car.

"Declan," she panted. "Please. Get off me. I can't breathe."

Rolling over on his back, he flung his arm over his face. "I can't move."

Gasping, Miranda slowly climbed to her feet and stood over him, hand extended. "Get up now, or so help me, I'll leave you out here all night."

With her assistance, Declan managed to stagger into her house as far as the living room sofa before collapsing.

Miranda hung his sheepskin jacket in the closet. Unlacing his hiking boots, she pulled them off and covered him with the fleece throw from the back of the couch. In the soft glow from the floor lamp, his face appeared untroubled. The wounded expression on his features earlier at the Wild Card had disappeared. Poor guy.

Impulsively, she leaned forward, smoothed back his thick hair and kissed his forehead. He briefly opened his eyes, and the corners of his mouth lifted. "You can be awfully sweet when you want to." He grimaced and turned on his side. "Oh, crap, not again."

She sprinted into the kitchen and grabbed the dishpan. After standing over him for what seemed like an eternity,

Miranda decided Declan was out, at least for the immediate future.

Shivering and suddenly unsteady on her feet, Miranda undressed in her bedroom, pulling on her flannel pjs and fuzzy socks. She wrapped her robe snugly around her and headed back into the living room, where she curled up in the easy chair within leaping distance of the couch, should Declan wake up.

A hot mug of tea would be nice, but walking into the kitchen seemed like too much effort.

She grabbed the crocheted throw draped behind her, tucked it around her feet, and opened the latest suspense novel she'd bought Saturday. After reading the same sentence for the third time, she rested the book in her lap and pondered the sleeping man sprawled on her sofa.

What was it about Declan that drew her in and made her forget all about her new resolutions?

It had been a long day, an even longer night, and she was too tired to try to unravel that mystery. Yawning, she tipped her head back against the firm upholstery and closed her eyes.

Little Jeremy sprawled behind her. He must have had another scary dream and crawled into bed with them.

The flannel sheets created a snug cocoon of warmth against the wintry night. She rolled over and gathered the four-year-old's small body against hers. He squirmed and snuggled close, wrapping his chubby fleece-clad arms around her neck.

Smiling in her sleep, she kissed the top of his head, inhaling the fresh, baby-shampooed scent of his silky hair. She rubbed light, reassuring circles over his back, chasing away his scary dream into the dark netherworld of his childish imagination.

Jeremy was the best thing that Scott had brought into their dried-out marriage. Though she hadn't given birth to him, the

toddler adored her as though she had. He belonged to her. Very
soon, he would be hers legally as well.

The child radiated too much heat. Disengaging herself from his
embrace, she eased over on her opposite side. Patting his small,
knobby knee, she breathed a contented sigh. As long as Jeremy
could reach out and touch her, he'd sleep soundly.

Miranda jolted awake, still curled in her wingback chair.
Declan slept on the sofa. Her contentment evaporated,
replaced with the cold, dimly-lit reality of her living room.

Her book thudded to the floor. Blinking, she licked her
lips, recalling the vivid heat of little Jeremy's body nestled
against hers, the fleecy texture of his blanket sleeper, his baby
soft cheek and the smell of his hair.

Rubbing her eyes with her knuckles, Miranda struggled
to contain her bleak reality. Jeremy was gone. Had he already
forgotten her? What if he was crying for her, wondering why
she'd left him?

Miranda stumbled out of the chair, landing on her hands
and knees, stifling the mournful cry rising in her throat.

Damn you Scott! I hope you rot in hell for what you're doing to
my little boy. My baby.

She lurched down the hall to her bedroom. Clutching a
pillow against her breasts, she surrendered to racking sobs.

She'd survive being tossed aside like a crumpled piece of
trash by Scott and losing her house, but giving up sweet little
Jeremy left a stabbing emptiness in her heart. Picturing the
upheaval and confusion the toddler was experiencing
devoured her from the inside out. Miranda wasn't sure she'd
ever get over losing Jeremy, but legally she had no choice.

CHAPTER 8

*T*he hammering chime of a clock woke him. Declan's head throbbed and his mouth tasted dry as sawdust. He was lying on a narrow sofa beneath a soft blanket.

Rising on his elbow, he located the offensive timepiece on the mantel over the fireplace. He narrowed his focus. Three in the morning? Light pooled from a floor lamp behind a solitary wingback chair. On the carpet in front of the chair lay a colorful knitted throw, reminding him of one his mother had. A paperback book, lying askew not far from the blanket caught his attention.

Furrowing his brow, Declan sat up slowly. His stocking-clad feet kicked an empty dishpan and the throw slid off his shoulders.

Cradling his aching head between his hands, he took a couple of deep breaths. Snatches of memory came flooding back: the arctic wind whipping inside Miranda's car, her urgent drill-sergeant's voice, and her strong, slender arms wrapped around him. There'd been the grating sound of a key, a lock popping open and warm air that smelled like apples.

Miranda had tucked a blanket around him and planted a chaste kiss on his forehead, her lips soft, her beautiful green eyes tender.

Declan smiled, touching the spot with his fingers. Another confusing memory tumbled over and merged with the one before it. His puzzled gaze returned to the chair, the blanket and the book.

It hadn't been a dream after all. He'd heard the book hit the floor, along with a choked sob that could only have been Miranda's, and then the clock had let loose, yanking him awake.

Declan cautiously turned. Leaning against the back of the couch, he knelt on the sofa cushions. The open arch with darkness beyond must lead to Miranda's bedroom.

His outraged stomach clenched. Declan gripped the furniture's nubby fabric and lowered his head until the queasiness passed. He worked his way around the sofa and down the hall, the wood floor creaking underfoot. He stopped short of the bedroom. If she was sleeping, he didn't want to wake her.

The muffled sound of weeping swept that concern aside. A plug-in nightlight revealed her tightly curled form on the bed, her face buried in a pillow she clutched to her chest.

Declan pressed the heels of his hands to his aching head. After the Wild Card, had he said or done something else stupid? He stood, rooted to the floor, flexing and unflexing his fingers. "Miranda?"

Miranda froze. "Declan."

She scrambled upright, pulling her hair back, staring at him, her lips parted.

Her sweet face, ravaged by tears, tugged a profound caring response he'd never experienced before. His misery receded, drowned by hers. Shrugging, he gave her a small smile, and sitting on the edge of the bed, opened his arms. He didn't know what else to do.

Miranda's features crumpled. "Oh, Declan."

She launched herself into his embrace, her startling impact nearly knocking them both off the bed.

Miranda clung to him, her arms locked around his chest. She buried her face in the crook of his neck, her gut-wrenching sobs ringing in his skull. He set his jaw, determined to muscle through his pain to alleviate hers.

Declan jockeyed his position until the two of them lay prone on the mattress. He folded his body protectively around her. "If it's me, I'm sorry about tonight. Shhh."

Pressing his lips against the smooth skin at her temple, he inhaled her flowery scent. He kissed her wet cheeks, tasting the salt of her tears.

He rested his head against hers, stealing comfort in their shared anguish. What was tearing her up inside? He didn't know and he didn't care. Right now, it was enough to be needed.

Eventually, her weeping subsided into weak hiccups. She nestled closer, her breath tickling his ear. "Please stay. I'm afraid the dream might come back."

A dream had caused her sadness. She wanted him to stay. Declan nuzzled her collarbone, so tempted to explore further, grateful for her multi-layers of clothing and his own alcohol-induced limitations. Better to save her petal-soft skin and the alluring curves of her slender body buried beneath her fluffy robe for another time.

After everything with Tom, did he even want to get involved with Miranda right now? He couldn't afford to make another mistake.

Yet, she fascinated him. In spite of their differences she'd rescued him twice now. Hadn't Dad taught him to judge people by their actions, not their words?

Her respiration had evened out. Declan caressed her cheek with his thumb. He knew hardly anything about this complicated woman who'd invaded his heart.

Tomorrow would come soon enough and reality with it. He'd go home, get some sleep and look at all his options before making any decisions. Period.

He moved to rise. She pulled him back down beside her. "Please. I don't want to be alone, not tonight."

Her quavering voice threatened more tears. Declan stroked her hair and pressed his forehead to hers. God, he wanted to kiss her. He wanted to see her again. "All right, I'll stay. On one condition."

She nodded eagerly, clueless as to how enticing she looked.

"Have dinner at my place this weekend. I'll call." A pleasant lethargy claimed him. His limbs liquefied and his eyes drifted shut.

❦

Declan woke early, parched and aching all over. The light edging around the closed blinds was too bright. He blinked and turned his head.

Oh, shit.

Miranda's face was inches from his. Her long pale lashes fluttered. She frowned, and a soft sigh escaped her parted lips—generous rosy lips that begged to be kissed.

Damn, he wanted her, and his body agreed. What a horn dog. *A horn dog with a hangover, you dumb shit.*

Declan inched his hand from beneath the covers. If she happened to wake up…

His stomach cramped, reminding him he was in no shape

to follow through on anything. He needed aspirin and something bubbly.

Miranda slept on, oblivious. Her tangled copper hair framed her delicate features. Freckles sprinkled her cheeks and the bridge of her nose.

Oh baby.

His smile twisted into a grimace. Time to hit the john. He vaguely remembered getting up once after Miranda had finally dozed off.

Declan lifted the comforter and planted his foot on the carpet. Rolling off the mattress, he stood, holding his breath. He'd slept in his clothes.

Jesus. It took him back to college and those wasted weekends. He never could do the hard stuff, like Tom had.

The bastard.

Screw Tom.

Dragging his hand along the wall for support, Declan stumbled into the bathroom. After he'd washed his hands and rinsed out his mouth, he opened the medicine cabinet.

He needed something for the pain. He'd write Miranda a note and apologize. Head down to avoid the light, he grabbed a bottle and peered at the label. Antacid. The next bottle stopped him cold.

Xanax filled six months ago at a pharmacy in Madison, Wisconsin. For acute anxiety. One one-milligram tablet every four hours as needed.

He wasn't familiar with the dosage, but Xanax was serious stuff. Miranda had mentioned she ran to relieve stress.

What the hell kind of stress?

Declan replaced the amber container and continued looking. He noted a partially filled disc of birth control pills from the local drugstore. Good to know.

He sighed and rubbed his pounding temples. Stop snooping. Find the aspirin and mind your own business.

The aspirin was one shelf up. He shook three tablets into his palm, switched off the light and headed for the kitchen.

The small house was quiet, except for the seismic ticking of the clock. His brains were likely to explode if it struck the hour before he made his escape.

Declan padded into Miranda's kitchen, shielding his eyes. Intense sunlight streamed through a greenhouse window and lit the room. Any other time, he would've been impressed, but not today.

The fridge sat on the far wall all the way across the tiled floor. Every freaking thing gleamed, the fridge, the ceramic tiles. He needed a pair of shades.

Licking his lips, he searched the cool interior hoping for soda or sparkling water.

No such luck. Several small blue cartons lined a shelf in the door. Coconut water was supposed to be good for a person. He might as well try it and see if it worked for a hung-over person.

Popping the aspirin, Declan washed the tablets down with a couple of hefty swigs.

The water didn't taste much like coconut, but the cold liquid appeased his thirst. Still holding the waxed container, Declan closed the fridge and spotted a magnet.

Orange-green- and red-streaked popsicle sticks framed a chubby little face wearing a mini Packer's ball cap and a wide, happy grin. Declan carefully peeled the magnet off and turned it over. Dated last year:

Jeremy Benedict, 3 yrs old, Busy Badger Day Care.
Miranda had a kid?

He frowned, repositioning the magnet. He knew she'd been married. He'd found that out when Tom had vetted her, but he didn't remember anything about kids. He'd have to check out the ex later.

Hopefully, the aspirin would kick in soon. Exhaustion was setting in. He was tempted to crawl back into bed with Miranda, but that wouldn't be smart. He'd already caused her enough trouble.

The clock went off, chiming seven, each reverberating peal hammering his skull. Wincing, Declan covered his ears. He needed a shower and his own bed.

Write a note and find your stuff.

Amid the neatly piled clutter next to her laptop, he discovered the backside of a used billing envelope with his name, all caps, printed in red ink.

A nice surprise. She'd been thinking about him, too.

Smiling, he penned a short note next to his name, adding a quick sketch.

She'd put his other clothing in the front closet. Slipping on his jacket, Declan found his phone tucked in one pocket, his keys in the other.

Sitting on the sofa, he laced up his boots. Miranda had agreed to dinner at his house, and he'd hold her to it. He had too many questions only she could answer.

CHAPTER 9

*F*riday, following their *unforgettable* night together, Miranda stood in front of the full-length oval cheval mirror in her bedroom and critically regarded her reflection. She'd chosen to wear one of her favorite outfits, a filmy green skirt with a matching blouse in a subtle floral print.

She rubbed her bare arms and frowned. The short sleeves did nothing to hide her freckles. It wasn't like Declan hadn't seen them at the run. Besides, tonight's dinner was no big deal. They were having a casual, home-cooked meal at his place.

Miranda walked into the bathroom. He'd underlined casual three times in the note he'd left her. Snatching the brush off the edge of the sink, she pulled it through her hair, until static crackled.

Once Declan had agreed to stay, she'd finally been able to fall asleep, his warm body curled around hers. The circular pressure of his hand between her shoulder blades had been comforting.

She'd slept late and found Declan's note on the coffee table beneath an empty coconut water carton.

He'd printed in small block letters on the back of an envelope, apologizing for his drunken behavior the night before, and thanking her for *EVERYTHING*.

Miranda's cheeks heated. She dropped her brush in the drawer and glanced at the mirrored cabinet. The same silly envelope she'd doodled his name on, in red, all caps, and drawn a box around.

Next to the box, Declan had sketched a humorous rendition of a happy face emoji, complete with bendy arms, legs, and a pounding heart. Enclosed in a speech balloon, he'd written: "I asked you to have dinner with me and you said, yes!"

Declan had called later that day. His resonant voice had been persuasive enough, but most compelling of all had been the way he'd honored her request that night, staying when she'd asked, and holding her with tender, unconditional silence.

The pleasurable memory lingered as she applied powder, mascara and lip gloss.

Tucking her hair behind her ears, light caught the gleam of the diamond-studded hoops. Grandpa had given her and Nikki each a pair the first Christmas after Nikki's wedding.

They'd stood together in Grandpa's bathroom, Miranda peering over her cousin's shoulder as Nikki had slipped her earrings in.

Miranda had been close to tears. Nikki and Matt were married. She should've been happy for them, but instead she'd been consumed by a fierce jealousy that had shocked her.

As always, Nikki had read her mind. She'd turned from the mirror and hugged Miranda tightly, and then leaned back her sparkling green eyes smiling into hers.

"Mandy, you are one hot woman, and don't you forget it. You'll find a good man of your own, and you'll be as happy as I am. I know it."

Miranda snorted. Eventually, she'd found Scott and look how that scenario had played out.

Inhaling, Miranda smoothed her hands down her skirt. What was she thinking? Here she was, about to get involved with another man, investing him with unrealistic expectations.

Sure, Declan had stayed when she'd asked him. Held her in his arms all night with no demands, but that didn't mean he was any different from her ex-husband.

Hadn't she spun the same romantic fantasies about Scott?

The smart thing to do was to keep things light. Have fun, but to absolutely indulge in no more fairy tales.

Miranda touched one of the small, glittering earrings. Sorrow welled in her chest. Life was cruel. Just when you thought you had all the answers and had a plan, shit happened. Nikki had been the happiest she'd ever been that Christmas.

Switching off the bathroom light, Miranda returned to the bedroom for her shoes. Nikki's tearful voicemail still haunted her. "Mandy, call me. Please."

Miranda sagged against the door frame, massaging her temples. She couldn't change the past. She couldn't change a fricking thing.

Slipping on gold pumps, she snatched her clutch off the bed and snapped it open. The enameled lipstick case containing her Xanax was inside. She checked the contents. Four blue pills. She hadn't taken any since moving back to Colorado, but it didn't hurt to carry insurance.

Outside, a full moon illuminated the sky, a large, ripe melon magnified in the crisp, thin air. Miranda imagined Nikki looking down on her. Miranda searched the sky for answers. Answers to questions she'd already asked the universe hundreds of times. "I miss you so much. Grandpa does too."

The frosty air stirred. Miranda shivered and headed for her car. Winter lurked just around the corner. Long, dark days stretched ahead. If she didn't keep busy, if she didn't run, her unruly mind would take over, continually logging her losses: Nikki, Jeremy, her marriage.

Miranda backed out of the driveway into the street. She couldn't let that happen.

By the time she pulled up in front of Declan's and parked alongside his black pickup, her pulse thundered in her ears. She dug in her purse and opened the enameled case. Just one would take the edge off.

How many times had Miranda heard Deirdre and Nikki say those identical words? Miranda snapped the container closed, stuffed it back inside her clutch and confronted her reflection in the rear-view mirror.

She could do this.

Locking her car, she resolutely straightened her spine. Tonight was nothing special. Like Declan had said, he'd planned a casual home-cooked meal.

Before she could knock, the front door opened. Declan's tall, lean silhouette was backlit in the hospitable rectangle of light emanating from the room behind him.

"Welcome." Dazzled by his brilliant blue eyes, she stepped inside. His hands were warm when he grazed her shoulders while removing her coat.

Leading her into the sitting area, he handed her a large goblet containing a rich, ruby liquid. "It's a new red blend I discovered. Tell me what you think."

Miranda smiled. Swirling the wine, she closed her eyes and inhaled the full fruity aroma before taking a generous sip. She detected a hint of oak, followed by a pleasant after-taste of cherries.

Licking her lips, she met his probing gaze. "Very smooth and not too dry. I like it."

He grinned, his charming dimples still discernable beneath his five o'clock shadow.

"What smells so good?" She moved in the direction of the kitchen and the stainless-steel pot on the stovetop. The table in the dining area had been set for two, and a pair of ivory candles graced the center.

Romantic, even if it was staged.

Declan walked up to stand beside her. "It's a special chicken recipe. I thought about trout, but I wasn't sure if you liked fish."

He shrugged and shot her a beguiling smile. "I figured chicken was a safe bet."

Miranda resisted the urge to fan her hot cheeks. She sipped her wine and circled back into the spacious, high-ceilinged sitting area. The mission-style sofa and chair complemented the rustic walls. "Chicken is perfect. I hope you made a lot because I'm starving."

Declan snagged his own glass off the kitchen counter and indicated a seat for her on the couch. "I like a woman with a hearty appetite. Let's enjoy our wine." He arched a brow and grinned. "That is if you can restrain your hunger for a few more minutes."

She could control her appetite, but how long could she resist the teasing glint reflected in his eyes, the snug fit of his jeans and the intoxicating scent of his cologne?

He settled in the chair opposite her, crossing his long, denim-clad legs at the ankles. He wore gray socks and the same battered loafers he'd worn at the bookstore.

Perching on the sofa's firm cushion, she swallowed more wine, grateful for the warm glow that suffused her body and bolstered her shaky composure. "You give a whole new meaning to the term 'casual home-cooked meal'."

The dimples in his cheeks deepened. He cleared his throat and stared down at his glass. "I got a little carried away."

Say something, anything. "Spencer is a completely different town in the winter."

Miranda bit her lip and knocked back more wine. That was lame. She was out of practice. She hadn't gone out with anyone since Scott, hadn't even entertained the idea of sex.

Until tonight.

Declan looked at her and laughed. He drained his glass and stood up. "I can't wait. I haven't skied in years, so I'm looking forward to hitting the slopes. I never had the time when I lived in Boston." He extended his free hand. "More wine?"

Miranda peered at her glass, shocked it was empty. The wine was excellent, and, since she'd resisted taking the Xanax, she smiled up at him. "Thanks."

His fingers brushed hers and her stomach fluttered.

Oh, God. He moved with the fluid grace of an athlete.

Retrieving the bottle off the kitchen counter, he poured each of them a generous refill.

"Here you go." His low voice contained a sensual undertone. His eyes were as dark and fathomless as the midnight sky.

She drew a shallow breath. A pleasurable heaviness swelled beneath her ribs.

Reclaiming her glass, she intentionally covered his larger hand with hers, tightening the exquisite tension.

Declan didn't break their fiery contact. Instead, his gaze remained fixed on hers, asking silent questions that simultaneously thrilled and terrified her.

Releasing him, Miranda sipped another mouthful of wine. This time, beneath the tannins and the subtle note of cherries, she tasted the sweet promise of passion, as deep and rich as chocolate.

He sat next to her, fingering the thin gold chain around her neck, his light touch searing her flesh. "I like your necklace. It's a little feather, isn't it?"

The pressing heat of his thigh seeped through the thin fabric of her skirt to her skin.

"Yes." She barely had the breath to whisper. Raising her gaze to his, she glimpsed a caring expression beneath his obvious arousal.

"Miranda, I'm not the monster you think I am." His voice was kind.

Monster was definitely not an adjective she'd apply to him at the moment. She took another sip of wine. "I know that. I tend to overreact."

Declan took her glass and set it down on the table. He gently gripped her shoulders and pulled her closer. "You're passionate about what you believe in, and that's good. That's admirable."

Miranda closed her eyes against his dazzling smile.

He kissed her, moving his warm mouth over hers.

She sighed and stroked the nape of his neck, then fisted her fingers in his thick hair, and savored his minty breath tinged with wine.

He traced his index finger above the scoop neckline of her blouse, his light caress raising gooseflesh. Planting more kisses along her collarbone, he skimmed his palm over her breast. "You smell like flowers."

Arching her back, she bit her lip, but failed to repress the soft, needy cry that rose from her throat.

Declan's response was a low, satisfied sound. Abruptly, he broke contact, leaving her stunned.

He cupped her chin, his blazing gaze consuming hers. "If I don't check on dinner, the smoke alarm will go off."

The incessant ringing of the timer was barely audible above her rampaging heart.

Standing, he clasped his hands behind his head. Turning his back to her, he exhaled slowly. "Sorry, it's been a long time."

Her lips still tingled from his kisses. He'd unleashed a reckless side of her she didn't recognize.

Desire urged her to go to him, wrap her arms around his chest, slip her hand inside his pants and whisper, "It's been a long time for me, too."

Instinct cautioned her to wait, to take her cues from him. He'd gone to a lot of trouble to impress her. The meal was part of the ritual. Miranda smoothed her hair away from her hot face.

Declan donned an oven mitt, lifted the lid of the pot and gingerly sipped from a large wooden spoon. He waved her over. "Come taste this."

He blew on the steaming food before putting it to her lips. "What do you think?"

The tips of his fingers grazed her chin. She smiled up into his flushed face. If she told him what she was really thinking.

With difficulty she directed her focus from Declan to the stew.

The savory-smelling dish abounded with chunks of chicken, potato, carrot and the familiar flavor of another root vegetable.

Miranda tilted her head and assumed a grave expression. "You were playing with fire by adding the turnips."

Declan darted a sideways look at her before tossing the spoon into the sink.

The corners of her mouth twitched. "You're lucky that I happen to like turnips."

Arching a brow, Declan stepped close--so close she had to steel herself from retreating. Lowering his gaze, he toyed with a lock of her hair. "I knew all along. Passionate redheads with freckles are crazy about turnips."

He was teasing. In a hot, sexy way, but still. She'd put on layers of foundation and powder. She looked down at her bare arms. She should've worn longer sleeves.

Declan seized her hand. Turning it over, he pressed his lips in the hollow of her palm. "I'm sorry."

Delicious warmth flooded her body and stole her breath. "It's silly, I know, but all my life I've been teased about my freckles."

Even by her ex-husband. She didn't want to think about Scott.

Declan frowned, searching her face. "Miranda, I'm crazy about your freckles, your hair, everything about you."

He pulled her into his arms for a long, slow kiss, wiping all other thoughts away, and promising bone-melting passion.

Groaning, he released her and exhaled. "See what I mean? We'd better eat. Now."

Seating herself at the table, she watched as he lit the candles and retrieved their wine glasses.

He served their salads on china plates with a simple double-ringed pattern of jade and black. Drizzling the vinaigrette with expertise, he sat opposite her and shook out his napkin. *"Bon appetite."*

Miranda reached for a crusty French roll from the linen draped basket. She'd had nothing to eat since lunch, and the wine had already made her dizzy. She cut the pale green pepperoncini in half and impaled it with a forkful of greens. The pungent taste of vinegar and peppery arugula was a delicious combination.

The rich chicken stew was filling. Swallowing her last bite, Miranda wiped the corners of her mouth and collapsed back in her chair. "Wow, a talented architect, a world-class chef and a great kisser."

Declan flashed his appealing, lop-sided grin, an inscrutable expression in his eyes. "Did you just tell me you liked my Standing Bear design?"

Miranda sighed and examined the dark sediment in the bottom of her empty wine glass. "It wasn't your design I objected to. It was the project."

He studied her over the rim of his glass and said nothing.

"There's already too much commercial development in the mountains. As I said at the hearing, a casino would destroy Spencer's historical integrity and tarnish its small-town atmosphere." Leaning forward, she clasped his arm. "I want to pass Spencer's legacy on to the next generation."

Declan tightened his jaw. "Do you mean the legacy of the town or the legacy of your family?"

Stung, Miranda released her grip and sat up straight. "What does my family have to do with anything?"

Propping his elbow on the linen tablecloth, he rested his chin in his hand and shot her a sad smile. "It doesn't matter. The casino isn't going to happen."

Grandpa's previous revelation about Tom Nagle crossed her mind, driving an invisible wedge between them. She still hadn't told Declan she'd known and said nothing.

"I'm in the middle of a shit storm. I'm unemployed. I've had to borrow money from my parents and meet with bankers and lawyers, which only costs more money." He drained his glass. "I'd checked the references Tom gave me, but apparently I should've dug deeper." Declan pinched the bridge of his nose. Leaning back in his chair, he stared up at the ceiling.

This was the perfect opening. She should tell him now. Even though it wouldn't make any difference, she should admit she'd known about Tom and get it over with. Keeping secrets had never worked well in her experience. They always caught up with the one keeping them and made them pay.

Miranda got up from the table. Grasping his broad shoulders, she leaned over him. "I'm sorry, Declan."

She took both of his hands and squeezed them before kissing his cheek. Resting her forehead against his, she closed her eyes, absorbing his woodsy scent and the heated texture of his skin.

Her confession would only add to his misery. She ached to comfort him and ease his grief. "Would you be my escort at the Aspen Gold's Annual Halloween Ball?"

The impulsive question spilled out of her mouth before she'd had time to consider the consequences. Startled at her boldness she prattled on. "The gala raises money for the David Spencer Charitable Foundation. Grandpa started the event years ago. Aunt Cora's place has the best costumes in town."

Declan stiffened. Twisting out of her embrace, he stood, and his napkin fell on the floor. Stooping, he balled the linen material in his fist and pitched it on the table. "I'm not big on wealthy, high-society parties, philanthropic or otherwise. I went to enough of those in Boston."

Her face burned, and she dug her nails into her palms. She'd just made everything worse. But he'd insulted her family. He knew nothing about the foundation or the good work it did. Coming here tonight had been a mistake.

Stacking plates and silverware, she carted the dishes over to the sink. "Thanks for dinner."

"Miranda." His exasperated voice sounded close behind her.

Folding her arms, she turned and faced him.

"Please, sit down and hear me out."

She shook her head. "It's getting late and I really should."

"What I have to say won't take long. If you want to leave afterward, I won't stop you."

Ignoring his outstretched hand, Miranda marched past him, blew out the candles, and took her seat at the crumb-strewn table.

Declan sighed and joined her. He scrubbed a hand over his mouth, his gaze searching hers. "I'm sorry. I'm sorry for a lot of reasons."

He stared down at the table. "You've been nothing but helpful, and I've been wrong to throw it all back in your face. I'm mad as hell at Tom, and I'm twice as mad at myself for being so stupid. It has nothing to do with you, with Aunt Cora, or the historical society." Declan cleared his throat, a resigned smile softening his mouth. "I suppose I better find a costume. If your offer still stands."

Hope fluttered in her heart. She nodded, but she kept her mouth shut. She wasn't about to offer any more helpful suggestions.

He tugged his ear and grinned. "Okay. Now that's settled, will you please stay for chocolate mousse? It's my mom's recipe."

Damn him and his dimples.

She should leave now. Even though she was more than tempted to stay, she should go.

But he had apologized.

"Declan." She laughed and rubbed her stomach. "I would, but I don't have room, not even for chocolate mousse. I ate too much of your delicious stew."

A weak argument, but the only excuse she could muster at the moment.

Reaching across the table, he caught her wrist. "Then at least stay for coffee. I'll clean up and you can keep me company."

The friction of his thumb stroking the top of her hand promised more than company and coffee.

If she was going to stick to her resolution, now was the time to smile politely, thank him and leave.

She looked away, focusing on the cluttered counter, the empty wine bottle, the grocery list stuck to his fridge with a Red Sox magnet.

Declan remained silent, but he continued caressing her hand.

Heat invaded her body from his gentle, questing touch. "Miranda?"

His low-pitched voice and hopeful expression revealed the desire smoldering in his blue eyes.

Pleasure curled low in her belly. Her pulse throbbed in her ears, and her heart pounded against her ribcage. She drew in a shallow breath. "Coffee would be good."

CHAPTER 10

*D*eclan lightly stroked Miranda's trembling hand and assumed a soothing tone. "I'll have you out of here and home by midnight."

Emotions ran high in this woman. She looked everywhere except at him.

With effort, he repressed his burning desire to kiss the faint bluish tinge that pulsed at her temple, gather her in his arms and love her. He should wait. Make coffee and clean up the dishes.

Instead, he whispered her name.

Her gaze returned to his. She parted her rosy lips and his body immediately responded.

Declan rose. Edging around the table, he gently tugged her to her feet. He kissed her pounding pulse, close to the delicate shell of her ear, claimed her soft, yielding mouth and swallowed the sweet outburst of her breath. "Miranda," he whispered again.

It had been too long since he'd been with a woman, and he'd been wanting Miranda since she'd stepped up to the podium at City Hall, sparks flashing from her spectacled green eyes. Her fiery hair had been knotted at the base of her slender alabaster neck, highlighting the beautiful bone structure of her face.

Now, he reveled in her intoxicating floral scent, her silky-smooth skin. He wanted to take his time, savor each kiss, but the urgent pressure of Miranda's taut, willowy body against his signaled she was as ready for him as he was for her.

Declan groaned, probing the liquid warmth of her mouth with his tongue.

Thank you, sweet Jesus!

Miranda wrenched her lips from his, her expression startled.

Exhaling a long puff of air, he forced a reassuring smile. He swept her cheek with his thumb and trailed his touch over her delectable lips. "It's okay. I won't do anything you don't want me to."

Grasping her hand, he led her to the stairs leading up to the loft.

She halted, yanking free from his grip.

Declan closed his eyes, the sound of his surging blood rushing in his ears. His erection was painful, but he was determined to let Miranda make all the choices in what happened next. If anything.

His watch chimed a notification. Clutching the railing, Declan counted to ten before opening his eyes.

Miranda was still there, standing a hair's breadth away, pale and beautiful in the muted light.

Reaching out with tremulous fingers, she covered his hand, pressing his flesh into the wood banister, her gaze focused on his. "Declan, it's not that I don't want you." She bit her lip as if marshalling her thoughts.

Declan sucked in a deep breath, steeling himself against his body's urgent need.

Tears filled her eyes, and she bowed her head. "My life is so screwed up."

The wrenching agony in her voice matched his own confused reality. Wrapping his arms around her, he buried his face in her glossy tresses. "Welcome to the club," he whispered.

He hooked his arm around her waist and together they climbed the stairs.

Inside his bedroom, Declan slipped his hands under her blouse, beneath the sleek material of her bra and caressed the firm, rising mounds of her breasts.

He heard the soft catch of her breath. Her eyelids fluttered closed. Capturing her mouth, he ran both hands along the elastic waistband of her skirt.

Kneeling, he tugged the garment down her legs, reverently pressing slow kisses into her warm, bare flesh, until he'd exposed her stunning body from the waist down, clad only in delicate lace panties.

He cupped her bottom, his lips branding the velvety skin below her navel, relishing her muted cry.

Removing the satin undergarment, he tossed it aside, caressing the downy juncture between her thighs.

Miranda gasped. Fingers clamping his shoulders, she buckled, her boneless weight leaning into him. "Don't stop."

Elbows braced to support her, Declan glanced up, taking in her closed eyes, her high color, her eager, features. He'd take it slow, prolonging her pleasure and holding out as long as he was able, which promised to be brief, based on his current physical state.

"My bed." Scrambling to his feet, Declan walked her backward. He'd start with gentle, light, teasing kisses as he touched her.

Miranda fell back on the mattress, yanking him down on top of her. Lifting his sweater, she rubbed feverish hands down his back, inching below the waist of his jeans. "Your bed, my rules."

An exquisite spasm shot through him. Declan closed his eyes, allowed her to roll him over and tease him with her lips, her tongue and gentle nips of her teeth.

"Yes ma'am." Her initiative was a nice surprise, and he wasn't going to argue.

She unzipped his jeans and peeled them down over his hips, grazing his erection. He gulped air, nearly losing control, and just about did when she firmly took hold of him.

He formed the words in his brain, but before he could caution her or plead with her, she'd straddled him, easing him inside her.

"Your turn." Her breathless voice carried a hungry edge.

Declan ground his teeth and pulled out. "Don't go anywhere," he said against her ear.

Tight and throbbing, he located the condoms in his nightstand. He hoped to God they didn't have an expiration date. Ripping the wrapper open, he sheathed himself.

Miranda groaned and flung her arm in his direction. "What's taking so long?"

"Help me out here," he gasped, yanking his sweater over his head.

She scrambled across the mattress to assist.

Even though he was in lust and agony, Declan managed a winded laugh. "I meant you."

Her breathing fast and shallow Miranda watched him as he divested her of her top and clumsily unhooked her bra.

Tearing his gaze from the stunning curve of her breasts, he covered her mouth with his and slipped back inside her slick inviting core. He thrust deep, then deeper, swallowing her rising cries of pleasure, until she shuddered beneath him.

Her long legs circled him, gripped him close, adding to

the sweet mounting friction. Declan heard his own hoarse cry as he convulsed with an all-consuming release.

He collapsed, chest heaving, his heart slamming against his ribs, basking in the sensual heat of her smooth, bare flesh.

Making love with Miranda was different than with any woman he'd ever known before.

Declan nuzzled her throat, planting gentle kisses along her jaw until reaching the enchanting target of her mouth. The awesome intensity of their lovemaking possessed an alarming edge.

He had the crazy urge to thank Miranda for the generous act of giving her body to him, tell her how special she was. That he loved her?

Chill dude. Don't confuse love with great sex. It's been a long time since you've had any and your judgment hasn't been the best lately.

Instead, he rested his forehead against hers. "I feel like I've just finished the Boston Marathon. I can't move a muscle."

Her bewitching eyes fluttered open. She smiled sweetly and touched a finger to his lips. "Then don't. Don't move. We can stay like this forever."

Declan tenderly cradled her cheek and overruled caution. Right now he wanted to live in real time. Live in his bed with this amazing woman, forget his reckless mistakes and his precarious future. "I'd like nothing better," he whispered against the shell of her ear.

Miranda shivered, and with warm, pliable lips, tugged on his lower lip. "You make me want to do naughty, delicious things."

Declan grinned and gently tangled his fingers in her silky hair. "All good things come to those who wait." He couldn't stop kissing her. "I don't think you'll have to wait long."

Miranda groaned and wriggled out of his embrace. "I have to go." Wrapping her slim arms around herself, she sprinted toward the bathroom. "Brrrr. I'll be right back."

He gazed after her, noting the perfect proportion of her breasts, the way her hips flared from the narrow curve of her waist. He couldn't wait to touch her, taste her and make her call out his name again. "I'm counting on it."

Minutes later, she returned, wrapped in his red terrycloth bathrobe that had hung on the back of the door.

He silently cursed the bathrobe and schooled his expression to remain neutral.

She sat cross-legged on the bed and the corners of her mouth turned up. "Is everything you own Red Sox?"

Declan fisted his hands beneath the blankets. He itched to untie the robe, slip it off her shoulders and kiss her sweet pink lips so she'd stop asking questions.

Instead, he fingered the sash, keeping his attention riveted on the gray comforter. "The robe was a Christmas gift from my parents last year."

He tugged on the knotted belt, bringing Miranda close enough to smell that she'd washed with his soap.

Her fresh face glowed, her long lashes barely visible. Declan traced each pale eyebrow and rested his hands on her shoulders. She was beautiful, with or without makeup.

Miranda looked down and chewed on her lip. "I wish."

Her poignant expression aroused a protective tenderness that surprised and scared the shit out of him at the same time. "What?"

She drew a deep breath. "I wish I had a mom who built snow forts and shared recipes with me, and I wish I had a dad to go fishing with."

Declan glimpsed a skinny, freckle-faced girl with large green eyes and fiery-colored braids. He wrapped her in his arms and kissed the top of her head.

Miranda clung to him, hiding her face against his neck. "My mom has always been so needy. Deirdre wears people out, especially men—my real dad and all the other guys I called daddy. Even Hunter and Heath's." Miranda's voice trailed off.

"Hunter and Heath?" Declan rubbed her back in soothing circles.

"My twin brothers. Their father left when we were kids."

Miranda's soft breath pebbled his flesh, tightening his groin. He stroked her hair and forced his attention back to what she'd told him. "That's rough," he said.

"It was a bad time. Deirdre was in and out of rehab, and we had one nanny after another until I was ten. I told Grandpa I was old enough to take care of myself and my brothers. Grandpa stuck up for me."

Miranda's enormous eyes probed his. "Jakob Spencer may look like a ruthless businessman, but there's a soft side to him. He's always been there for me and for Nikki."

Declan had his doubts, but given Miranda's fragile, emotional state, he said nothing. What family secrets did she keep locked inside her?

He thought of the little boy in the magnet frame on her fridge, remembered the bottle of Xanax. He recalled the woman at the bookstore's snarky comments about Miranda's cousin, Nikki, mentioning Nikki's poor husband and two kids. "The other night, what was your dream about? Was it your cousin?"

❦

Miranda shook her head. Grief stabbed her and obliterated all other feelings. Jeremy's small, solid warmth and the heart-breaking fragrance of his baby shampoo still lingered in her memory.

Declan didn't know about Jeremy, but he'd heard about Nikki. Lauren had made sure of that.

Yet Declan's searching gaze, his low, caring voice tapped the dark secrets buried deep in her heart, coaxing her to confess.

She swallowed the lump in her throat and blinked back stinging tears. Her sorrow had only grown heavier, even after countless therapy sessions. Was she crying for Nikki or for sweet, little Jeremy? She'd lost them both.

"Shhh." He swiped his thumbs beneath her eyes, concern etching his handsome features. "It's okay, baby, you don't have to tell me anything."

The dam broke and the words tumbled out. Her voice sounded outside herself. "Nikki had tried to call me the day she killed herself. She'd texted me. We were so close, and I wasn't there for her."

Miranda rubbed her forehead. "I was at an academic retreat up in the woods. I sensed something was wrong, but I'd convinced myself Nikki was having another one of her episodes, like my mother. Both of them could suck the energy from a room."

Miranda fisted her hands. The warmth of Declan's body, the hair-roughened texture of his bare skin, and his musky fragrance was real, yet her mind was elsewhere, reliving that horrific day.

She swiped her face on the sleeve of his robe, stealing comfort in the steady rhythm of his heart, the soothing pressure of his hand on her back.

"The next afternoon, as we got closer to the airport, my phone started going off with notifications." Her tearful voice faded to a mere whisper. "I knew in my heart who was trying to reach me, but I made myself listen anyway.

"They were all texts and voicemails from Nikki, all

begging me to call back. Asking me if I was mad at her." Miranda pressed her face against Declan's chest and wept.

His muscular arms tightened around her.

Miranda's throat closed as though the words choked her in retribution. "The worst part was the way Nikki was found."

An agonizing explosion of pent-up breath escaped Miranda. "She'd hung herself in the barn. Her oldest boy was the one who found her. I know Nikki hadn't planned it that way. Matt's mother had picked up both the kids from school, but Stevie had forgotten something. That's when Zach noticed that the horses hadn't been turned out.

"He'd thought Nikki had forgotten again and ran into the barn." Miranda could barely get the words out. "No eight-year-old should have to find his mother that way."

The inescapable suffocating anguish gripped her. It didn't matter how many times she relived it.

Gradually her weeping subsided. Declan gently shifted her to lie back against the bank of pillows. She must look terrible.

His placid blue eyes expressed compassion. "I'll be right back. Will you be okay?"

Miranda nodded. "Could you please bring me some tissues?"

His engaging grin reassured her aching heart. "I've got something better in mind."

She stared after him, grateful for the distraction of his broad shoulders, the muscular contours of his glutes and calves. He contained strength, tenderness and good looks in one irresistible package.

Clutching the bedcovers, she turned her head. A small drafting table nestled between the beams of the outer wall. Framed architectural prints she couldn't quite make out in the dim light flanked the desk. Atop the chest of drawers on the opposite wall, a semicircle of Red Sox bobble heads paid homage to an autographed baseball displayed in a case.

Minutes later Declan returned and set a glass of amber liquid on the bedside table. He brandished a dark green washcloth, which he proceeded to dab gently over her face.

Miranda closed her eyes and inhaled. "It smells nice, like you." She covered his hand with hers.

"Feel better?"

Of all his smiles, she loved this shy, crooked smile the best. Nodding, she raised her gaze to his. "Thanks."

He removed the washcloth and handed her the glass. "Can you stay?"

The husky timbre of his voice, the memory of their shared passion and his tender reaction to her confession linked together.

After the smooth whiskey's initial bite, the liquor left a pleasant, glowing trail down her throat. Licking her lips, she passed the glass back to him and loosened the belt to slip his robe off her shoulders.

❦

Waking early the next morning, Miranda rose on her elbow. Declan slept on his stomach, sprawled over the bed. Dipping her head, she inhaled his musky scent. She kissed his heated skin, skimming her fingers along his spine, below his hips, then back up between his shoulder blades.

Declan stirred. "Ummm. That feels good."

Miranda repeated her caress. Draping her body over his, she pressed quick, tender kisses along the nape of his neck. "How does that feel?"

"Ummm, that feels even better. Do it again."

She laughed softly against his bare flesh. "Gladly."

She couldn't get enough of him.

He'd been gentle, infinitely attentive to her pleasure before his. So different from her ex. Last night had been what making love was all about.

Take a step back, Miranda. Don't make any more of this than a casual encounter with good sex.

She closed her eyes and rested her cheek against his back. It had been so much more than merely good sex.

Cupping his bare shoulder, she plunged her other hand beneath the bedclothes and intertwined her fingers with his. Miranda searched the finely-chiseled contours of his face.

In answer to her silent question, Declan grinned. He slowly rolled over, cradled the back of her head and claimed her mouth with his.

This time, their lovemaking was unhurried, with whispered endearments and shared smiles.

After another earth-shattering climax, she curled up on her side. Her eyes drifted shut. Declan had gone downstairs and had promised to return with coffee.

"Hey, sleepyhead. Are you going to snooze the day away?"

Declan's low voice and the pungent aroma of coffee roused her. She lifted her head and blinked up at him. He'd put on a pair of gray sweats and a blue t-shirt.

Miranda sat up and raked the hair out of her eyes. "How long were you gone?"

The pupils of his eyes dilated and he sighed. He rummaged in the chest of drawers and tossed a shirt at her. "That should keep you warm."

He cleared his throat and poured coffee from a carafe into two red mugs.

She glanced down at her bare breasts and couldn't resist a coy smile. She pulled the shirt over her head. The soft cotton fabric smelled like him. "The girls thank you."

He flashed his dimples and folded his arms. "I aim to please."

Miranda patted the rumpled duvet next to her. "I won't bite. Besides, I'm decent now."

"Not decent enough." Declan's naked expression mirrored his words. He sat on the edge of the bed. "I know what you're like under that shirt."

Reaching out, he ran his index finger along the tee's neckline, grazing her collarbone.

She closed her eyes, holding her breath, blood pooling in her most sensitive parts, building an exquisite tension.

Her reaction was crazy. He'd barely touched her.

Declan palmed her breast and she clutched his wrist.

Oh, God.

The mattress dipped. He covered her mouth with his and slid both hands beneath the shirt. "Screw the coffee."

She pushed him over on his back and cupped his face, his beard's roughened texture a pleasant abrasion against her open hands, his eyes so blue and deep. Why risk spoiling the rest of this morning together? Reality would set in soon enough.

His dreamy kisses, the mounting urgency of his touch, the low, needy sound in his throat and her keen cry of pleasure were all the reality she wanted to handle for now.

By the time they were ready to drink the coffee, it was cold, but, sated and wrapped in each other's arms, they both agreed that loving each other had been worth the sacrifice.

While Declan went downstairs to make breakfast, Miranda took a shower and dressed in the clothes she'd worn the night before.

Taking one last look around the bedroom, she shook her head in a vain attempt to dispel her niggling anxiety. Reality had arrived, just as she'd feared.

It had been a relief to unburden her secret to Declan, but her prior knowledge of Tom Nagle's duplicity and her failure to promptly inform Declan still gnawed at her conscience.

She squared her shoulders and descended the stairs. She'd tell him now, whatever the consequences.

Sunlight streamed into the great open room. The enticing smell of bacon hung in the air. The table was set for two, and Declan stood in front of the stove frying eggs, his dark hair tousled, his feet bare. He glanced up.

"Hey, beautiful."

His appreciative smile weakened her resolve. All was right with his world in the present moment. Why ruin it? If she told him now, nothing would change. Nagle would still be gone, along with Declan's investment and his hopes for the future. Even if she'd called Declan immediately after breakfast with Grandpa, there hadn't been enough time to change the way things had turned out.

Declan wore a puzzled expression. "Why the frown?"

"I was just thinking."

Tell him and get it over with.

"What were you thinking?" Declan set their plates on the table, his penetrating blue eyes a startling contrast to his unshaven face.

"Declan, I'm hungry. Breakfast will get cold. I'll tell you after we eat."

Taking her seat, she bit into a crisp piece of bacon, buying time. "This tastes great. Thanks."

"Miranda." His voice carried a distinct edge.

Relieved at her sudden burst of inspiration, the words tumbled out of her mouth. "I was trying to remember what costumes there were at Aunt Cora's that you might like, and I forgot to tell you that Halloween is also Grandpa's birthday."

She dunked her toast in the pierced egg yolk and took a

bite. "Grandpa wants to meet you. Besides Spencer, he has holdings all over Colorado. I'm sure he can find you a position."

The light in the room faded. A glance out the window over Declan's shoulder revealed thick, gray clouds scudding across the sky.

He rose from the table and stood with his back to her, his posture rigid, arms locked across his chest. "I can find my own position."

"Declan, I'm sorry. I didn't mean." Miranda stared down at her plate, wishing she could take back what she'd said.

Sighing, he raked a hand through his hair and turned to face her. "You don't get it, do you?"

Her half-eaten breakfast churned in her stomach. "Get what? You're talking in riddles and shutting me out."

She went to him, grasped both his hands and flinched. He might as well have been carved of marble. Miranda clamped down on her lower lip, but her eyes still filled with tears. He was Scott, all over again. Would she never learn?

Her self-directed fury and disgust erupted. "You're no different. You're worse. You just act nice and pretend to care. Hypocrite."

Miranda raised her open hand and swung her arm back.

❦

Declan caught her wrist. Her pulse throbbed beneath his fingers.

Adrenaline fueled her anger and made her stronger than he'd expected.

Her emerald eyes glittered in her pale face. "Let me go."

She spat the words, like the hiss of an angry cat. Instead of releasing her, Declan pulled her against him, enduring her thrashing arms and pounding fists. He squeezed his eyes shut and pressed his lips to the top of her head. He'd been unfair. He'd intentionally hurt her because her misguided words had hurt him.

As he'd cooked their meal this morning, he'd expected the intimacy they'd been sharing to continue. Instead, Miranda had been secretive, evading his questions. Last night, her gushing invitation to her grandfather's ball had sounded calculated, a lot like his obscenely rich clients in Boston with their phony social norms.

"I'm sorry baby." He held her until she sagged against him and was quiet. Tipping her flushed face up to his, he read her stricken expression. Hadn't she'd come to his rescue more than once? Hadn't she trusted him enough to share her deepest secret? Hadn't she generously given him her body?

He'd do whatever it took to alleviate her wounded heart, even if that meant enduring another pompous charity gala and making nice with her wealthy grandfather. "Does your invitation still stand?"

An hour later, Declan watched Miranda back out of the yard and disappear down his rutted drive. He released a long breath and collapsed to sit on the top step of the porch.

Low, gray clouds had obliterated the sun. A cutting wind whipped the long-needled pines and stung his face.

Miranda had thanked him. She'd promised to text him about the ball later. Her courteous smile and awkward response to his fleeting kiss had amplified his misgivings.

He should've let things be. Now he was obligated to attend another endless social event, rubbing elbows with Spencer's elite. It would be on a smaller scale than Boston's snobby affairs, but just as aggravating.

He missed Miranda. He longed to recapture last night, but last night had been a fleeting illusion. Nothing had changed. He'd still been swindled, still had no job and no savings.

It was probably better this way. He had a lot of work ahead of him and he didn't need any distractions, least of all her.

Declan slowly climbed to his feet, walked inside and slammed the door.

CHAPTER 11

*M*iranda drove directly from Declan's to The Attic. Aunt Cora had always been more like her mother than Deirdre.

As teens, she and Nikki had often taken refuge in the weathered Victorian structure. Aunt Cora could be trusted to listen, withhold judgment, and give advice only if specifically asked.

Climbing the chipped, blue-painted steps, Miranda wasn't sure how the older woman would react to the news that she'd slept with "the enemy," but she needed to talk and sort out her muddled emotions.

Other than her therapist, she'd trusted nobody else with her secrets.

Until last night.

Miranda lightly rubbed her lips. Declan's tender kisses, his reverent touch, his caring response to her grief for Nikki had contrasted sharply with his icy reserve at breakfast this morning.

But that was on her. She should have told him the truth,

instead of babbling on about Grandpa's birthday and how influential Jakob Spencer was.

Miranda sighed. The truth would've probably produced the same reaction. Declan seemed particularly sensitive when it came to Grandpa, and he hadn't even met him yet.

It was a given that once she walked through Aunt Cora's daffodil yellow door, what was left of the morning would fade to afternoon, and the day would be sucked away.

But this was important—even more important than protecting Spencer. This was her life. Miranda's mind boiled over with images of Declan, of Nikki's funeral, of Matt and the forlorn faces of Nikki's two little boys.

Grasping the antique knob, Miranda pushed open the door and the familiar sound of chimes announced her arrival.

She hung her coat on the rack and paused in the entry-way, drifting back in time. Sweet and spicy smells hovered in the warm, dust-laden air. The staircase rose in front of her, the carpeted risers leading to a shadowed landing.

She walked past the ticking sentinel of the grandfather clock into the brightly lit shop. The Attic was a fascinating jumble of furniture, knickknacks and books.

Aunt Cora stepped out from behind the counter, reading glasses perched on her nose. Her long silver-streaked hair was braided and pinned up in her customary coronet. Bohemian leather sandals peeked out beneath the long hem of her floral print skirt.

Eyes wide, she clasped a stack of flour cloth dish towels to her chest. "Good God Almighty, Miranda. I was just thinking about you, and now here you are."

The emotional turmoil of the last twenty-four hours, and Miranda's ever-present, consuming anxiety fractured. Tears pricked behind her eyes. "I had to see you, Auntie. You're the only one in Spencer that I can talk to."

Aunt Cora dropped the towels on a nearby glass tabletop and enveloped Miranda in a warm patchouli-scented hug.

Miranda closed her eyes and swallowed. Next to Grandpa, this woman was her rock and always had been.

Nikki's, too.

"Well, Miss Mandy," she said bussing Miranda's cheek. "This calls for a pot of tea and my special iced lemon cookies."

Nodding, Miranda clung to the tall, spare woman. She was reluctant to break the tenuous thread that connected the two of them and embraced the spirit of a third.

Aunt Cora held Miranda at arm's length. Her wise brown eyes searched Miranda's face. "I've been thinking about Nikki, too."

Clasping Cora's cool hand, Miranda followed the woman beyond the sliding pocket doors that led to the kitchen. She sank onto one of the four chairs at the round maple table. The wooden lazy Susan was still in its place.

Smiling, she grasped one of the squat ceramic corn-ear shakers, its surface smooth and nubby at the same time.

How many times had she and Nikki sat here after school, devouring cookies, transforming the lazy Susan into a "spinning wheel" to tell their fortunes?

The plastic honey bear, with its yellow pointed cap, was the arrow. Salt was yes and pepper was no.

Miranda carefully replaced the salt shaker next to the matching sugar bowl, chipped and cracked where it had been glued.

Nikki's face filled her mind, her cousin's wide smile and bubbly laugh ethereal, yet tangible in the spice-scented room.

Aunt Cora filled the ancient teakettle with water. She set it atop a blue ring of flame on the old white enamel- and-chrome gas stove. "I've felt her presence." She sighed as she fished a plate out of the cupboard above the yellow countertop and plunked it down next to a large round tin. "Sometimes I think I'm losing my marbles."

"Nikki was happy here," Miranda said. "Like I am. We both felt safe."

A serene peace wrapped itself around her. Dust motes danced in the sunlight that filtered in through the paned glass over the sink.

The teakettle whistled. Cora poured steaming water into the blue paisley teapot and covered it with the faded gingham cozy. She took a carton of half-and-half out of the fridge and filled the corn pitcher.

The cup and saucer she placed in front of Miranda was painted with delicate pansies.

Miranda cradled the fragile china between her hands. "My favorite teacup."

Her throat tightened and her eyes filled with grateful tears. She set the cup carefully back in its saucer. "I need to talk about Nikki." Her voice quavered. "About a lot of things."

Cora fished in the pocket of her skirt and handed Miranda a square of embroidered cloth. "It's been a few years, but I'm still in the habit of keeping a hanky tucked close. Between you two girls."

"I miss Nikki so much." Miranda choked and fisted the handkerchief hard against her forehead. "I should've been there for her. Matt would still have his wife, and the boys would still have their mother if I had been."

Numerous clocks chimed the hour. One after another, striking different tones. Miranda looked up.

A single tear glistened on Cora's cheek.

The same grief shone in the woman's watery eyes that Miranda bore in her heart. Cora sighed heavily and rose from the table. "Be right back."

She disappeared in the direction of the bathroom. The

familiar honk of Aunt Cora blowing her nose was followed by the sound of running water.

Miranda poured tea into her cup and reached for the cream. A ripple of cold air swept past her. Gooseflesh traveled along her arms. She froze, clutching the pitcher.

Bright sun shone through the window over the kitchen sink. Miranda blinked and glimpsed Nikki's wavering reflection in the dust motes dancing in the light. A wave of heat suffused Miranda's body. Slowly, she set the pitcher down on the table. Her eyes drifted shut and she relaxed back against the chair, her spine fluid.

It's cool, Mandy. I'm happy now. You and Matt belong together. He needs a good woman and my boys need a good mother. Ask Aunt Cora. She knows. Love you.

Miranda shivered and opened her eyes. Dust motes still floated in the sunlight, but Nikki was gone.

Cora had returned. The older woman leaned against the counter, her expression watchful.

"Nikki said to ask you about Matt and the boys… that you know." Miranda's voice sounded outside herself.

Cora nodded and sat down at the table. She poured herself some tea. "I've only really seen Nikki once. I was baking a batch of those damn cookies and, as I took the sheet out of the oven, I suddenly felt something right behind me. I looked over my shoulder and there she was."

She shook her head and raised her cup to her lips. "Damn if I didn't hear her voice, clear as a bell say 'I sure miss your lemon cookies, Aunt Cora.' And then she was gone. I damn near had a stroke."

Cora gulped her tea, a distant expression in her eyes. "It was all I could do to hang onto the cookie sheet."

"Did she say anything else?" Reaching for the round tin, Miranda helped herself to another lemony delight. She broke off a piece and let the buttery, tart taste dissolve on her tongue.

The woman waved her arm in dismissal and grabbed a cookie for herself.

Miranda frowned and sighed. She knew better than to push. "Never mind."

The sun had shifted. The path of light and the fine particles of dust had vanished, although Nikki's words still echoed in Miranda's mind.

She'd foolishly thought that telling Declan last night would somehow make her guilt vanish.

Hardly. All it took was coming back here, connecting with deep-seated memories that she and Nikki had shared.

Cora leaned across the table and grasped both Miranda's hands in hers. "Mandy, over the years, I've watched you follow at Nikki's heels like a devoted puppy, always ready to jump when she said jump. I know I'm a busybody." She snorted softly. "I prefer to think it's because I'm observant and want to help. In this case, it's because I love you."

The woman's grip tightened. "Oh yes, I loved Nikki, too. There was no knowing that girl and not loving her, but she had a way of taking love and hoarding it." Releasing Miranda's hands, Cora sighed and shook her head, sadness mirrored in her eyes. "The girl didn't know how to give back what she received. Forgive me for saying this, but that flaw runs deep in the blood. Your grandmother Marguerite left her mark in one way or another on all three of her daughters."

Miranda couldn't argue with that statement. Even as a child she'd observed Grandmother's cold attitude toward her mother and her two aunts. She and Nikki had always been a little scared of Grandmother and her mean streak.

"What I'm trying to say, Mandy, is that you have the right

to live your own life, not your mother's, or your brothers', or your grandfather's—and certainly not Nicole's.

"You're under no obligation to take on Matt and those two little boys, regardless of your feelings. Regardless of what you think Nikki may have said to you or what you think you should do.

"Mandy, I love you like my own and I'm glad you've moved back to Spencer, but it's time for you to live your own life and find your own happiness."

The woman's eyes brimmed with emotion and Miranda felt the answering sting of tears. She'd always known the woman had loved her and Nikki, but "talk is cheap" had always been Cora's declaration, and this was the first time Aunt Cora had actually said it.

It was a sad fact, but Miranda could probably count on the fingers of one hand how many times in her life she'd been told she was loved.

Grandpa's way had always been with quick hugs and chucks of her chin. Maybe that was why she and Nikki had told each other millions of times. Maybe they had both needed to make up for what they'd been lacking.

The chime rang. Footsteps and voices sounded on the other side of the door.

Cora rose to her feet, dabbing a napkin at her eyes and mouth. "Think about what I said."

She left Miranda alone at the kitchen table, a faint whiff of patchouli in her wake.

Miranda rinsed out the china cups and, covering the tin of cookies, replaced them on the cluttered counter.

When she went to put the pitcher of cream into the fridge, her attention was drawn to two Christmas cards hanging at skewed angles on the white enameled door.

She recognized last year's card with Scott, Jeremy and herself, all wearing Santa hats, sitting in front of the decorated tree. Jeremy sat cuddled in her lap. Miranda closed her eyes and recalled the heat of his small sturdy body and his little boy smell. Her hazy dream of the other night returned.

She missed Jeremy's chubby face, his wide, happy grin and his infectious giggle. Most of all she missed his exuberant hugs and kisses.

Miranda shuddered to think how Jeremy would grow up without her influence. Was anyone giving him the attention the sweet, affectionate toddler deserved? Did anyone read him bedtime stories or play trains with him? He could very well turn out to be as self-centered and manipulative as his father.

Hugging herself, Miranda inhaled deeply and moved on to the other card. The image was just as painful and unforgettable.

Wearing cowboy hats and flanked by two black labs, Matt, Nikki, Zach and Stevie were perched on the rustic steps of their massive log home.

She'd received hers only weeks before Nikki's death. *Nikki's last Christmas.*

Miranda examined the card, as she'd done numerous times before, peering beyond Nikki's fixed smile and her flawless makeup for a clue to her cousin's desperate state of mind. As often as she'd studied the photo she'd detected nothing of the impending tragedy.

A wiry tortoiseshell cat crept into the kitchen and curled its warm furry body around her legs.

"Agnes." Miranda crouched down and rubbed the flat of her hand along the feline's arched back. "Hi, kitty," she cooed, reverting back to when Agnes was a kitten and she and Nikki had played with her.

Agnes had always preferred Miranda over Nikki, and Aunt Cora's tortie had been a secret source of comfort when Nikki and Matt had hooked up.

"There they are!" Aunt Cora hustled back into the kitchen and plucked her reading glasses up from the counter. "Right where I left them." She rolled her eyes and sighed, casting Miranda an exasperated grin. "I lose the damned things at least six times a day."

Pausing on her way back out to the shop, she said. "I see Agnes has found you. Help yourself to another cup of tea and more cookies."

The door chimed again. Laughing feminine voices and booted footsteps echoed in the entryway.

Aunt Cora rolled her eyes again and shrugged. "Better yet, come out and give me a hand. It's turning out to be one of those crazy days." She cocked her head and the corners of her mouth lifted in a knowing smile. "You're a bit over-dressed, but no matter."

She perched the glasses back on the bridge of her nose and swept out of the kitchen. "Good morning, welcome to Aunt Cora's Attic, where treasures lie in wait to be discovered."

Miranda's face burned at her recollection of last night's lovemaking. "Nothing gets past Auntie. Isn't that right, kitty? Gotta go help in the shop."

Agnes meowed and pounced on Miranda's ankle. The tortie's front paws batted her shoe and the top of her foot.

Miranda laughed and bent to pet the demanding feline.

Although she hadn't had the opportunity to talk to Aunt Cora about sleeping with Declan and her scrambled emotions, it was enough to simply be here. Aunt Cora and the cherished memories this house contained grounded Miranda, infusing her with the serenity and strength she desperately needed.

Auntie was right, and her advice echoed that of Miranda's wellness coach. No matter how much they needed her, taking on Matt, Zach and Stevie was not her responsibility.

Not taking on others' problems would also include her family and anyone else, particularly Declan.

Her first priority was to care for herself and look after her own happiness.

"Easier said than done," she confided to Agnes, stroking the cat from her bony little head to the tip of her erect tail.

Agnes mewed and wandered over to her bowls.

Rising to her feet, Miranda wiped her hands down her skirt and crossed the entryway into the shop, now teeming with browsing customers.

CHAPTER 12

*M*iranda peered at her laptop, checking for typos on the David Spencer memorial application. Her gaze drifted and her hand hovered over her phone. She hadn't heard from Declan since the morning she'd left his cabin.

She'd lost it, foolishly equating his stony silence with her ex, projecting her misplaced rage on poor Declan, who had enough of his own troubles to deal with.

Where had that anger come from, anyway? She'd thought the past months of rigorous therapy had purged Scott out of her mind.

Miranda had spent the last five agonizing days replaying her hysterical response in her head. Declan's forceful grip on her wrist had stopped her hand from connecting with his face. Thank God.

He'd pulled her tight against the muscular strength of his lean body, weakening the impact of her thrashing blows. Cradling her in his arms, he'd kissed the top of her head and apologized in his low, soothing voice.

Declan had apologized and, instead of apologizing in

turn, she'd acted the wounded victim. Miranda sighed and forced her attention back to the glowing screen of her laptop. She still hadn't told him about Grandpa's investigation regarding Tom, which had precipitated the whole muddled mess.

Her phone buzzed with a text.

Heart soaring, Miranda seized the phone and clasped it to her chest. She'd tell Declan she was sorry. She'd invite him here for dinner. He could spend the night. Smiling, she looked down at the screen.

Hey Mandy. What's up? My boys are asking.

Not Matt. Not now.

Miranda squeezed her eyes shut and massaged her temple. She wanted to cry. She pictured Zach and Stevie's forlorn little faces at Nikki's funeral.

A familiar weight settled on Miranda's chest. It didn't matter what Aunt Cora had said. She'd promised Nikki she'd take care of them, and she would.

Slumping back in her chair, she thumbed her response.

Sorry. Been busy.

Meet me at 7 Wild Card?

Miranda straightened and raked her hair away from her face. This invite sounded more about Matt than Zach and Stevie.

At the service, Matt had looked just as bewildered as his boys, standing stiffly in a suit and tie.

Though Nikki's spirit—or whatever it was—had said she and Matt belonged together, Miranda had never promised Nikki she'd take care of Matt.

There had once been a time when she would have done so gladly, but, as Grandpa was so fond of saying, that ship had sailed.

And now there was Declan.

Too many complications. Miranda's pulse accelerated. Tightening her trembling grip on the phone, she managed a deep breath. She couldn't think about any of them right now.

She'd set strict boundaries. A quick beer and home by nine. Another text.

Yes or no?

Miranda rubbed her forehead. She didn't have to meet him tonight. Another time would be better for her, but he had his business and the kids.

Blinking rapidly, Miranda thumbed *yes*. She swallowed the rising lump in her throat, tried to quell her pounding heart and shoved Declan to the back of her mind.

She couldn't deal with both men at the same time.

❦

It seemed she'd been spending a lot of time at the Wild Card lately. Unlike dressing up for dinner with Declan, tonight Miranda had donned jeans and a flannel shirt, plaiting her hair in a simple French braid down her back.

She'd swirled powder over her freckles, spiked her lashes with black mascara and called it good.

Matt was like family, she told herself as she walked from the brisk, starlit night into the warm, noisy restaurant.

So why was her stomach fluttering?

Ace stood behind the bar, washing glasses. He grinned, inclining his head in the direction of the booths located in the back.

Matt was staring down into the brown depths of his glass mug as she approached. His dark beard was neatly trimmed and his mahogany hair looked wispy and damp, as though he'd just showered.

"Hey," she said, smiling.

Startled, he glanced up. His slow, well-remembered grin deepened the tiny lines around his warm hazel eyes. His eyes appeared hollow with dark circles of exhaustion.

He stood and enveloped her in a bone-crushing hug, lifting her off her feet and pulling her disturbingly close against his broad chest.

"Hey, yourself," he murmured, burying his face against her neck.

Miranda closed her eyes and breathed in a nostalgic mix of spicy cologne and leather, calling to mind summers long gone.

Grandpa's long white barn, halters hanging beside spacious stalls. The sweet, dusty fragrance of hay and alfalfa. Those carefree days, when the three of them were kids, hanging out at the stable or up at the shack.

Matt's lips grazed the sensitive skin behind her ear, sending an involuntary shiver shooting through her.

She stiffened and pushed back, her face growing hot.

"Sorry," Matt muttered, his complexion ruddy above his sheepish grin. He set her back on her feet and held her at arm's length. "I couldn't help myself."

Neither could she, apparently. Sliding into the booth opposite him, Miranda touched her earlobe, remembering that summer afternoon up at the shack and the one secret kiss they'd shared.

So much of what they'd shared had included Nikki.

Except that kiss, which was better forgotten, but which Miranda had kept locked in her heart, unwilling to put to rest.

That one sweet kiss remained, an old dream, comforting to cling to after Scott had left and she was feeling lonely.

She reached for the plastic-coated menu propped behind the condiment basket.

Matt plucked the menu out of her grip. "What's the frown and the big sigh for?"

His narrowed gaze searched hers. Miranda snatched the menu back and reached for his beer. Raising the mug to her lips, she drank, partly to deflect his question, partly because she suddenly craved a buzz.

Swallowing, she replaced the glass on the table and half rose, peering down at the object resting on the bench seat next to him. "Oh my God, Matthew. Is that the same hat you wore in high school?"

Reaching for the distinctive fedora, he smoothed the brim with his fingers, regarding it fondly. "Yup, it's an archeological artifact itself by now and part of my brand. You should check out my new website. A lot of the tech guys I've taken out suggested I needed an online presence."

"For your outfitting business?"

Matt nodded and flagged down their server, who he seemed to know on a first-name basis.

Miranda ordered the same dark draft and a basket of chicken tenders, with fries and coleslaw. "I'm hungry," she said in response to his raised brows. "We can share."

She directed a pointed glance at the empty shot glass

sitting beside his mug. "You need to eat too. Especially since you're having another one of those."

Matt shrugged and tilted his head, regarded her again with that unsettling, brain-probing look. "You've changed, Mandy."

Miranda thought of Nikki's suicide. The life she'd left behind in Wisconsin, her broken marriage and losing Jeremy. Melancholy seeped into her bones. "We've all changed, Matt. Shit happens. The people we love leave us." That sounded pretty bleak, even to her own ears.

She forced a smile, squeezing one of his large, calloused hands in hers. "Tell me about the boys."

Matt's answering grin lit his face. He absently rubbed his thumb over her knuckles. ""Stevie's doing great. That kid would eat, drink and sleep with the horses if I'd let him. He'd rather be out in the barn than at school, but he's getting good grades. He's only six and placed first in his division at the state fair. He wants to compete at the stock show in January."

The server reappeared with their drinks.

"Wow, that's great." Miranda eased her hand from Matt's. She sipped the cold, pleasantly bitter brew, grateful for the interruption. Being here with him ignited too many buried feelings and memories.

"Zach's another story." Exhaling a long breath, he downed the whiskey and chased it with a robust swallow of brew.

Matt grimaced and cleared his throat. "That boy is a handful right now. He's acting out at school and his teacher is threatening to expel him. He always was closest to his mama. I've got him in counseling."

Miranda knew all this, thanks to Lauren, but hearing the pain in Matt's voice squeezed her heart. If Matt started crying, she'd dissolve along with him.

He rubbed a hand down his face. "I hired a tutor, but

nothing seems to be working. There's nothing dumb about that boy."

Matt sat back as the server set a steaming basket of chicken and fries on the table, along with plates and a bowl of ranch dressing.

"Anything else?" The woman's gaze was directed at Matt, who was busy filling his plate.

"Water would be great," Miranda said.

The woman's attention remained focused on Matt. Miranda nudged Matt's leg.

He glanced up and flashed the server a contrite grin. "I'd better have a cup of coffee. I have some bookwork to do and it's going to be a late night. Thanks, Dawn."

"Sure." Bright spots of color highlighted her cheeks. She looked at Miranda, then back to Matt. "Who's your friend?"

Matt exhaled through pursed lips, his expression guarded. "Dawn, meet Mandy. Mandy, meet Dawn."

How involved was Matt with this person? Why had he suggested they meet here? Miranda nodded, forcing a cordial smile. "Matt and I are related by marriage. His wife and I were cousins. We go all the way back to kindergarten."

"Hey, Dawn." A burly dude with red suspenders at one of the nearby tables hoisted his arm. We need another pitcher."

Dawn turned her head. "Be right there."

Her lips tightened. Averting her gaze, she collected Matt's empty mug and shot glasses. "I'll charge everything to your account, like usual."

She spun on her heel and ambled toward the other table, her tight jeans emphasizing her voluptuous curves.

Miranda lowered her gaze. After her fling with Declan last Saturday night, who was she to judge Matt?

Yet, she blamed him for suggesting they meet here, for resurrecting her buried feelings, and, as ridiculous as it seemed, for replacing Nikki.

"I hope she realizes I'm not here to steal her man." Miranda couldn't bite back the remark or her sarcastic tone.

Matt drank his beer and focused on his mug. "Sorry about that. Dawn and I have gone out a couple of times. I guess we should've met somewhere else."

"Yes, we should've." She popped a salty fry into her mouth and looked in the direction Dawn had disappeared.

Matt seized both of her hands in his. "Look at me, Mandy." He swallowed, and his hazel eyes grew liquid. "It's been bad since Nikki died. Especially for Zach. It gets busy. I've got my outfitting business to run. I'm away for days at a time, then it's back home to my two boys who need me and can't understand why their mama left them."

He dropped her hands like a hot potato and lapsed into silence as Dawn returned with Miranda's water and a white ceramic mug of coffee along with a check for Matt to sign.

The woman's expression momentarily softened. "Tell Zach and Stevie I said 'hi.'"

Matt scrawled his signature and gave the server a weary smile. "I will. Thanks Dawn. We'll probably see you Monday, as usual."

"Sure thing." Dawn squeezed Matt's forearm. She took the receipt from him and slanted Miranda a furtive glance before walking away.

Miranda sipped her water. "Sorry I snapped at you."

He scratched his bearded jaw and glanced down at the table. "Yeah, we come here Mondays and Thursdays. I'm not much of a cook, and Dawn looks out for us."

Matt slid the basket of food in Miranda's direction. "It's getting cold, better eat up."

Miranda sighed and dunked a breaded piece of chicken in the ranch dressing. "Leave it to Nikki to leave a train wreck in her wake."

Matt nodded glumly. Head down, he drenched his fries with catsup and cleaned his plate in record time.

Reaching again for her hand, he gripped her fingers painfully tight. "Look Mandy, I'm home next week 'til Friday. I wondered if you'd come over and have supper with me and the boys. Nothing fancy. Grilled cheese, spaghetti, or pizza is about all they'll eat."

Her heart contracted at his hopeful, eager expression. She couldn't say no.

"No strings, Mandy. I promise."

Miranda smiled and nodded. In spite of Matt's good intentions, she suspected there were plenty of strings attached.

CHAPTER 13

*T*he high beams of her headlights barely illuminated the winding road. Miranda's heart pounded wildly and seemed too big for her ribcage, making it hard to breathe.

She'd run earlier in the day, but by the time she was on her way to Matt's, her anxious mind was already spinning what-if scenarios. Reminding herself of the pills tucked in her purse failed to reassure her.

She hadn't had sufficient time to sort out her jumbled emotions after meeting Matt at the Wild Card. Tonight's dinner with him and the boys only promised to further complicate her already over-complicated life.

And then there was Declan to consider. She still hadn't heard from him and continually found herself searching for his black truck on the streets around town. Twice she'd almost texted him. The decisive woman she'd been before Scott had done a number on her would've already contacted Declan and resolved the issue by now.

Licking her lips, Miranda slowed down and stole quick glances at her phone's glowing screen. The volume was maxed and she hadn't heard anything. Had she missed the turn?

She had to stop thinking about Declan and concentrate on the road before she got lost.

She was ready to pull over and text Matt when her app squawked and her headlights lit up the arrowed sign advertising Timberline Outfitters.

A gravel road climbed to an assortment of well-lit buildings, dominated by a sprawling log home. Two huge, barking labs rushed up to her vehicle and prowled just outside her door.

Matt had cautioned Miranda to stay put until he came out and corralled them. "They're good dogs with family and friends, but they've been trained to guard the property and protect us."

Miranda froze against the seat and rubbed the tingling scar on her arm. Large, noisy dogs reminded her of Conan.

The Doberman had already been part of the family when she'd married Scott and become Jeremy's new mommy. Regardless of Miranda's objections, Scott had refused to part with his beloved dog.

It had been frustrating enough cleaning up after the animal had tracked dirty paw prints all over the carpet, or after ripping a pillow to shreds, but she'd drawn the line when the canine beast had cornered Jeremy.

The toddler had innocently picked up Conan's rawhide bone while the dog had been eating.

Startled by Jeremy's terrified scream and the dog's guttural snarl, Miranda had sprinted into the laundry room. She was bitten as she snatched the small boy away from the animal's bared teeth.

It was only after driving Jeremy over to Scott's parents that Miranda realized she'd been bitten badly enough to need stitches. She and Jeremy had stayed with his grandparents until Scott had found Conan a new home.

Gripping the steering wheel with trembling hands, she fought to control her panic. She was safe inside the car. Conan was long gone.

A side door to the log home opened, and both the boys ran out, their high voices barely audible above the ruckus.

The taller of the two approached her car, while the smaller boy issued a command in conjunction with a short, sharp gesture. Immediately, the dogs stopped barking and rushed to the child's side.

Out of the corner of her eye, Miranda glimpsed Matt approaching, but her attention fixed on the child feverishly tugging on the door handle.

Zach's resemblance to Nikki was uncanny. The reminder must be painful for Matt.

Once both the animals were secured on leashes, Miranda cautiously stepped outside the security of the car and extended her hand. "Hi, Zach. Remember me? I'm-."

"Mandy," Zach said, cutting her off. He pumped her hand, flashing an impish grin. "If you're nice to me, I'll tell Harry and Sally to stand down and they won't eat you."

"Zachary. That's enough. Where are your manners?" Matt tousled his older son's hair.

Zach dodged behind his father and ran back toward the house. "Last one in is a rotten egg!"

Matt sighed and gave Miranda an exasperated glance. "Stevie, bring Harry and Sally down so they can meet your cousin, Miranda."

It looked more like the dogs were bringing Stevie down the slope toward her. As he approached, the boy issued another order and gave a couple of quick tugs on the animals' leashes.

Both dogs obediently sat on their haunches, panting and whining while keenly focused on Miranda.

"Stevie's going to ease up on them a little. Just stand still and let them sniff you." The comforting pressure of his fingers on her upper arm reassured her.

Heart thudding in her ears, Miranda swallowed. She had nothing to be afraid of. She had nothing....

The labs circled her, sticking their cold wet noses against her open palms.

Matt chuckled. "They've decided you're not a threat."

"Or dinner, I hope." She exhaled, resisting the urge to yank her hands out of their reach and wipe the dog slime off on her jeans.

"Harry, sit. Sally, sit." Digging into his pocket, Matt gave each dog a treat. "Stevie, once I get Miranda in the house, you can release them." He ruffled the small boy's hair, as he'd done to Zach. "Good job, buddy."

Stevie's wide smile revealed a missing tooth. "Hey, Dad, can we have chocolate milk tonight?"

"We'll see, son."

In the light from the bulb over the door, Miranda noted the same dark circles of exhaustion beneath Matt's eyes that she'd noticed the other night at the Wild Card.

As though reading her mind, Matt turned his face away and ushered her inside.

He halted in the doorway. "Dammit, Zach!"

A jumble of coats, boots and backpacks littered the mudroom.

Closing his eyes, Matt clasped both hands behind his neck and exhaled sharply.

In the awkward silence that followed, Miranda clenched her jaw and stared down at the toes of her boots.

A fresh wave of anger swept over her. How could Nikki abandon this good man and her two little boys?

The apparition at Aunt Cora's came to mind. Even in death, Nikki was counting on her to step in and rescue them.

She shouldn't have come tonight. She shouldn't have met Matt at the Wild Card. She shouldn't have slept with Declan.

Matt gently grasped her hand. "You okay? You look like you want to run for the hills." He grimaced. "I don't blame you."

Beneath the concern reflected in the depths of his hazel eyes, Miranda read his silent, desperate plea. "I'm good," she said, faking it.

His fingers tightened around hers. "It's all part of parenting, right?" Kicking a pair of boots clear of their path, Matt escorted her through the minefield into the kitchen. "Watch your step."

The dark wood floor encompassed a dining area, an island, stainless steel appliances, rustic hickory cabinets and granite countertops. Zach was studiously setting four plates on the rectangular hickory table.

Miranda caught the familiar glimmer of defiance, so like Nikki's, in Zach's green eyes. "Nice kitchen."

Matt pulled open one door of the enormous side-by-side and peered into the fridge. "It always looks good after the cleaning crew comes. What would you like? I have a great local microbrew, or wine—."

"I'll have chocolate milk," Zach interrupted, shooting Miranda another puckish grin before fixing a rebellious stare on his father.

"You're pushing it, Zachary," Matt said, his mouth a grim line. He pulled out a gallon of chocolate milk and glanced over his shoulder at Miranda.

"I think I'll save my beer for dinner," Miranda said.

Stevie thundered into the kitchen and glared at his brother. "Dad, Zach messed up the mudroom!"

"Dad," Zach mimicked, pointing dramatically at his brother's feet, "Stevie forgot to take his boots off. Again."

Stevie's face flushed red. He uttered a high-pitched yell and rushed the older boy.

Matt waded into the tangle of thrashing arms and legs, wedging his body between the boys. "That's enough."

He gripped Zach's shoulder and nudged the boy forward. "Stevie, please go take your boots off and wash your hands. You can keep cousin Miranda company, while Zachary and I have a talk upstairs."

Miranda flashed Matt a supportive smile.

Zach squirmed. "Ow, let go, you're hurting my arm!"

"Then keep moving. Back in my day it would've been your backside." Matt released the boy's arm and followed him from the room, trailing close behind.

"Mom said spanking is child abuse." Zach's protests gradually faded, ending with the distant sound of a door closing.

Stevie pulled a stool up to the sink and turned on the water. "Zach gets in trouble all the time." Hands dripping, he hopped down and swiped them on the towel draped over the oven handle.

"Wanna glass of chocolate milk?" His round face was transparent with hope. With his small thumbs hooked in the belt loops of his jeans, Stevie looked like a mini-Matt.

Miranda grinned. "Sure, if it won't spoil your dinner. I don't want you to get in trouble too."

Scrambling up on the granite counter, Stevie fished two plastic glasses out of the cupboard. "Naw, I always clean my plate. Poppy says I eat like a ranch hand. Besides, Mommy used to sometimes let me and Zach have a little glass of chocolate milk before we ate. She said it was a pair of teeth."

Aperitif.

Miranda folded her arms at Stevie's childish reference, sadness welling up within her. Nikki had often indulged in an aperitif before a meal, sometimes skipping the meal altogether.

Looking at Stevie, Miranda thought of Jeremy. Her throat constricted and tears pricked behind her eyes. Did her sweet little boy still remember her?

Miranda cleared her throat. Crouching so her face was level with Stevie's, she lowered her voice in a conspiratorial tone. "Can I tell you a secret? Milk gives me a tummy ache, so is it okay with you if I have water instead?"

Stevie nodded, a beaming smile lighting up his freckled face. "Sure thing. I'll get you some while you get my chocolate milk. Please," he said, with an appealing shrug.

Miranda gave his bony little shoulder a gentle squeeze. "Thanks."

She and Stevie had finished their drinks when a chastised Zach shuffled back through the kitchen on his way to the mudroom. Matt followed, a weary frown etching his features.

"What the—? Everything's all picked up." Zach's howl split the air.

Bolting out of the walk-in pantry, Matt glanced at Stevie, who held out both hands, palms up. "I just thought I'd help so we could eat sooner."

Zach stomped back into the kitchen and collapsed onto his chair with an exaggerated sigh. Crossing his arms, he scowled at his father. "Now what?"

Bending down, Matt retrieved an electric griddle from a lower cupboard. He set it on the island's broad countertop and plugged it in. "You can help Stevie muck out stalls tomorrow morning."

Flinging his head back, Zach uttered a melodramatic groan. "Oh my God! It'll take all day." He glared at his younger brother. "Stevie, you butt. You did that on purpose."

"That's enough, Zachary." Matt's voice carried a steely edge.

Zach slumped in his chair and sulked in silence.

Miranda glanced from Zach's stormy countenance to Stevie, nonchalantly licking the cloudy rim of his empty glass.

Matt shot her a halfhearted smile. He sliced several pieces off a giant red-wrapped brick of cheddar and nodded at her. "Want a refill?"

"I think I'm ready for that beer." She scooted back from the table. "You want one?"

He tilted his head in Zach's direction and grinned. "Do you even have to ask? Thanks." Pulling a stack of bread out of the wrapper, he assembled a row of sandwiches in front of him. "The opener's behind me. Here."

She took it from his hand. The corners of his mouth lifted and the gold-green color of his eyes brightened. Scooping a generous dollop of butter out of a plastic tub, he paused, staring down at the counter. "It's good to have you back, Mandy."

Miranda retreated behind the refrigerator door. She bit her lower lip and frowned. Had Nikki had been at work here, too? What ideas had she put in Matt's head?

She took out the chocolate milk and two amber bottles. Uncapping the beers, she handed one to Matt, who immediately took a healthy pull.

"Drinks all round," she said, filling both the boys' glasses before setting down the gallon jug and lifting her beer. "Here's to good times and chocolate milk!" She tapped her bottle to Zach's glass.

The boy stared daggers at her before lapsing back into his sulky pout.

Miranda turned to Stevie and tapped his glass.

"Good times and chocolate milk," Stevie echoed in a loud,

enthusiastic voice, jerking his glass high. Milk sloshed onto his hand and trickled down the sleeve of his red shirt.

Zach broke into a hearty belly laugh and pointed at his brother. "Good one, Stevie."

Smiling to himself, Stevie grabbed the wad of paper towels Matt handed him.

An affectionate glance passed between father and son. "Better go change your shirt, buddy." Matt slapped sandwiches on the electric griddle.

Zach downed his milk in a series of noisy, continuous gulps, ending with a loud belch. He slid Miranda a sly smirk before glaring at his father's back.

Matt opened the oven door and stirred the fries. Walking over to the table, he wrapped both arms around his older son. Hoisting Zach off the chair, he set the boy on his feet.

"Mandy, do me a favor and keep an eye on the food. It looks like Zachary and I need to have another talk."

Zach's smirk remained in place as Matt walked him out of the kitchen.

Stevie padded back into the room and heaved a hearty sigh. "No matter how hard I try to help, Zach still gets in trouble."

Miranda took both the boy's small, damp hands in hers and met his troubled gaze. "You have a big heart, Stevie. Zach is very lucky to have you as his brother."

Stevie nodded and rewarded her with another heart-warming gap-toothed grin.

She gave the boy another quick hug. "We'd better check on those sandwiches. You can help me flip them over."

The sandwiches had been grilled to perfection by the time Matt reappeared with a scowling, but subdued Zach.

Miranda opened the oven door. Squinting against the blistering heat, she slid the cookie sheet full of fries out and set it on top of the stove, then refilled the boys' glasses.

Stevie's eyes widened, and he gaped from her to his father. "Wow! We sometimes get seconds, but never three times."

Miranda laughed and stroked his straw-colored hair. What a little sweetheart.

Matt stared hard at Zach, until the sullen boy uncrossed his arms and shrugged. "Thanks."

She opened her paper napkin and placed it in her lap. She wished she could comfort Zach with a loving hug and tell him everything was going to be okay, but it was an outright lie and cold comfort to this grieving child.

Mercifully the meal passed uneventfully. Zach wolfed his fries down before eating his sandwich. Stevie studiously imitated his older brother, smacking his lips and wiping the back of his hand across his mouth.

A frown momentarily creased Matt's brow. He glanced at Miranda and scratched his jaw.

She shot him an understanding smile. He had to pick his battles, particularly with Zach.

Washing down the last bite of her thick, buttery sandwich with the rest of her beer, Miranda pushed her plate away. "I am so full I could."

"Bust a gut, is what we say." Zach cast a longing look at the fries remaining on her plate. "Can I have those?"

"Zachary." Matt's astounded tone punctuated his irritated expression. "How many times?"

"What? That's what you always do when it's just the three of us. You used to do it when Mom was still here, too."

Miranda gave Matt a pleading look. "I really can't eat another bite. How about we split them between you and Stevie, if it's okay with your dad?"

Zach rolled his eyes and gave a theatrical sigh. "Just once could I please not have to share? Why do I have to have a brother anyway? I wish Mom was here instead."

Stevie stared down at his plate. His lip quivered and he blinked long, fair lashes. A single tear rolled down his cheek. "Can I please be excused?"

Matt jerked to his feet. Zach flinched, but his father didn't look his way. Matt gently tugged the boy out of his chair. "Come on son, let's go upstairs while Zach clears the table and loads the dishwasher."

"But the chart says it's my turn." Stevie choked and wiped his nose on his shirtsleeve.

"I know, buddy, but you can have your turn tomorrow." He lifted Stevie in his arms and dropped a kiss on top of the boy's head.

Stevie turned his tear-streaked face back at Miranda. "Don't leave 'til we get back, okay?"

Miranda shook her emphatically. "No way. I'll be here."

Matt shot her a grateful smile as he carried Stevie from the room. "Thanks, Mandy."

She responded with a reassuring thumbs-up. Stevie was such a sweet little guy.

Zach shoved all the plates off the table. Silverware clattered on the floor. Fries flew everywhere. He stared at her insolently. "I'm not sorry either!"

A broken sob issued from his throat and his face crumpled. He huddled on the floor and buried his head in his skinny arms. "I hate life. It sucks."

Instinctively, Miranda got down on the floor and wrapped her arms around him. "Shhhhh. It's all right. It's all right, Zach."

He stiffened and shook his head furiously. "No. It isn't. It isn't all right."

Her throat tightened. "I know, Zach," she whispered and rested her head against the boy's. His hair smelled like it needed washing.

Zach twisted out of her arms. He stood over her and

clenched his fists. "Go away. Leave us alone. Leave my dad alone. He doesn't love you. He still loves my mom."

The boy tore out of the kitchen. His thudding footsteps echoed up the stairs and a door slammed.

The room swam back into focus. It looked like a frat house after a food fight. Heaving a sigh, Miranda collected the scattered plates. They were the durable kind and all intact, thank goodness.

She made it her mission to search and recover each one of the crinkled potatoes spread all over the dark planks. Action was preferable to thinking. The crushing weight of Nikki's loss, as unbearable as it was for her, paled in comparison to the devastating impact Nikki's abrupt death was having on Matt and the boys.

Especially on Zach. Not only did he look like his mother, but he appeared as volatile and high-strung as Nikki had been. What if he didn't have the right counselor? What if he didn't respond? He'd found his mother hanging in the barn. What kind of lasting psychological damage had that done?

Miranda's chest constricted and she drew a shallow breath followed by another. Even though she'd already had a beer, one Xanax might relax her enough to keep from bolting out the door.

Matt was still upstairs. She hurried into the mudroom. Her purse was hanging on the hook under her coat.

Her phone. She'd forgotten all about it. Declan might have texted—or called. She took a quick peek at the screen. Damn. Several notifications, but nothing from him.

Clutching her purse, she walked over to the entrance to the kitchen and listened. Nothing.

She unzipped the narrow compartment and froze. The pocket was empty and her pills were gone. Miranda searched her purse again and rifled her coat pockets. There were more pills at home, but that wasn't the point. What if

Zach—? She didn't even want to consider the possibility. If the boy had taken her Xanax, she needed to tell Matt. Now. Pressing her hand over her pounding heart, Miranda raced across the kitchen and almost collided with him in the doorway.

He reflexively reached out and gripped her by the arms. "Mandy, what's—?

"I think Zach took my pills. I just checked my purse and they're missing." Her voice sounded high, thin and desperate.

Matt released her and dug in the back pocket of his jeans. He shook the bottle, causing a violent rattling noise. "You mean these?"

Miranda held out her hand. "Yes. Where did you find them?"

He opened the bottle and stared down at the contents, his lips pursed. "I've seen these before."

I don't take them all the time. They're just in case."

He nodded sagely. "I've heard that before, too."

"I'm nothing like Nikki." Miranda folded her arms, heat rising in her face.

"Zach told me they fell out of your coat pocket and that he was going to hide them to help you." Matt's voice was calm. "That's how I know he likes you."

Miranda wasn't as sure of that as Matt was. She'd glimpsed the naked rage on the boy's face before he ran out of the kitchen. She couldn't tear her gaze from the container in his hand. "They didn't fall out of my coat pocket. They were zipped inside my purse. I don't think stealing someone's pills constitutes affection. It's a good thing you have him in therapy."

Matt's complexion paled and he narrowed his eyes. "What Zach did was wrong. I'll give you that, and I apologize, but dammit, Miranda, this shit is dangerous. Do you really want to turn out like Nikki...or your mother?" He slammed the bottle down on the granite countertop. "Take your damn pills."

It was as though he'd slapped her. She hadn't taken any because of her mother and Nikki. In the back of her mind she was afraid she was bipolar or crazy like Deirdre. She didn't need Matt being her conscience—making her feel bad about herself. "It's not your place to judge me." Her voice shook, and she dashed her hand across her wet eyes. "I thought you were my friend. Friends don't judge friends."

"It's because I'm your friend and because I care about you that I'm telling you this. I can't believe I'm doing this all over again. I'm not judging you, Mandy!"

He lifted his arms high in the air and let them fall at his sides. "It's because I—I don't want to lose you, too. Nikki knew we'd kissed up at the shack. She even told me more than once that if anything ever happened to her."

Miranda didn't want hear what Matt was about to say next. She just wanted to get her pills and go home. She'd had enough drama for one evening.

"You're absolutely right, Matt," she interrupted, snatching the bottle and stuffing it deep in the pocket of her jeans. "I don't want to turn out like Nikki or—" She gave a harsh, jaded laugh. "Or God forbid, like Deirdre. I've been in therapy, and this prescription was written under a psychiatrist's supervision."

He said nothing, an eloquent plea still evident in his expressive eyes.

There was nothing she could do, nothing she could say that would convince him that she was telling the truth. It would be better for both of them if she left now.

Miranda forced a smile. "I've taken up running, and it's helped me cope with my anxiety and—other issues. So, thanks for dinner and tell Stevie and Zach." Her voice trailed off into silence. "Tell them thanks, too." Hollow words for two hurting little boys.

Her eyes stung with fresh tears. She and Matt shared too much where Nikki was concerned.

She held her purse by the strap and struggled to get her other arm into her coat sleeve as she walked toward the door. Matt caught up to her and followed her outside into the frosty night. "Mandy."

"Please." Her breath puffed a cloud of vapor in the air. "Matt, please, go back in the house. You have no shoes on, no coat. You can't afford to get sick."

"I can't afford to let you go."

Miranda slid into her car, but before she could hit the lock button, Matt slipped into the seat beside hers. They were separated only by the console. "I know this is probably not the right time and sure as hell isn't the right place, but I'm not letting you go until we talk this out."

The cold penetrated the double layers of her coat. He had to be freezing. She turned the car on, switching the heat on high.

The outside light over the door to the house illuminated the determined set of his jaw and his intense gaze.

Matt leaned over and grasped the wheel. Miranda shrank against the door. The darkness, the close confines of the car triggered the vivid and terrifying memory of Scott's final brutal rage. He'd put his face so close to hers that his sour breath had cast furious spittle in her face.

"Jeremy isn't even legally yours, you bitch! So don't even think about suing for custody."

He'd gripped her upper arm in a crushing hold that had left a deep purple bruise on her pale flesh for a week. "I'd kill both you and Jeremy before I'd let you take him away from me."

Terror had paralyzed her vocal chords. She still remembered the scream trapped in her throat.

"Mandy, please, what in the hell is wrong with you?" Matt's pleading voice brought her back to the present, but the memory left her trembling.

"Don't look at me like that. I'm not going to hurt you, honey." He released the steering wheel and sagged back against the seat, his expression incredulous. "Son of a bitch, you were staring at me like I was an axe murderer."

Miranda chewed on her lower lip and rubbed her temples. Another flashback? She was on the verge of bursting into tears. Matt couldn't understand because he didn't know. Nobody knew, except her shrink, and Miranda wanted to keep it that way.

Matt expelled a resigned breath. When he finally spoke again, his voice was quiet. "Look, I'm sorry. I didn't mean to push you." He gave a bitter laugh. "My timing always seems to stink. 'Bye, Mandy."

"It's not you, Matt." She couldn't keep her voice from shaking. "It's me. It's not you." She swallowed in a vain attempt to steady her breathing. Head down, she sucked in air and gripped the steering wheel. "I've got a lot going on right now. I-I need time and space. Please. Please." Her voice dissolved into a whisper. "Please."

She jerked at the gentle pressure of his large hand on her shoulder. "I'll give you all the time and space you need, Mandy. I meant every word I said tonight."

Matt opened the passenger door, admitting a frigid blast of air, and then he was gone.

Miranda sighed and gazed out the windshield at the log-sided house. The light in the mudroom window went dark.

She put the car in gear and drove slowly back down the gravel drive. She'd made her share of mistakes in the past, but after tonight's events, coming back to Spencer seemed like the biggest mistake she'd made yet.

Instead of reclaiming her life, she'd managed to complicate and derail her recovery. Taking on the historical society's cause for Aunt Cora had led to sleeping with Declan, and if that wasn't bad enough, she'd just topped it off by adding this convoluted situation with Matt, Zach and Stevie into the mix.

Matt's biting words about turning out like Nikki and Deirdre haunted her. Maybe he was right. What would he say if he knew she'd slept with a man she barely knew?

CHAPTER 14

*W*ith Miranda clinging to his arm, Declan trudged up the steps leading to the brightly lit veranda of the Aspen Gold Lodge. It was going to be a long evening.

Miranda had called three weeks ago while he'd been driving to Denver. Her voicemail had sounded impersonal and scripted. He'd listened to it so many times, he'd memorized it.

"This is Miranda Buffet. I'm calling to confirm that you'll be escorting me to the Aspen Gold's Halloween Ball at the end of the month. If you are unwilling to attend, I understand. Please call or text me back at your earliest convenience."

She'd given him an out, but at the time he'd been so happy to hear her voice he'd immediately called, and then texted when it went to voicemail. He had accepted her invitation.

He'd missed her. He'd replayed their lovemaking over and over in his head. Her winsome, heart-shaped face and mossy green eyes had bewitched him.

The very same bewitching creature now accompanied

him as they approached the ornate front doors which, if memory served him right, led into an opulent lobby.

"Declan, this is a party, not an execution." Miranda's eyes sparkled, her cheeks pink. A black shoulder-length wig concealed her rich copper-colored hair.

"We make a dashing couple, don't you think? I've loved Grandpa's Halloween ball since Nikki and I were toddlers," Miranda chuckled. "The two of us took playing dress-up to a completely new level."

Declan smiled. He tipped the brim of his magician's hat and swirled his cape. Her enthusiasm was irresistible. Correction, *she* was irresistible. He was willing to come with her tonight and endure another endless charity gala because he wanted to believe that the night they'd shared had been more than sex.

Did she believe that?

Though he'd been busy sending online resumes and interviewing the past six weeks, he'd been unable to erase the memory of Miranda lying in his bed after their lovemaking, her long, fiery hair against her pale shoulders, her provocative eyes intent on his as they'd talked nonstop into the morning.

"Hello. Earth to Declan. I love it when you get that sexy look in your gorgeous blue eyes, but this is not the time or the place." Miranda's full red lips curved in a teasing smile.

Grinning, he slipped her coat off her shoulders and swallowed hard, tempted to cover her back up again. "Sorry, I couldn't help myself."

Miranda's shiny red, blue and gold costume was low cut on top and short on the bottom. His gaze drifted over the evident gooseflesh that dimpled the enticing expanse of her cleavage. White stars amplified the snug-fitting blue shorts, which barely covered her charming derriere and the tempting curve of her hips. Her slender, shapely legs appeared longer in the knee-high red boots. A searing flash of heat surged through his lower extremities.

"Do you like it?" Miranda's flush deepened and her thick black lashes fluttered. "I hope you don't mind. It's very daring and not something I would normally wear, but Nikki and I idolized Wonder Woman when were kids."

She hugged herself and stared down at her toes.

Like it? He liked it so much he wanted to drag her into the nearest alcove and ravish her senseless behind the potted fall foliage.

What he didn't like was sharing the tempting vision she presented. Every man within fifty feet of them was already ogling her, but the last thing Declan wanted to do was make her feel self-conscious. He'd never seen her happier. Resting his hands on the cool, soft skin of her bare shoulders, he planted a proprietary kiss on her hot cheek. "You definitely do the costume justice."

Inclining her head in his direction, her lashes dipped and lifted. The sultry expression in her eyes brimmed with an intimate promise.

"There you are." A tall, muscular man possessing a deep commanding voice strode up to them.

The pirate's green eyes, a masculine version of Miranda's, were trained on Declan.

"Heath?" She laughed, wrinkling her nose delightfully and launching her scantily-clad self into the pirate's arms.

He enveloped her in a brief hug, then held her out at arm's length and examined her costume. "On you, that outfit should be illegal, and I don't know where in the hell you're going to put my security pin."

Miranda's smile faltered. Her face turned the color of a ripe strawberry. She raised her charming chin. "I know the perfect place to put your f-ing pin."

A good-natured guffaw rumbled from Heath's broad

chest, and he released her. "Now that's the big sister I know and love."

She inclined her head. "Declan, meet my brother, Heath Lawe. Heath, my guest, Declan Elliot."

In a breathless voice she gushed on: "Declan's a talented architect from Boston. His designs are incredible, and he's looking for work."

Miranda's brother extended his hand. "Declan. Interesting name."

The man had a firm grip. His watchful gaze scanned Declan in a swift assessment and then shifted back to his sister.

Heath grasped her arm. "Time to go, Mandy. Deke's waiting on you. We're supposed to grab Jack and Ryder before meeting up with the old man."

Declan flexed his fingers and mentally counted to ten. He'd been inspected and dismissed before. The term, "interesting," had been applied to his name before. It echoed the superior attitude of his frat brothers and had followed him into his professional life. What stung was Miranda's humiliating introduction.

He thought he'd made it clear that he could find his own job. He'd meant the designs he'd shown her for her eyes alone.

Like it or not, he wasn't about to be summarily dismissed again. Declan cleared his throat and stepped forward, invading their tight, intimate circle. His gaze intercepted Miranda's.

She laid a palm on her brother's chest. "Hey, Heath, give us a minute."

Heath glanced at his watch. "That's about all the time you have. You know how the old man is about being late."

Miranda clasped Declan's hand in both of hers and gave him an apologetic smile. "I'm sorry. I was so excited about tonight, I forgot to tell you that Grandpa called at the last minute this afternoon and asked me to help him greet guests." The contrite expression in her emerald eyes pleaded with him to understand. "It should only take about an hour and then we'll have the whole rest of the evening together."

She glanced back at her brother and sighed, dropping her voice. "I'd forgotten all about helping Heath out with his security system. All I have to do is wear a pin of some kind, so that won't take any time at all."

With soft fingers, she squeezed Declan's hand. "I'll make it up to you."

Over her shoulder, the pirate shifted from one high black boot to the other, his arms crossed, his lips pursed.

Declan smiled to himself. It wouldn't hurt the smug bastard to wait another thirty seconds. He returned her squeeze and leaned closer, inhaling an enticing whiff of her exotic floral scent. "I'll be thinking of ways you can make it up to me while you're gone."

He brushed his lips against her temple, stirring the delicate crystal globe that dangled from her earlobe. "Go with the buccaneer before he runs me through."

She closed her eyes and shivered, clamping her hands around his. Loosening her grip, she trailed her fingers across his palm. "An hour, I promise."

His body tightened in response. Exhaling, he widened his stance.

Other than the color of their eyes, he didn't see much resemblance between Miranda and her brother. Miranda's willowy form reminded him of the graceful, sculpted lines of a figurine. Heath Lawe was built like the Parthenon.

Watching her stride beside her brother, Declan's gaze gravitated below the curve of her waist, to the tantalizing sway of her hips.

Another quick glance around confirmed his ugly suspicion. The other male guests in the immediate vicinity shared his appreciation of that particular part of Miranda's delectable anatomy.

Declan frowned and craned his neck. Where were those waiters with the champagne?

God, he hated affairs like this. He didn't know anybody here, but he'd bet they were all in the top one percent of the wealthiest people in the state.

He lifted his white cuff and set a notification on his watch. He'd get a drink and scope the place out. If Miranda wasn't finished in fifty-seven minutes, he'd go through the receiving line alone and personally introduce himself to Jakob Spencer, regardless of the social consequences.

Hell, he was as good as the rest of them. He could just act as entitled as Miranda's overbearing brother and Spencer's wealthy patriarch.

❖

"He's an improvement on the midget."

Miranda's lips twitched. Both Heath and Hunter stood a good head taller than her ex. Her brothers had applied the wicked nickname to Scott from day one. "I think so."

"That's obvious." Heath shot her a teasing grin. "Your 'talented architect' is almost as tall as I am, but I'd still whip his ass."

She upped her pace and ignored his jibe. Heath lived to debate and she wouldn't give her younger brother the satisfaction.

He playfully tugged her wig. "Hey, Alex is at the kid's party and I'm too busy with security tonight to spend much time with Cassie. I thought maybe she could hang out with you. If Devlin doesn't mind."

"It's Declan. Of course Cassie's welcome to join us."

Her brother scanned the crowd. "The dude's kind of got a touchy attitude, doesn't he?" Heath chuckled and tugged her wig again. "Extremely territorial. He gave a low whistle and shook his head. "It might have something to do with your hot costume."

Miranda slugged his rock-hard arm. "Stop! And leave my wig alone. Why don't you go help Grandpa? I'll check in with Deke and track down Jack and Ryder."

Fifteen minutes later, Deke had finished briefing her about her security pin, and Miranda wandered among the costumed guests, searching for her cousins.

Deke's expression had been comical as he'd looked her over to find a place to put the tiny pin. He'd finally thrown his arms up in the air and handed it to her. "Just put it wherever."

Her initial excitement was fading, replaced with the familiar suffocating blanket of anxiety.

Declan was being a good sport about everything, but she'd read the flash of irritation in his eyes and noted the tight set of his jaw. She couldn't blame him. She was upset at herself for spacing off everything and neglecting to tell him about Grandpa's request ahead of time.

It was also obvious that Declan and Heath had gotten off on the wrong foot. God knew, Heath could be curt, especially when he was focused on an assignment like tonight's trial run of the lodge's security system.

Intense focus was a Spencer family trait that she and her twin brothers possessed in an unhealthy amount.

Her wellness coach was right. Trying to appease her grandfather, her brother and Declan was exhausting. If juggling those three wasn't enough, Matt was sure to be here somewhere and running into him was inevitable.

She couldn't worry about that right now. Retracing her steps, she finally spotted Jack leaving Deke's station to join

Kate and Ryder, the latter appearing captivated by his exotic-looking companion.

Intercepting Jack, Miranda signaled Ryder to follow. She led the way toward the reception line. "Sorry dudes. We're already late and Grandpa's going to be grumpy."

Jack frowned, but dutifully followed Ryder.

Grandpa stood at the head of the line, his posture confident and erect. His white hair was impeccably styled and he sported his customary tux.

Willa stood next to Grandpa, and beside her, Heath. Jack and Ryder seamlessly took their places after Heath.

Miranda had always dreaded the social tradition of greeting and exchanging pleasantries with one guest after another. She'd be under the town's microscope tonight.

Drawing a deep breath, she slipped into line next to Grandpa and plastered on her best, hospitable smile.

Heath rolled his eyes.

Grandpa swept a quick glance over her. His bushy brows came together, the same disapproving look Miranda remembered from childhood. He switched his attention from her to the two couples who'd just filed in through the arched doorway.

Once the guests moved on, she enveloped her grandfather in a quick hug. "Sorry, Grandpa."

The older man's large, warm hands grasped hers. "Your brother already filled me in. I see what he meant about your costume. There's certainly not much left to the imagination."

He darted his keen green eyes behind her. "Where's your guest?"

Damn. Where had her brains disappeared to? She'd been so flustered, she'd forgotten to bring Declan and make her introductions. So much for making a good first impression.

Miranda studied the toes of her red boots, her mind raced to come up with some idiotic excuse. She glanced up,

prepared to confess her stupidity and, like magic, the next
guest coming through the line was Declan. She resisted the
impulse to leap into his arms and kiss him.

"He's right here. Grandpa, I'd like you to meet my guest
for the evening, Declan Elliot. Declan, my grandfather, Jakob
Spencer."

Declan extended his hand, his earlier scowl replaced by a
polite smile. "Sir."

Jakob shook hands, his shrewd gaze appraising. "Mr.
Elliot. I'll cut Mandy loose as soon as most of my guests
arrive."

"Yes, sir." Declan's tone was cordial enough, but the
muscle in his jaw twitched. Turning his attention on her, he
enveloped her hand in his and leaned close, pressing cool lips
against her cheek, before moving on to Heath.

Miranda raised her palm to her tingling face and stared at
Declan's handsome profile.

His contact with her brother was mercifully brief and
civil. Jack pumped Declan's hand with a friendly grin.
Declan's rigid pose softened and he responded with an easy
smile.

"Miranda," Her grandfather's brusque tone jarred her
concentration. His mild expression indicated the couple
standing in front of her. "Please welcome Mr. and Mrs. Bill
Martin."

❦

Declan stood on the periphery of the dance floor and sipped
his third--or was it his fourth?--glass of champagne. It had
better be his last, at least until after he'd eaten something. He
released his pent-up breath and flexed his fingers. Another
glance at his watch would only underscore how long he'd
been waiting.

The reception line was still going strong. Miranda had been too busy flirting with a guy dressed like Buffalo Bill to look up and notice him, but her pirate of a brother had tipped his head in Miranda's direction and shot Declan an arrogant smirk.

Declan swigged a healthy dose of champagne and clenched his jaw. As desirable and tempting as Miranda was, he should never have agreed to come. He tugged his ear and focused on the decorated ballroom. Anything to pass the time.

The backdrop surrounding the elevated bandstand was sufficiently spooky with stark fluorescent trees and a giant full moon. Three witches in full flight were silhouetted against its glowing surface. The chandelier overhead shone with a muted green radiance, illuminating a dark purple and gold curtain.

"Declan, I'm sorry it took so long."

He glanced over his shoulder. Miranda's breathless apology was reflected in her anxious heart-shaped face. Stroking his arm, she linked her fingers with his, reminding him of the night she'd spent in his bed.

God help him!

He grinned to counteract his heated reaction. Heart pounding, he tipped his flute to her delectable lips. "Have a sip."

Miranda swallowed, tilting the glass higher. "Thanks, I'm dying of thirst. Oops!"

"Oh my, you've got champagne. Everywhere." Releasing her hand, he whipped a scarlet handkerchief from the pocket of his costume. Dabbing her mouth and chin, he eyed the sparkling droplets on her cleavage. If they were alone in his bed instead of stuck at this party, he'd take his tongue and—.

Miranda snatched the handkerchief from his grasp and pressed it to her chest. "I've got it."

Declan blinked and examined the nearly-empty flute.

He finished it off and cleared his throat. "Another dead soldier, as my dad would say."

A server bearing a loaded tray approached.

Declan reached for a refill. With an indulgent grin, Miranda lightly smacked his hand and towed him after her. "You might want to eat something first. We're supposed to find our seats. Grandpa has reserved tables for the family."

Minutes later, he was seated right next to the old man. Declan peered around Jacob. Miranda sat between Aunt Cora and Jakob's striking lady. Spencer had introduced the silver-haired woman sitting on the other side of him as Willa Samuels.

Declan returned Miranda's frown and popped a stuffed mushroom into his mouth. Yeah, he was buzzed, but she had nothing to worry about. The Wild Card had been a momentary descent into despair.

At the Boston firm, he'd been expected to attend any number of formal occasions, more than he wanted to count. He'd been buzzed plenty times before. His privileged frat brothers at Princeton had initiated him into the finer points of drinking.

"The mushrooms are good, but the steak tartare on toast is one of our specialties. We use nothing but locally raised, grass-fed beef." Jakob Spencer licked his lips and helped himself to two of the meaty appetizers. "Take a few. They're delicious."

Declan nodded and faked another polite smile as he filled his small plate from the silver tray Jakob held out to him. "Thank you."

The old man was right. The savory meat dissolved in his mouth. Declan devoured everything on his plate and sipped his water, hoping another tray of food would show up soon.

He stole another glance at Miranda. He couldn't wait to

get her out on the dance floor. She'd promised to make all this up to him, and he'd mulled over a host of sensuous possibilities.

Two in particular. He'd whisper them into her ear, making her close her eyes and shiver like she had earlier.

Aunt Cora was an unexpected surprise. The hippie woman wore her hair up in a stylish nineteenth century pompadour and her floor-length gown complemented her tall, angular frame. Her brown eyes sparkled, and her lips were tinted a becoming pink. She had an attractive smile and seemed at home amidst the snobs, probably because she couldn't care less what they thought.

Declan chuckled to himself. Cora Fleming was beginning to grow on him.

Jakob leaned his way. "I heard about Snow Peak Properties. I won't lie. I'm relieved. A casino is the last kind of enterprise Spencer needs. Otherwise, I would've already built it."

There it was. Jakob Spencer's real reason for sitting him where he had. Declan stared at the older man in stony silence.

Spencer's piercing gaze never wavered. "Hear me out, Mr. Elliot. This isn't personal, this is business. I can always use a good architect."

He clapped Declan on the back. "I have a couple of projects in mind. Stop by my office next week if you're interested."

"Sure." Declan managed a brittle smile and knocked back the rest of his water. He wouldn't go there right now. Thinking about working for Miranda's grandfather would ruin his plans for later.

As soon as this ordeal was over.

Jakob rose from his chair. "Excuse me. It looks as though

my daughter wants something." He gripped Declan's shoulder. "Think about what I said."

❧

Miranda nibbled on the appetizers on her plate and sipped champagne. Even though the receiving line was behind her and the bubbly was kicking in, she was still on diplomatic duty.

Grandpa had deliberately seated Declan beside himself, and she'd been casting stealthy glances up the table while conversing with Aunt Cora.

Though most of Jakob's attention had been transfixed on Willa, Miranda knew from past experience that he'd eventually accomplish whatever his objective was concerning Declan.

Grandpa leaned closer to Declan and said something. She stopped breathing and fisted the napkin in her lap.

Aunt Cora squeezed Miranda's arm reassuringly with a gloved hand. "Looks like Mr. Elliot is holding his own with the old fart." She glanced at Miranda's plate and arched a penciled brow. "If you want to drink you better eat more."

"I know, but Declan's on edge and Grandpa can be so ruthless." Leaning over the table so the excess tomato concoction dropped on her plate, Miranda sighed and dutifully bit into a heaped bruschetta.

"Honey, you don't have any control over what's going on between those two." Cora curled her arm around Miranda's shoulders. "As hard as it is, you have to trust your man."

Miranda nodded and sipped more champagne.

"Excuse me." Willa leaned over on Miranda's other side, her luminous violet eyes reflecting genuine warmth. "Cora, I haven't had a chance to tell you how glad I am that you and Jakob have settled your differences. I'm so happy you could join us. Your costume is stunning, and so are you. I love your hair. Did you do that yourself?"

Aunt Cora's brown eyes shone and a becoming flush graced her high cheekbones. "I took a picture with me and showed it to Claudia over at the beauty shop. That girl can work miracles!"

Willa's musical laugh was contagious. Miranda actually savored the stuffed mushroom and relaxed against the back of her chair.

The charming artist had sure worked miracles with Grandpa. Miranda had never seen him so content. Never in her wildest dreams would she have connected the word "content" with Jakob Spencer.

Both Willa and Cora got up from the table to visit the ladies room. Miranda rested her chin in her hand and smiled wistfully after the two older women, an ache in her chest. That could've been her and Nikki someday.

Sighing, she drained her glass and glanced at the other end of the deserted table. Declan was leaning back in his chair absently rubbing his ear. His transparent blue gaze was focused on her.

Frowning, he picked up his glass and walked down to where she sat. Sitting in Aunt Cora's chair, he scooted closer. "You okay?"

Miranda pressed her lips together and nodded. He'd been looking at her with such longing. Desire, yes, but an unguarded tenderness that clutched her heart and made her want to weep.

She wished they were alone so she could tell him what she'd been thinking, share everything she was feeling.

Swallowing hard, she directed her attention to the lavish autumn centerpiece. A tear escaped from the corner of her eye. She quickly brushed it away and shrugged. "Sometimes thoughts of Nikki just pop out of nowhere."

Declan grasped her hand and raised it to his lips. "I know," he said.

Conversation around them hushed. Someone whispered, "Aunt Cora and Willa?"

Miranda blinked, still reeling from Declan's tenderness, his unspoken declaration. She reluctantly shifted her attention to the two women entering the ballroom from a side door. "Oh my God. Declan, look."

"Who's that with Cora?" Declan slipped an arm around her and peered over her shoulder. His breath fanned her cheek.

Miranda rested comfortably against him. "It's Willa. She's Winifred."

"Who's Winifred?"

"She's one of the witch sisters in the movie, *Hocus Pocus*. Miranda turned to gape at Declan. "You've never seen the movie?"

Declan's interest was riveted on Willa. "I don't think so. I'd remember if I had. Wow, she's like some alternate universe version of the Queen of Hearts with buck teeth."

Miranda laughed. "I never looked at Winifred that way, but you have a point. I'll have to remember to tell Grandpa.

"*Hocus Pocus* is his favorite lame Halloween movie. From the time we were kids, we've watched it every year. It's tradition."

Miranda clung to Declan's arm and pointed. "The twenties flapper is my Aunt Zoe. Ryder's mom. She's the glue that keeps all of us cousins together."

"Your aunt sounds like a very special lady," Declan said. He kissed the top of her head. "Ugh. I'll be glad when you can lose the wig."

Zoe led Aunt Cora and the costumed Willa over to the head table. She spotted Miranda and waved before saying something to Jack and Kate.

Aunt Cora dropped into the seat on Miranda's other side. A wide grin stretched across her face. She looked ten years younger and ready to burst.

Miranda narrowed her gaze. "Aunt Cora, you're up to something."

The lights dimmed. A spotlight skipped across the curtain behind the stage. A twang cut the air, silencing conversation. The curtain parted, and there was Grandpa—wearing a costume.

A collective gasp was followed by a swelling murmur and applause.

It was Grandpa, but it was hard to reconcile the wild-haired, ragged zombie shuffling to the middle of the stage with Jakob Spencer.

Aunt Cora poked Miranda with her elbow and chortled. "Billy and Winifred. Well done. I told Jakob he'd shock the hell out of everyone."

Miranda rolled her eyes and leaned closer to Declan. "I should've guessed. All I can say is Grandpa must really love Willa a lot because he's never dressed in costume before. Not for anyone."

Jakob made a show of cutting the "stitching" around his mouth. Smiling broadly, he welcomed everybody to the Aspen Gold Halloween Gala. He pitched the historical society and donations for the one-room schoolhouse restoration project.

Aunt Cora beamed and nudged Miranda for a discreet high five. "All our determination and hard work is going to pay off."

Miranda glanced at Declan. He shrugged. A corner of his mouth quirked with a resigned smile. She squeezed his hand, and he squeezed back.

The bandleader raised his arms and the smoky strains of

a sax, accompanied by a bass, launched into a slow, rich melody.

Grandpa came down from the stage and held out his hand to Willa. She met him in the center of the dance floor. Removing her buck teeth she stepped into Grandpa's outstretched arms for a long, loving kiss.

Miranda watched the couple dance, acutely aware of Declan behind her. He lightly skimmed his fingers across her bare back. She shivered and her skin broke out in pleasurable goosebumps.

He chuckled softly. "I've been thinking of all the ways you can make it up to me."

A server placed fresh sparkling flutes of champagne on the table.

Miranda sipped the effervescent wine and struggled to slow her racing heart. Although she loved this party and celebrated Grandpa's newfound happiness, in her mind the gala was over. She was lying in Declan's arms, surrendering to his tender kisses.

The music faded and someone handed Grandpa a mic. "I'd like to invite our families to join us."

Declan gently pried the champagne flute out of her grasp. "Let's dance." Leading her out onto the floor, he wrapped his arm around her and pulled her close.

Miranda clasped her hands behind his neck, closed her eyes and swayed in a warm sensual haze of champagne, music and Declan's woodsy scent.

His hot breath tickled her ear. "Okay, I'm starting to enjoy myself." Pressing his hand against the small of her back, he aligned her body along the sculpted length of his.

"I'm glad." She was dying to ask him about Grandpa, but why risk spoiling everything? Bold with champagne, she kissed the roughened texture of his throat and flattened her palm over the hammering beat of his heart.

Every square inch of her body hummed with sensual alertness. The magic of the night stretched ahead of them, brimming with promise and passion.

The music abruptly came to a halt. A screen descended from the high ceiling, and a scene from the movie flickered behind the live band.

Still holding her, Declan expelled a frustrated breath. "Now what?"

Miranda giggled like a silly schoolgirl. The champagne and the steady pressure Declan applied along her spine made her giddy. She stood on tiptoe, her lips grazing his ear and launched into her best Winifred imitation. "I put a spell on you. And now you're mine."

The band merged with the projected group on the screen and burst in a spirited rendition of the song from the movie.

Miranda moved her hips and stepped up her rhythm to the music's brisk tempo.

Declan half-grinned and looked from her to the costumed guests rocking out around them. He shook his head and gently grasped her arm. "Let's sit this one out."

"Why?" She dropped into the chair he'd pulled out for her.

Declan flashed his dimples and lightly traced her collarbone with a warm finger. He casually reached for her drink and emptied half its contents.

"Hey, you." Miranda reached out, waggling her fingers for her glass. She licked her numb lips. "I think you've had quite enough. You're a little bit tipsy, Mr. Elliot."

She turned to see if Aunt Cora had witnessed his brazen flirtation.

Cora was watching Grandpa and Willa enthusiastically dancing among the other guests. Heartache stamped her features.

She absently toyed with the filigreed chain that lay

beneath her amethyst pendant. The same vulnerable, unfocused expression had blurred her features that afternoon at the schoolhouse. Her gloved fingers had fiddled with the necklace hidden beneath her wooly scarf.

Aunt Cora had been in love.

She and Nikki had always suspected it. Miranda was sure of it now.

"They make a cute couple." Declan's low-pitched remark was sincere.

Miranda stared at him, struggling to wrap her mind around her epiphany.

"Your grandpa and his lady." Declan cleared his throat. "Excuse me, I mean Billy and Winifred."

He circled his arms around her and rested his chin on the top of her head.

She laughed, covering his hands with hers. "They do."

He chose that moment to plant his lips between her bare shoulder blades. An erotic jolt coursed through her. Her backward glance collided with his. The message she read in his liquid gaze was unmistakable.

Declan nodded in Aunt Cora's direction. "Excuse us."

Miranda's pulse quickened as he led her out on the parquet floor. "How come you only like to dance to the slow songs?"

"Why do you think?" Declan drew her into his embrace, brushing his lips briefly against her temple.

Miranda nestled against him. She wanted this dance to last forever. "I'm going to practice living in the moment."

"Practice all you want, sweetheart." Under her cheek, Declan's chest heaved with silent laughter. He pulled her closer and swung her a little off balance. "Practice all you want."

Smiling, she buried her fingers in his thick hair and

stroked the back of his neck. "Ummm, I'm glad you lost the hat."

"Now who's tipsy?" His chuckle sounded a little breathless. One of his hands slipped lower on her waist.

"A little bit, maybe." Miranda nuzzled his wiry jaw. His beard tickled her lips. "You smell nice, too."

Declan gazed down at her. "I like it when you're a little tipsy." He stroked her cheek, grazing her lips with his thumb. "You're not on your guard as much."

She closed her eyes and swayed with the melody. The nice thing about champagne was it blurred all the sharp edges of her life. The lyrics to the song were about dreams. Tonight she felt as though all her dreams were within her grasp.

"Remember when you said you'd make it up to me?" Declan's low, husky tone reminded her of his bedroom, the moonlight spilling over his face, his broad shoulders, his narrow hips.

"Excuse me." Matt's familiar voice intruded, shattering her pleasurable fantasy.

Running into him had been inevitable, but why now?

CHAPTER 15

*D*eclan released her with a forced smile. "Ah, an outlaw from your checkered past. I told you all the boys would want to dance with you-even the bank robbers."

Matt shot Declan an annoyed look. "We're old friends." Hooking his arm around her, he swept her closer and transitioned into a smooth box step.

Miranda turned her head. Where was Declan? She dropped a step and trod on Matt's boots. "Sorry. When did you learn to dance? You used to hate it."

His gaze focused elsewhere and he loosened his hold a notch. "I still don't like it. Nikki signed us up for ballroom dancing. She said it was something we could do together besides fight."

Exhaling a heavy sigh, he searched Miranda's face. "What's going on with the magician?"

Miranda stiffened. "What do you mean?"

Matt frowned. "I'm your friend and I'm asking because I care about you. You told me you needed time, but that wasn't the whole truth was it? It's obvious the two of you have some history together."

A wave of heat flooded her chest and scorched her cheeks. What would he think of her if he knew just how much history she and Declan shared? "Matt, it's complicated."

"Look at me, Mandy." Matt's expression was earnest. "I'm worried about you. The episode with the pills the other night at the house was troubling enough. Now you're picking up strangers."

"Picking up strangers?" Miranda lowered her voice. "You're making me sound like Deirdre all over again. The magician's name happens to be Declan and he isn't a stranger."

"Okay. So where did you meet Declan and how long have you known him?"

"Matthew. We're dancing." Friend or not, she wanted to tell him that it was none of his business. She appreciated his concern. She owed him an explanation, but now was not the time or the place. She didn't have the energy to argue about pills, or Deirdre, or Nikki. Besides, he didn't need one more thing to cope with. Miranda pictured Zach and Stevie's confused, childish faces. A razor-sharp pang of guilt stabbed her and her shoulders sagged.

"Matt, please stop pressuring me. Like I told you before, I do need time. I need time to get my own life straight. Her adrenaline level spiked and her voice shook. She tapped her index finger against her chest. My life, Matt. Not yours, not even Zach and Stevie's, not Nikki's last wishes, but my life!"

Unloading all her emotional baggage on Matt wasn't fair. If she was being honest with herself, she should be pounding this truth home to Declan as well. Where was he anyway?

Matt's tight-lipped expression reminded her of that night in the kitchen when she'd accused Zach of taking her pills.

Miranda was vaguely aware that the music had ended and they'd stopped dancing. She raised her hands as though to cradle his bearded face, then dropped her arms at her sides. "Matt, I'm sorry."

He looked incredibly sad and infinitely tired. "I'm sorry too." As he walked off the dance floor, Miranda was reminded of the adolescent boy he'd been that afternoon, long ago up at the shack. After he'd kissed her and apologized.

He'd apologized because he hadn't meant to kiss her in the first place. Nikki had hurt him. He'd been stung and angry. The dream Miranda had nursed and carried around in her memory had been an illusion, a teenage girl's fantasy.

The band launched into a vigorous rock-and-roll classic. Miranda threaded her way back to their table. Declan would be waiting for her. She'd soothe his injured pride and later tonight, lying in bed with his arms around her, she'd tell him all about Matt and finally lay that tattered memory to rest.

❧

Declan paused at the edge of the dance floor, hands tightly fisted in his pockets. The same dude in the receiving line that Miranda had flirted with earlier was dancing with his girl. What really grated was that the *outlaw* had cut in, interrupting their private, erotic interlude.

Rubbing his neck, Declan recalled Miranda's feather-soft kisses along his jaw. He'd slipped his palm down her back to the hollow just above the curve of her bottom, pressing that delectable part of her slender body against his.

Declan would ask around and find out who the guy was. Aunt Cora would know. He suspected the outlaw was Matt Chandler, but he wanted to confirm it.

He cast one last glance over his shoulder in time to catch

Miranda stumble and step on the cowboy's fancy boots. Declan grinned. He'd let Miranda dance with her outlaw friend. In the meantime, he'd grab something to drink before going back to their table.

Later tonight, they could continue their interlude where they'd left off. He could wait. Miranda would make tolerating this ordeal worth it.

He headed in the direction of one of the bars. Remembering his last visit to the Wild Card and how he'd felt the morning after, he ordered a soda instead.

"Declan." It was Jack, the guy dressed like Ricky Ricardo, along with the tall, ghostly-looking cowboy. Miranda's cousins.

"Remember us from the reception line? I'm Jack and the marshal here is Ryder Barlow, also known as 'Mr. Hollywood.'"

"Knock it off, Jack." Affectionate exasperation laced Ryder's voice.

He shook Declan's hand, his expression amiable. "Good to meet you again."

Jack shrugged and flashed Declan a good-natured grin. "Why don't you grab a beer with us? Kate and Vianna went to the ladies room."

The guy meant well, but Declan wasn't in the mood to socialize. Miranda was probably already back at their table, waiting for him. Nevertheless, he momentarily stifled his impatience and dredged up a smile. "I'd better not. I've already drunk a shitload of champagne."

"Okay. Finish what you're having then. We told the girls we'd meet them here, so grab a table with Ryder, and I'll get the beers."

Declan frowned at Jack's retreating figure, costumed in the puffy-sleeved shirt and fitted Cuban trousers. "He sure has the Spencer DNA."

Ryder laughed and slapped his thigh. "Exactly." His green eyes reflected ironic amusement. "We're actually likeable once you get to know us. Let's grab that table and talk for a few minutes. If that's okay with you."

Declan nodded and trailed behind Barlow. At least one Spencer had a sense of humor.

He'd sit with them until his drink was gone and then cut out. "I've got about fifteen minutes."

"Yeah, before Mandy comes looking for you." Jack ambled toward them, bearing two pints of amber brew.

Ryder shook his head and sipped his beer. "We heard about your business partner ripping you off. It's probably a good thing he split. Mandy's always been the nicest of our bunch, but trust me, the way she'd looked, that jerk wouldn't want to meet up with her anytime soon."

Declan's gut clenched. Why did Miranda have to go around sharing his disgrace with all her rich relatives? He glanced at his half-empty drink. He'd kill it off with a couple more swallows and leave. He'd text Miranda, offer some excuse and talk to her tomorrow after he cooled off. His erotic plans for later tonight had just been cancelled.

"When did you talk to her?" It didn't matter much anymore. It was more to make conversation until he could split.

Ryder tipped his glass and licked his upper lip. "Ran into her over at Pearl's the other day."

"Yup." Jack looked at Declan and grinned. "She's pretty damn sweet on you. She talked you up and asked us to spread the word around."

"Until you can get back on your feet," Ryder interjected, belching softly behind his fist.

Humiliating rage rose in Declan's chest. He wanted to heave the rest of his drink across the room. Instead he clenched his jaw and pasted a smile on his face. "She's quite the promoter, isn't she?"

Jack looked at Declan thoughtfully over the rim of his glass. "It's more about loyalty than promotion."

He shot Declan a sympathetic glance and sighed. "What happened to you was damn rotten. The old man should've at least given you a head's up."

"What do you mean?" Nerves strung tight, Declan braced his shoulders. He forced a bitter sounding laugh. "Sounds like the whole f-ing town knew I was conned, except me."

Ryder shifted in his chair and shook his head, his gaze candid. "Not really. Nobody really knew except Grandad. He makes it his business to know everything that can possibly affect Spencer or the family. He'd vetted your partner, and you've been under his magnifying glass as well. We in the family refer to it as loving manipulation."

Jack glanced at Ryder. "Some of us call it something a lot stronger."

Declan drained his glass. "So, Mr. Spencer told you."

Ryder shook his head and took a swig of his beer. "Mandy told us she'd found out when she'd had breakfast with Grandad and Willa. She said she was going to tell you." His eyes widened and he looked from Declan to Jack. "Shit."

Jack gave a low whistle and stared down at the littered tabletop. "Shit is right," he said, under his breath.

Declan lifted his cuff. He glanced at the black face of his watch, rose to his feet and gave both men a stiff smile. "I'm sure she meant to. We haven't seen a whole lot of each other the past week and tonight's been pretty crazy."

Ryder leaned forward. "How about getting together soon? Jack and I have an idea we'd like to run past you."

Swallowing the bile rising in his throat, Declan held out his hand. "You have a card?"

Ryder opened his wallet and produced one slightly creased business card. He grimaced. "From my Hollywood days. Use the cell number."

Declan stuck the card in his pocket. He shook Ryder's hand, then Jack's. "Thanks. I'll be in touch."

He strode rapidly through the lobby, training his gaze above everyone's heads. Once he was out the door and onto the wide veranda, he sucked in deep, chilling gulps of mountain air.

Tipping the valet, he climbed into the privacy of his truck and shifted into gear. Tomorrow, he'd text Ryder a short, polite message declining their invitation. Well intentioned or not, he didn't need anyone's pity.

Declan stopped at his house briefly to change out of the silly costume and pack an overnight bag.

He'd been gut-punched enough tonight. First, with Miranda's arrogant brother, then old man Spencer, rubbing it in. Telling him it wasn't personal and throwing a job in his face, like tossing a dog a bone. That was choice.

Declan shut his eyes briefly, before backing out of his drive. And Miranda. Spreading his humiliation all over town and begging jobs for him after he'd told her repeatedly that he was capable of finding his own work. Pulling out on the highway, he laughed out loud and tried to subdue the lump rising in his throat, making his eyes water. Miranda had the Spencer DNA in spades.

He wanted to go home. Talk to his mom and dad. Put as much distance between himself and Miranda as possible.

Rounding a curve in the road and leaving the scattered lights of the town behind him, he recalled his parents once advising him to remember that when you marry, not only do you marry your wife, but you marry her family.

The musicians struck up another slow, romantic song. Clamping her trembling hands together, Miranda sat at the table and tried to remain calm. She'd been waiting over thirty minutes for Declan to return from wherever he'd been. She glanced down at the blank face of her phone. Still no text. No calls. He'd looked a little irked when Matt had cut in on their dance, but he hadn't seemed too upset. She and Matt hadn't been dancing that close. They'd argued more than they'd danced. Besides, Declan could've cut back in if he'd wanted to.

Cora's solicitous voice sounded at her elbow. "I asked around, but nobody can recall seeing a magician answering his description. I can't locate Deke or your brother either. Honey, have you tried contacting him?"

Miranda shook her head and gazed over at the dance floor. The swaying couples wavered in her vision. Blinking, she pressed her lips together and cleared her throat. "I probably should." She cleared her throat again and met the older woman's compassionate brown eyes. "Declan is my escort. I shouldn't have to track him down."

Cora sighed and taking the seat next to hers, squeezed her hand sympathetically. "I know."

"Miranda." She looked up to see Aunt Zoe approaching, her face creased with anxiety.

She reflexively put her hand to her chest. "What?"

Zoe leaned closer and lowered her voice. "Dad has been having some pain in his arm and we're taking him to the ER."

Miranda attempted to stand.

Zoe laid a restraining hand on her shoulder. "We don't know anything yet, but your grandpa insisted that this remains quiet and that you continue hosting the party in his absence.

"Most of the guests are enjoying themselves and the main

events are over, so all you have to do is make the rounds maybe once more.

"Ryder and Jack are coming with me. You should let Heath and Deke know, but nobody else."

Zoe's gaze included Cora.

"As soon as I hear anything, I'll let you know."

Miranda clutched the back of the chair, concern for her grandfather overriding everything else that had happened tonight. "What if someone asks about Grandpa?"

"Just tell them that he and Willa were feeling a little tired after all the excitement and decided to call it a night. Thank them for coming and urge them to remain and enjoy themselves."

Miranda nodded and looked anxiously at Cora.

"I'll stay as long as you need me, Mandy."

Zoe smiled with relief at both of them. "Thank you. I'd better go."

Miranda followed her aunt outside in time to see Grandpa being assisted into a red pickup. She sprinted down the walk and caught a brief, but alarming glimpse of Jakob's ashen features.

"Grandpa, I want to go with you." She felt eight years old again, fear of losing the one person she'd always been able to count on mushrooming in her chest.

Zoe hugged her. "Your grandpa needs you here, sweetheart. Live up to that Wonder Woman costume and make him even more proud of you than he already is."

Miranda stood and watched the taillights disappear down the drive and through the gates.

Back inside the ballroom, the gala was still in full swing. The band continued to play. Miranda made the rounds, stopping at tables and checking in with the guests. Thank God nobody even mentioned Grandpa except to remark that he and Willa made a beautiful couple.

She searched the room and the remaining guests, desperate to spot Declan. Had he gone home, leaving her stranded? Deserting her when she needed him most? Blinking back tears, she carried on, trying not to think about Grandpa, trying to contain her escalating anxiety.

It wasn't much longer before Heath strode up to her table and excused them both.

Miranda latched onto his hand. "Where've you been? Grandpa."

"I know. Ryder called me." Heath's handsome face was tense. "Listen, I need to get back to Cassie as soon as I can. Besides the old man, we have a critical security situation. It's Cassie's little boy." He closed his eyes and raked a large hand through his hair. "Alex is missing and we think he's been abducted. I just put out an amber alert."

Miranda impulsively wrapped her arms around her brother's neck and gave him a hard, reassuring hug. "Oh, Heath. I'm sorry. Is there anything?"

"Just keep on doing what you're doing." He pecked Miranda on the cheek. "Gotta get back to Cassie. I just wanted to let you know."

Miranda wandered over to the dessert table and poured herself a cup of coffee. She sipped the hot, acrid brew and tried not to think about Grandpa, Alex or Declan. At this point, there was nothing she could do for any of them but wait.

Aunt Zoe called. Grandpa was resting comfortably in the hospital. He'd suffered a mild heart attack and would be admitted for observation and tests.

Ryder had also called and apologized. He'd accidentally mentioned to Declan that she'd known about the rotten partner. He'd thought Declan already knew.

Miranda had reassured Ryder that no harm had been

done. She'd straighten things out with Declan tomorrow. In her heart she seriously doubted he'd want to talk to her, but she'd try anyway.

She rubbed her throbbing temples and wished she could shed her ridiculous costume, especially the boots which encased her aching feet. All she wanted to do was go home, pull the covers over her head and stay there.

Deke had called with nothing further to report regarding Alex's abduction.

She drifted aimlessly through the dwindling clumps of people. The pressure in her chest eased when she spotted Aunt Cora. The woman was conversing with two older men, dressed identically in coat and tails down to their spats.

The taller of the two glanced up as she approached. His warm gray eyes crinkled. "And here she is. Wonder Woman herself."

He bowed. "Stuart Fiske, aka Fred Astaire. It's a pleasure to meet you."

Miranda smiled and grasped his warm hand. Her throat tightened. He reminded her of Grandpa.

Aunt Cora slipped a comforting arm around her shoulders. "Honey, you look exhausted. Are you about ready to leave? Jesse and Stuart have offered to give both of us a ride home."

Hands in his pockets, Jesse nodded and stepped forward with a friendly grin. "It's no trouble. I live right across the street from Cora."

"The Websters have lived there for as long as I can remember. Jesse and I grew up together."

Cora squeezed her arm. "It looks like the party's breaking up, and there's nothing else for you to do. I've already talked to Zoe," she added, lowering her voice.

Miranda nodded and teetered on rubbery legs. A nauseating wave of fatigue swamped her. She'd done all she could. She'd have to rely on Heath, Deke and the sheriff's department to find Alex.

As it turned out, she couldn't rely on Declan at all.

CHAPTER 16

*D*eclan arrived at Pearl's Cafe early. It had been nearly a week since the Halloween ball. He'd agreed to meet Jackson Samuels and Ryder Barlow to discuss converting the Michaels ranch into a therapeutic horse center. Not seeing either one of them, he picked a booth in the back and ordered coffee.

The prospect was less than exciting, but after thinking about it and bouncing it off Mom and Dad, it made sense to work on this project until he found something else.

He'd made the first cut with the Portland firm, which was encouraging, but distressing to his parents.

The two architectural firms to which he'd submitted resumes in Denver still hadn't contacted him. He might have to relocate.

Designing his own projects and creative control would have to be tabled until he'd paid off his parents and replaced all the money he'd lost.

After the fiasco with Miranda so soon after being swindled, Declan had seriously considered packing up and relocating, at least to Denver. But he liked Spencer. He loved the mountains, and he couldn't put Miranda out of his mind no matter how hard he'd tried to forget.

She'd wormed her way into his heart with her deep green eyes, charming freckled nose and passionate nature.

Ryder slid into the booth across from him, his complexion ruddy from the cold.

"Jack just texted me. He'll be late. Had a last-minute emergency call. He said to go ahead and give you a general idea of what we're thinking."

Declan nodded. "Sounds good."

The waitress brought two mugs of steaming coffee. Ryder didn't order anything else. "I already ate one of Vianna's cinnamon rolls," he said with a wide grin. He shot Declan a rueful look. "It's getting to be a habit. If I'm not careful, I'll be fifty pounds heavier by spring."

Ryder took a cautious sip of his coffee. "It's not a big project. Not compared with what you're probably used to, but it's big for us.

"Since we want to add to the existing buildings on the ranch, we're looking for a design that goes with what's already there." Ryder sat back and folded his hands, resting them on the table.

Setting his mug out of the way, Declan opened his portfolio to a blank sheet of yellow legal paper. He rolled his mechanical pencil between his fingers, itching to start sketching.

The equine project and Ryder's enthusiasm sparked his interest. This was what he'd dreamed of doing. Working with clients who had their own vision and translating that personal vision into reality. "So, what's already there?"

Ryder smiled and consulted his phone in response. "I took pictures. We've got the main house, the barn, a bunk house and a corral. Michaels' was a working ranch for decades until recently."

Declan rapidly roughed out each building on a separate page, with sure straight graphite lines. "What kind of condition are the buildings in, would you say?"

"They're pretty good on the surface." Ryder's phone pinged. He scanned the screen and thumbed a response. "Jack's got another emergency." Ryder's expression was apologetic. "Sorry about that."

The waitress served Declan's order and refilled their cups.

"Shit happens." Declan laid the pad on the seat next to him and bent his attention to his food, listening as Ryder waxed enthusiastically how he and Jack wanted to provide medical services for horses and help emotionally disturbed kids, using equine therapy.

At one point, Declan determined that along with the hallmark green eyes, passion must be a dominant Spencer trait.

Sopping up the remaining traces of egg yolk with his toast, he jotted down a couple of ideas on the pad, still on the seat next to him.

He wiped his mouth with his napkin and took a swallow of coffee. "I'd like to walk around the property with you and Jack and check things out. Before submitting my designs I usually give my clients a couple of choices based on what we all come up with."

"Sounds great." Ryder consulted his phone. "I'll set a day up with Jack and get back to you. How's next week?"

"How's later this week? My appointment book is wide open these days. Business and personal. But you already know that." Declan studied the grounds in the bottom of his cup before setting it down on the tabletop. "Sorry, I acted like a jerk at your grandfather's party. How's he doing, by the way?"

What he really wanted to know was how Miranda was.

"Grandad's good." Ryder smiled. Narrowing his green eyes, he tilted his head. "I'm not so sure about Mandy. She was a trooper, staying behind to hostess the party after we left. She kept grandad's condition and the kidnapping under wraps."

Declan frowned and rubbed his jaw. "I should've stayed. I was so angry I wasn't thinking straight." He didn't want to discuss the subject with Ryder any further. This was a business meeting and his feelings were personal. "I guess I figured she'd get a ride home from her friend, Matt."

"Wrong." Ryder withdrew a twenty from his wallet and slapped it down on the table between them. "Matt wasn't the ass you were, my friend, but he left before everything happened."

The man's stinging comment pricked Declan's conscience. He forced himself to look Ryder in the face. "Miranda has talked about Chandler's two boys and his wife's death, but what about Matt and Miranda?"

Ryder held up a hand. "Stop right there." He pitched his voice lower. "There's history between them, but not the kind you seem to think.

"Our cousin, Nikki was Matt's wife and mother to those two little boys. Nikki was always wild, beautiful to look at, exciting to be around, but not the domestic type." He sighed and a sad expression crossed his features.

Remembering the night she'd sobbed in his arms, Declan cleared his throat and rubbed his mouth. "Miranda told me."

Ryder's green eyes clouded. "I wasn't in Spencer when Nikki killed herself, but my mom dealt with it firsthand. She said the worst part was how it affected the kids.

"Stevie was inconsolable, but Zach. Zach went quiet. He turned it all inward.

"Mom said the family knew things were shaky between

them—we all knew Nikki. Matt learned who she was the hard way. I think he probably tried his best." Ryder's voice trailed off and a distant look shone in his eyes. "His outfitting business occupies most of his time, but he's still dedicated to making a normal life for those boys."

Declan sipped his coffee, turning over Ryder's revelation in his mind. "So, if I'm understanding you, Miranda is just being a good friend?" He shook his head and gave a rueful laugh. "It's none of my business anymore, but watching them out there on the dance floor, I sensed a deeper connection."

Ryder leaned forward and leveled his piercing green gaze at Declan. "Well, there's only one way to find out for sure, and that's to ask Mandy directly. And apologize for being an ass while you're at it."

Declan snorted and looked away. "That's not happening. Besides, I don't have time for romance, especially now. I've got too much work ahead of me."

He rose to his feet and tapped the twenty-dollar bill. "Thanks for breakfast. I'll mock up a couple of rough ideas, but I'd like to take a look at the ranch as soon as possible."

Ryder stood and drained his cup. "Yeah, I'll talk to Jack and one of us will get back to you sometime today. They're talking serious snow later this week. It'll be easier to get up there and move around before then."

"Sounds good." Declan pumped Ryder's hand, slipped on his shades and walked outside. He filled his lungs with Spencer's thin, exhilarating air and studied the vivid blue sky. Hard to believe winter was just around the corner, but the surrounding peaks were already capped with snow.

This project with Ryder and Jack could put him in a position to forge new contacts and get more business. Hopefully, he'd have the opportunity to help move Spencer into the future, with sustainable design and construction practices, while still keeping the town's historical integrity.

Declan smiled to himself. He understood Miranda's passion. He couldn't forget Miranda Buffet, with her copper-colored hair. He recalled the night he'd made love to her, the way her mercurial green eyes had shifted color like the rushing waters of a sunlit stream. The satiny smoothness of her rose petal skin and the softness of her lips were stamped in his memory.

He stopped short, nearly colliding with a woman stepping up on the curb. Apologizing, he unlocked the door to his truck and climbed in behind the wheel.

Even though Ryder had dispelled a romantic connection between Miranda and Matt, dramatic images from the ball still occupied Declan's mind. He liked to think he was a man who didn't hold a grudge, but in Jakob Spencer's case the old man's conceit still gnawed at his gut.

Declan switched on the ignition and slowly backed into the busy street. What he'd told Ryder was the honest truth. He had no time for romance. But he had to admit that whether he had the time for romance or not, a day didn't go by that he didn't wonder where Miranda was, what she was doing and hoped he'd run into her around Spencer.

At the next intersection, he braked for a couple holding hands and lost in their private conversation. Dammit. Ryder was right. No more pussyfooting around, as Dad would say. He'd call Miranda and apologize. If she forgave him, maybe they could move on from there. It was time to make decisions, not only about his professional life, but his personal life as well.

He had resumes out in Denver, the horse project here in Spencer. He'd lost a bundle with his business venture, but a weight had been lifted from his shoulders.

Miranda's white CR-V wasn't in her driveway. Impulsively, he headed west and drove past The Attic. She wasn't at

Aunt Cora's either. He pulled into the lot at the Wild Card. She could be any number of places in Spencer.

It might be better not to see her until he'd taken time to think about what he wanted to say.

Sitting in the ticking silence of his truck, he stared down at his phone. It wouldn't hurt to text her. A text would be less aggressive than a phone call.

Sucking in a deep breath, Declan tapped the screen.

Where are you?

He exhaled. Slipping the phone in the pocket of his jacket, he jumped out of his truck and walked toward the bar's entrance, hope high in his heart. He'd grab some ribs, a couple of beers and see what happened next.

❦

Miranda yawned and squinted at the glowing laptop screen. She'd worked on this grant all week and wanted it finished tonight. She'd read it over before giving it to Aunt Cora. Hopefully another pair of eyes would catch any typos or other mistakes.

Her mind drifted to Declan. Where was he? What was he doing?

Several times last week she'd talked herself out of calling him to demand an explanation for his unexpected departure and his rude behavior. It was better this way, she'd reasoned. She had to untangle her own life before jumping into someone else's.

Miranda's phone vibrated on the table at her elbow and

chimed her mother's distinctive ringtone. She sighed and rolled her eyes.

She couldn't handle dealing with her mother. Not yet. She'd been putting off talking to Deirdre, but she'd definitely call her next week after she'd finished the grant and the environmental impact report on the Michaels' Ranch that she'd agreed to do for Jack and Ryder.

A clipped sheaf of papers on the other side of the laptop reminded her that she still had to go over bids on moving the schoolhouse.

It was going on eight o'clock. She grabbed her mug, and stuffing the protein bar wrappers inside the half-empty yogurt container, strode into the kitchen.

While waiting for water to boil, she rummaged through her tea cupboard for chai. She heard her phone above the rising sound of the electric kettle and jogged into the living room.

She'd left messages with key committee people earlier this afternoon, and the call could be from one of them.

By the time she slid her thumb across the screen, the caller had disconnected.

Miranda chewed on her lower lip and carried her phone back into the kitchen. She had two voicemails.

Denver Metro Hospital had called both times, and they wanted her to call them back immediately. Miranda tapped call back, and winding her hair around her fingers, she tried to silence the alarm bells clanging in her mind.

A disembodied female voice answered and put her on hold.

She paced the length of the kitchen, one yellow wall to the other, and then back again, endeavoring to breathe slow and deep. *Slow and deep. Don't panic, don't think.*

Confronted with the wall again, panic swamped her. She closed her eyes. *Don't think, don't think.*

"May I help you?" The woman's harried tone was laced with weariness.

Miranda pressed her spine against the wall and slid down until she was crouched against the floorboards while she identified herself and listened.

The hospital had located her number as Deirdre's emergency contact. Her mother had suffered a stroke. Her vitals were stable, but her speech was impaired. She'd gotten agitated and had been sedated.

Miranda scribbled down Deirdre's room number. She poured her tea into a travel mug, tossed a couple of bananas and energy bars into a backpack with a bottle of water and switched off the light.

Stuffing extra clothes and toiletries from the bathroom on top, she ran the backpack, along with her laptop, out to the car.

Fifteen minutes later the road was a blur of snowflakes lit by the car's headlights. She muttered a soft curse. With any luck, the weather would be better once she hit the interstate.

Using bluetooth she'd called Aunt Cora and told the woman where she was going and that she'd keep her informed.

It wasn't until Miranda had reached I-25 that she realized she'd forgotten her pills.

She shrugged. Too late now. She hadn't taken a Xanax since she'd moved to Spencer anyway, not even on the horrible night of the Halloween ball.

She'd dealt with Grandpa's heart attack and his emergency trip to the hospital. She'd gone through Alex's kidnapping and Declan's shocking departure. She'd survived without the pills then, and she'd get by without them tonight.

Clutching the steering wheel, she resolutely fixed her eyes on the wet highway in front of her.

She should have answered when Deirdre had called

earlier in the week. She should have called when Deirdre had texted her the next day.

Not for the first time, Miranda wished her brothers lived closer so they could help take some of the burden and responsibility of Deirdre off her shoulders.

Too bad Deirdre and Sal weren't married, so he could deal with her mother's health issues.

Which reminded her, she'd better call Heath and Hunter, Grandpa and Aunt Zoe too.

Jakob had assured her he was fine, but his little episode, as he'd called it, had emphasized his age and fragility.

She smiled, remembering Grandpa's public proclamation of his love for Willa and their engagement.

Miranda upped the volume on her radio and sipped the hot, fragrant tea in her travel mug. She'd dealt with her mother's emergencies before and she'd do it again. Besides, it made more sense to wait and see how Deirdre was before calling and sending everyone into a panic.

But a stroke was different from a drug overdose or an alcoholic fugue. Strokes were for old people. Deirdre wasn't old enough. Miranda gnawed the inside of her cheek, recalling her childhood terror of losing her mother.

"Declan." She whispered his name above the steady swipe of the windshield wipers. Her mind drifted to his warm smile, his tender touch when they'd made love, the way he'd looked at her when they'd danced at the ball and his disappointed expression when Matt had tapped him on the shoulder and cut in.

Matt, on the other hand... Miranda tightened her grip on the steering wheel. The trouble was, it wasn't only Matt she had to think about. Zach and Stevie hovered in the background, and superimposed over the man and his two little boys was Nikki's spirit.

Miranda turned her attention back to the interstate. At

this lower elevation, the snow had turned to rain. Large, heavy splats of water pelted the windshield so fast and furiously she cranked up the wipers. She clutched the wheel and peered ahead, striving to keep her vehicle on the road until she reached the hospital.

The door opened on the sixth floor. She clenched her fists and, breathing deeply, forced her attention on the present. She willed herself to not even think about the possibility of losing her mother.

In spite of Deirdre's past transgressions, the woman was still her mother. She needed her and this time she truly was ill.

Deirdre looked small and washed out lying in the hospital bed under the dim light. The left side of her face, closest to the light was slack, her mouth slightly turned down. She snored softly above the steady, monotonous beep of the monitors. Without makeup, she appeared older and more vulnerable.

Miranda resisted the impulse to smooth Deirdre's straw-colored hair off her brow and whisper in her mother's ear that she was here. She didn't want to disturb the woman's peace. Instead, she sat on a nearby chair, pulled her laptop out and settled in for the rest of the night. She might as well work on finishing the grant. It would keep her anxious mind occupied.

Less than an hour later an alarm sounded. Miranda frowned and turned, looking for a nurse.

Her mother groaned.

Miranda rose and pressed the call button.

Deirdre's blue-green eyes opened wide. She latched onto Miranda's arm and uttered high-pitched cries.

In spite of the terror that gripped her heart, Miranda remained outwardly calm. She squeezed her mother's hand

and smiled. "I'm here, Mom. Everything's okay. The nurse should be here any second."

Raising the head of the bed slightly, she gently massaged her mother's cold hand. Where in the hell was the nurse?

Deirdre mumbled, a thin trickle of saliva leaking out of the corner of her cosmetically enhanced lips.

A young male nurse with kind brown eyes entered the room. He blinked at Miranda in surprise, then smiled as he replaced the empty IV bag and addressed Deirdre. "This must be your daughter."

Deirdre nodded and gave him a weak smile. "Mm, Mm—"

Watching and listening to Deirdre struggling to talk, it was hard for Miranda to connect this woman to her glamorous mother.

The nurse lifted Deirdre's hand and put two of his blunt fingers against the frail, blue lines of her wrist. He studied his watch as Deirdre stared up at him, fluttering the lashes of her good eye.

The man couldn't be much older than her brothers. His nametag identified him as Dean.

Dean wheeled the computer over and entered the data. Finished, he leaned over the bed and gave Deirdre a caring smile. "Mrs. Lawe, I'm going to ask you a few questions. I'd like you to nod your head for yes and shake your head for no. Is that okay with you?"

Deirdre nodded.

"Great." Dean's smile encompassed Miranda. He plucked a tissue from the nearby box and dabbed the corner of Deirdre's mouth. "Are you comfortable?"

Deirdre nodded.

"Any pain?"

She shook her head.

"Any anxiety?"

Deirdre shifted her childlike gaze up at Miranda and flashed a lopsided smile before shaking her head.

Tears stung Miranda's eyes unexpectedly. Her heart swelled with love. Her mother was trying so hard to be brave.

Dean shot a grin at Miranda and patted Deirdre's arm reassuringly. "Excellent."

Miranda brushed away the tear that had escaped the corner of her eye and smiled back in gratitude. She cleared her throat. "Is there someone I can talk to?"

He slid the computer cart out of the way. "Her doctor will be by tomorrow morning." He bent over Deirdre's bed one last time. "Get some rest, Mrs. Lawe, and don't forget to press the button if you need anything."

Her mother nodded and gave Dean a thumbs up with her functional hand.

He returned her gesture. "Thatta girl." He glanced at Miranda. "Are you staying tonight?"

"Yes."

"I'll have a recliner and some bedding brought in."

"Thanks." The adrenaline that had enabled her to make the long drive down from Spencer and contain her rampant panic in order to reassure her mother suddenly fled, leaving her spent. A place to lie down and a pillow to rest her head on sounded heavenly.

As soon as Dean left the room, Deirdre swung her good arm back and forth in the air, making mumbling sounds.

Miranda patted her mother's arm, imitating Dean's comforting gesture. "Shhh, it's okay."

She leaned closer and lightly kissed Deirdre's brow. She'd done the same thing in the past when Jeremy had suffered his night terrors. She cupped her mother's soft cheek. "I'm here, Mom, and I won't leave you."

Deirdre gripped Miranda's arm, and tears leaked from her eyes.

Blinking back sudden tears of her own, Miranda gazed down into her mother's anxious face and forced a confident smile.

Miranda remained in the same position until Deirdre's fingers relaxed and she fell asleep. Holding her breath, Miranda gently lowered her mother's arm and carefully slipped her hand free. She straightened her stiff back and repressed a groan.

Moving quietly around the room to ease her aching muscles, she cleared used tissues and empty paper cups off the bedside table before resuming her work on the grant.

She cringed and put her fingers to her lips when two orderlies brought in the recliner and bedding.

Sighing, she rubbed her burning eyes and shut the laptop. She rose stiffly and glanced at Deirdre. Thankfully, her mother was still sleeping, the slack side of her face hidden from view.

Miranda peered out at the rainy darkness overlooking a dimly-lit parking lot. Bare saplings with fragile, spindly trunks twisted in the wind.

The room was tiny and overheated. She was alone, isolated in this big city so far from Spencer except for her frail mother lying in the bed behind her.

Miranda hugged herself and, closing her eyes, she conjured up Declan: the handsome, chiseled contour of his face; the hair-roughened texture of his cheeks and chin compared to the incredible warm softness of his mouth. She touched her own lips, recalling his kisses and how gently he had caressed her with his long fingers.

He had texted her earlier. *Where are you?*

She palmed her phone and studied the lit screen. *At hospital.*

·   ·   ·

Right now, she didn't have the will or the energy to explain what had happened. Calling him would be easier, but she couldn't call him from here. She was too exhausted to think straight, and it made more sense to wait until she'd had some sleep. She shouldn't talk to Declan until she had her wits about her.

After all, he'd walked out on her without any apparent reason. Truth be told, she'd spent most of the time that night stressing over his abrupt departure and it still grated on her nerves.

Miranda sighed and glanced from Deirdre's bed to the recliner. She should try to get some sleep before her mother woke up and needed something. Instead, she picked up a dog-eared fan magazine that had been left on the bedside table and flipped through the pages. How anyone could occupy their time and interest reading about how famous people lived their lives was beyond her. She tossed the magazine back.

A cup of coffee sounded good. There was a station down the hall that offered coffee, tea or cocoa, along with an ice machine and a fridge full of juice boxes. Anything to escape this stuffy, overly-warm room and move around.

Miranda ended up sitting in the deserted visitor's lounge, clutching a paper cup in both hands. She stared down into the coffee's black, oily surface.

Taking care of Deirdre was the last thing she needed on top of everything else in her life right now, but her mother's childish trust and lopsided smile came to mind. Deirdre was counting on her support. Miranda would put her life on hold and do what she had to do.

She closed her eyes and surrendered to the sweet lethargy that stole through her, liquefying her bones. She should go back to the room, where the recliner was.

Her phone chimed. Miranda started, frowning down at

the cup she still held in her hands. She blinked and gazed around the deserted lounge. She should get back in case Deirdre woke up. Her phone chimed again. She set the cup down and retrieved the device from the depths of her purse. *Declan again.*

Can't stop thinking about you.

CHAPTER 17

*M*iranda straightened and set aside the paper cup. She read his text in the cloud bubble again, afraid she was hallucinating. Her heart fluttered and beat faster.

Another chime.

How are you?

Relief flooded through her, she wasn't alone after all. She longed to see his face and feel his arms wrapped tight around her.

Biting her lower lip, she thumbed her screen.

I'm fine now. Smiley emoji.

"We need to talk! I'm at the Wild Card."

.   .   .

Her heart sank and tears stung her scratchy eyes. She wanted
to bolt out of the hospital and drive back to Spencer, to the
Wild Card where Declan was, to someone she could lean on
for a change.

Miranda closed her eyes. A wave of guilt washed over her.
She couldn't ignore her mother's helplessness, and her hand
still throbbed from Deirdre's desperate grip.

I'm in Denver. My mom's in the hospital.

Miranda's empty stomach clenched and gurgled. She needed
to eat something.

Another chime.

Which hospital?

She rubbed her temples. She should let her family know
before telling Declan anything more. That would involve
phone calls and more energy than she possessed at the
moment.

Once the family knew, she'd text Declan back. Maybe
he'd come. She longed to rest her head against the
comforting wall of his chest and hear the deep reassuring
timbre of his voice.

There were bananas and protein bars in her bag in
Deirdre's room, but Miranda craved chocolate. She fed a
dollar bill into the vending machine adjacent to the drinks
station, tore the wrapper off a Hershey bar and popped two

creamy squares onto her tongue on her way back to the lounge.

She'd call Heath and Aunt Zoe first. She dreaded calling Grandpa. He'd insisted he was good as new, but he tired easily and, though he wouldn't admit it, he'd slowed down a bit. It would be worse though if he found out she'd known but hadn't told him.

Forty-five minutes later, she plodded toward the elevator to return to her mother's room. Mercifully, all the calls had been brief. Grandpa had already gone to bed, so she'd spoken with Willa. Heath had initially been skeptical, but at the mention of the stroke he'd softened his attitude and offered to call Hunter. She'd thanked him repeatedly until he'd cut her off, told her he loved her too and hung up.

Her phone vibrated. Aunt Cora.

"Mandy honey, you sound exhausted."

Stinging tears sprang to Miranda's eyes. "I am. It's been a long—" She swallowed, not able to trust her quavering voice.

Cora cleared her throat. "I can imagine. Mandy, I just talked to Claire about tomorrow night's hearing, and she's taking care of it. So please don't worry."

Miranda nodded and swallowed. "Thanks." She wiped beneath her eyes and whispered. "I appreciate it."

"Honey, is there anything else I can do on this end?"

"No." Miranda shook her head, frantic to disconnect before she dissolved into a weeping mess. "I—I need to go now."

"All right, but you call me if you need anything. I mean it. I don't mean to make you cry, but I love you like my own. You know that. Goodbye."

Somehow, Miranda made it to the nearest restroom, stumbled inside the furthest of the three stalls and sobbed softly until she had no tears left.

Finally, she composed herself, splashed cold water on her

face and headed back to her mother's room. Deirdre might be awake and looking for her.

Thankfully, Deirdre was still sleeping and the room was a blessed cocoon of silence.

Miranda finished her muffin and peeled the banana. Her eyes drifted closed. She was still holding the banana when a nurse came in to check on her mother.

Blinking awake, she realized she hadn't texted Declan back. She laid the banana on the arm of the recliner and fumbled in her purse. Her phone was nearly dead, and she'd left her charge cord out in the car.

❁

Declan drained the rest of his beer and checked his phone again. Nothing. He rubbed the back of his stiff neck. It'd been nearly two hours since he last heard from Miranda. He'd eaten maybe half of the ribs on his plate before pushing it aside. He was tempted to signal Ace for another beer but ordered coffee instead. As soon as he heard from her, he'd be out of here and on his way to the hospital.

Ace was asking who he liked to win Sunday's game when his phone vibrated.

Sorry. Fell asleep. Mom is okay. At Denver Metro. Will talk to Dr. in the am. Call you tomorrow.

An hour later Declan accelerated onto the highway. He'd showered and packed a few things before heading out. He played the hospital scenario over in his head.

He'd take Miranda into his arms, look into her beautiful green eyes and tell her he was sorry for running out on her at the ball. He'd kiss her soft, sweet lips, tell her he loved her and that he'd give her as much time as she needed to sort out her life.

As Declan wound his way down the canyon, his traitorous mind reviewed what Ryder had told him about Matt Chandler at breakfast. The man had gone through hell with his unstable wife, yet he was a good dad to his two little boys and he owned a successful outfitting business.

Compared to Miranda's childhood friend, Declan was a naïve idiot who'd invested his life savings in a fake company and lost everything.

Miranda was part of the richest family in the state. What could she possibly see in him? Besides that, instead of standing by her at the ball while her grandfather had been rushed to the hospital, he'd deserted her. Why would she even listen to his apology, let alone forgive him?

Declan clenched his jaw and tightened his grip on the wheel. It didn't matter. It didn't change how he felt. All that mattered was getting to her as soon as possible and letting her know he was there for her.

❦

After the first, younger nurse had checked Deirdre's vitals, Miranda had sent Declan a text updating her mother's condition. She must've drifted off again because the next time she opened her eyes, the nurse tapping entries on the computer was older and shorter.

Deirdre stayed alert. Her pale face reflected the television's flickering light. Occasionally she'd laugh, a low liquid chuckle.

Miranda's head sagged and her eyelids drooped. She was too tired to stay awake and keep her mother company. She licked her dry lips and longed to stretch her cramped legs.

She should wash her face, brush her teeth and try to get some more sleep.

Her mother tapped the white board the occupational therapist had given her earlier. "Ma, ma, mar…"

"Just a minute," Miranda muttered under her breath. Sighing, she levered her stiff body out of the chair and pitched her voice louder. "Give me a second, Mom."

Deirdre slowly and laboriously printed: tomorrow.

"Yes. Tomorrow. Dean told me the doctor will be in tomorrow." Miranda emphasized and enunciated the last sentence, forcing a reassuring smile.

Her mother grunted satisfaction and wiped the board with short, clumsy movements, leaving most of the blue letters she'd written still visible.

Her heavy, breathless sigh at the simple exertion filled Miranda with despair.

The therapist had explained that Deirdre would be severely frustrated if the only way she could communicate all her questions and fears would be to try to write letters when her brain moved faster than her body.

Miranda steadied the board, plucked another tissue, and wiped the white surface clean.

Deirdre uttered a short, deep guttural noise and slowly the crooked letters took shape. Spencer.

Clenching her hands until her fingers ached, Miranda struggled to keep from crying. The stroke had compromised her mother's short-term memory.

"Yes, mom. There's a very nice rehab center in Spencer, very close to where I live. That way, I can come and see you every day."

Deirdre nodded stiffly and mumbled something that sounded like, "morrow," and "Spe, Spe…"

Miranda smiled into her mother's trusting face and planted a gentle kiss on the woman's brow before taking the white board from her and placing it on the bedside table.

"I'm putting the board here until tomorrow, and I'm going to get ready for bed. I'm beat."

To her amazement Deirdre nodded and lifted her good arm up and out. Miranda embraced her mother's frail body.

Deirdre made a light smacking noise with her lips and it sounded as though she said, "Nite, nite," without the ts.

"Night, Mom." Miranda's heart contracted and her throat swelled. "Love you."

Miranda was brushing her teeth, her mouth full of mint foam, when she thought she heard her phone chime. She finished quickly.

Declan had texted.

In the parking lot by the ER.

Miranda's heart lurched. "Oh my God," she whispered. With trembling thumbs, she texted:

Coming down. Meet u er.

The television still flickered, but Deirdre's eyes were closed and she snored softly. Miranda crept out into the hall and jogged to the nearest stairwell, adrenaline overriding her exhaustion.

She took the stairs as fast as she dared, her flat palm sweeping the rail. He was here. He'd come.

The hospital was an endless maze of corridors, signs and arrows. After what seemed like forever, she rounded the corner leading to the ER. Pausing at the door, she peered through the glass panel, her shallow breath coming in short, quick gasps.

Declan stood with his back to her. His long, lean body looked hot in a snug T-shirt and fitted jeans. Holding herself in check, she yanked open the door.

He turned. His blue eyes widened and the corners of his mouth tilted in a crooked grin.

Sprinting across the room, she launched herself into his arms, burying her face in the crook of his neck. "Declan. Thank you. Thank you for coming."

He hugged her tightly. His thudding heart echoed hers. "I had to. It's been hell without you." He expelled a long sigh. "Mandy."

His voice caressed her name. His lips grazed her cheek, her temple. He rubbed her back between her shoulder blades.

All the bottled-up anxiety concerning her mother suddenly flooded to the surface. Declan was all she'd needed.

Miranda nodded, tried to choke back her tears and failed.

Declan shifted his feet, swaying slightly back and forth. "Shhh. It's okay, baby. It's okay."

Eyes closed, nose pressed against his chest, she inhaled a shallow, trembling breath, then another. He smelled clean and woodsy. She focused on the beat of his heart, his strong arms around her.

Lifting her head, she smiled. His thick, black hair stuck out in wisps around his ears. She cupped his smooth-shaven jaw, drowning in his brilliant blue eyes.

She could stay in his arms forever.

Declan tugged her ponytail. He lightly tapped her chin and grinned. "You look cute in your sweats."

God, she'd missed his dimples.

His grin faded and his gaze dropped.

Heat bathed her cheeks. She rose on her toes to meet his

kiss. The touch of his mouth was like a transfusion. He cradled the back of her head, keeping delicious contact between them.

The muscles of his body tensed. He drew her even closer, close enough to feel his arousal.

Declan broke the kiss first, his gaze consuming hers, his pupils so dilated they appeared black. "Wow!" he murmured. "Wow."

He closed his eyes and exhaled through pursed lips. "Wow," he said again and looked around the room.

Arms still locked around him, Miranda followed his gaze. The ER was packed. Heat scorched her face.

Most people immediately glanced down at their phones. An older woman, rocking a fretful toddler, glassy-eyed with fever, smiled at them. A security guard, arms folded, regarded them sternly. Behind the low counter, a nurse entered data on the computer in front of her.

The sliding doors whooshed open and a very pregnant woman, clinging to the arm of a half-awake man, shuffled toward the desk.

Gently gripping both of Miranda's arms, Declan turned her around, facing away from him. "Let's sit down. Lead the way."

She glanced back at him over her shoulder and he gave her a gentle nudge. "Please, I haven't been this embarrassed since high school."

They took seats as far from everyone else as they could. Head bent, Declan held her hand in both of his. He said nothing.

Miranda remained quiet, sensing he needed the time he was taking. Now that her adrenaline rush was over, fatigue lapped at the edges of her awareness.

He stroked the top of her hand, lifting his sympathetic gaze to hers. "How's your mom doing?"

Miranda's eyes filled unexpectedly with tears. "Deirdre looks so fragile and her face is droopy on one side." She swallowed. "Sorry, I'm really, really tired and emotional." She offered him a tremulous smile. "The nurse said Mom's vitals are stable and the doctor will be in to see her tomorrow."

Declan nodded. "Good to hear." Leaning forward, he flattened his palms on his thighs. "Miranda, I want to explain about that night at the ball. I'm not good at fancy social events, and there was a Spencer family group dynamic going on."

Miranda sighed. "There always is when all of us get together."

Declan reached for both her hands, his expression solemn. "I'm sorry I walked out on you at the ball. I was an ass. Ryder told me so yesterday."

A crushing wave of weariness swept through her. She wanted to listen to him. She wanted to acknowledge his apology, but gazing around the room at the sick and injured people waiting to be treated reminded her she was at the hospital and Deirdre had suffered a stroke. She reached over and squeezed his forearm. "Declan, I'm sorry, but I need to go back upstairs to Mom's room in case she wakes up and needs me."

A muscle jumped in his jaw. "Ryder's told me a lot of things, Miranda."

It was as though a pail of icy water had been tossed in her face. She thought back to that day she'd encountered Jack and Ryder at Pearl's. What had they talked about? What was it she knew about keeping secrets?

She searched the troubled depths of his eyes, a tight knot forming in the pit of her stomach. "What did Ryder say?"

Declan dropped his voice so low she leaned closer to hear him above the room's bustling atmosphere. "Why didn't you warn me after your grandfather told you that Tom Nagle was going to con me?"

Keeping secrets never ends well. Despair and its cold certainty gripped her heart. Miranda's pulse pounded in her ears. "Declan, I was going to tell you, but by the time I found out that Grandpa had vetted Tom and Snow Peak, it was already too late. It wouldn't have made any difference."

Declan frowned and stared down at his clasped hands. "You knew when you ran into me at the Wild Card. You knew when we had dinner at my house." He flashed an incredulous glance at her. "Jesus, Miranda, you sure as hell knew while we were making love in my bed." Leaning back in his chair, he briefly closed his eyes. "You didn't say a word."

"Declan, I'm sorry. I tried more than once to tell you, but—"

Tight-lipped, he held up his palm. "I left the ball that night because I'd been gut-punched." He sighed. "Mandy, I know you mean well and you're trying to help me, but I don't need you or your grandfather interfering in my life."

"Interfering?" Miranda stood up too fast and spots floated in her field of vision. She swayed and reached out to steady herself.

Declan sprang to his feet and caught her arm. "Sit down before you faint."

Miranda twisted out of his grasp. "Leave me alone."

The nurse at the front desk glanced over before resuming her strokes on the keyboard.

"Interference. That's choice. You're the one who walked out on me without so much as a text. I was under the absurd delusion that you drove down from Spencer because you wanted to support me." She fisted her hands at her sides.

She shuddered, remembering the comfort of his embrace,

his sweet kisses, the way he'd breathed her name. He wasn't any different than her ex after all.

Shaking her head, Miranda swayed again and caught herself. "I'm going back upstairs to hopefully get some sleep before my mother wakes up again."

Another wave of tears threatened.

Declan reached for her. "Mandy, please."

She backed away from him. Squaring her shoulders, she glared into Declan's bewildered face. "Don't ever, ever call me Mandy again."

Turning her back to him, Miranda was aware that most of the people in the room were watching. She was too tired to care. She lifted her chin and marched across the room towards the door she'd come through earlier, raising her arm in a halfhearted wave.

The door closed with a thud. Her knees buckled and a sob escaped her throat. Clinging to the cold, steel rail, she resolutely climbed the concrete steps up to the sixth floor.

❦

Declan stared at the door long after Miranda had disappeared. He'd screwed up again. He'd noted the blue-tinged smudges beneath her eyes and instead of taking care of her and putting her needs first, he'd single-mindedly pursued his personal agenda.

He had driven down to apologize, to stay with her at the hospital. He hadn't meant to blurt his accusations out without giving her time to respond, and he certainly hadn't meant to bring Mandy and her grandfather's interference into his argument, but it was the truth. Jakob Spencer did interfere. The old man had probably interfered all his life. Mandy's interference was because she cared.

Declan recalled how thrilled she'd been to see him.

Her saucy ponytail and no makeup made her pale face more vulnerable.

Miranda had trusted him with her loving heart, and he'd acted like a selfish ass. *Again*.

Swearing softly, Declan snagged his coat off the chair. He'd try texting her tomorrow. Remembering her livid expression, she probably wouldn't even read it. Hell, she'd probably delete him from her contacts.

Declan recalled nuzzling Miranda's petal-soft cheek, kissing the shell of her ear. Basking in a sensual haze of desire, he'd involuntarily called her Mandy. A smile had parted her lips. Yet seconds before she'd stormed out of the ER, Miranda had told him in no uncertain terms to never call her Mandy again.

Zipping up his jacket, Declan stepped out into the frigid night. Maybe his vision of moving Spencer forward into the future wouldn't work out after all. It might be better to leave the town, put the bitter experience of his failed business behind him, and forget Miranda altogether.

❦

The following morning, a tall, middle-aged man wearing dark horn-rimmed glasses and alligator boots walked through the door into Deirdre's room.

"Dr. Bell," he said, extending his hand.

Miranda bit back the anxious questions she'd written down last night. She waited while he examined her mother and asked Deirdre more questions.

Deirdre gave the doctor the same skewed smile and fluttered lashes she'd given the male nurse the night before.

Anything in pants.

Guilt stabbed Miranda and she softened her heart. Self-centered and addicted as she may be, this frail woman was still her mother.

When Dr. Bell had finished, he picked up the electronic tablet from the bedside table and scanned Miranda's questions. He looked from Miranda to Deirdre. "Mrs. Lawe, I'd like to visit with you and your daughter about your condition and recovery."

Deirdre's features twisted. She shook her head, her good eye closed, the other disturbingly at half-mast. The sounds she made were obviously her protest.

Miranda inwardly flinched.

"Please don't try to talk," she wanted to say. Instead, she gently took her mother's cool hand and used the same soothing tone she'd often used to calm Jeremy.

"It's okay, Mom. I'll visit with Dr. Bell and then we'll talk about everything later, like we used to."

Her mother squeezed Miranda's hand, a relieved expression on the functional half of her face.

Miranda followed the doctor out into the hallway, a thousand more questions running through her head, most of them having nothing to do with her mother's medical condition.

How was she supposed to start her own life over when she now had to care for her disabled mother?

CHAPTER 18

*D*eclan parked his truck in front of Aunt Cora's Attic. Turning off the ignition, he sat in the ticking silence and fading warmth of the cab. Ryder was right. He was an ass. Instead of apologizing for his rude behavior and comforting Miranda at the hospital, instead of noting her exhaustion, he'd peppered her with his grievances and accused her and her grandfather of interfering in his life.

Now, here he was, about to bare his soul to a woman he hardly knew, a woman who until recently he'd regarded as his primary opponent, but the woman who appeared to know and love Miranda best. Miranda's warm, natural response to Cora's attentive supervision the night of the ball and their easy conversation during dinner had been proof of that.

The intense connection he and Miranda had shared that night in his loft was still stuck in his head. He'd been craving that intimacy with her day and night ever since. Intimacy even more than the sex.

Checking his phone's blank screen again, he raked a hand through his hair.

Still nothing from her.

No celebrated Colorado sunshine this morning either. The bleak street was deserted, the houses and cars cloaked in snow.

Declan rubbed his forehead and thumped the steering wheel. What the hell was he thinking? The shop didn't open for another two hours. If he knocked on the door now, Aunt Cora would take one look at him and probably slam it in his face.

As he considered other possible options, the door opened. A bundled-up woman cautiously backed out of the house, hauling a shovel. She went to work, clearing a path across the snow-drifted porch.

An opportunity made in heaven.

Declan ducked his bare head against the frigid air and trudged up the buried walkway. He gently pried the shovel from her grasp, smiling into her wide-eyed features above the scarf shielding her mouth. "Here, let me do that."

Cora stepped back and planted her gloved hands on her hips, her voice muffled. "For God's sake, son, where's your hat and gloves? You're going to catch pneumonia."

Declan heaved a scoop of heavy wet snow. It landed in the yard with a satisfying thud. "They're still packed in a box somewhere."

"Well, you'd better find them fast. This is the first of many good snowfalls you'll see before spring."

She rubbed her arms vigorously and stamped her feet. "Come on in when you're done. The least I can do is make you some breakfast."

"Thanks." Declan flung another shovelful after the last. Part of the problem was solved. He still wasn't sure about the formidable woman's reception, but he'd walk through fire if it helped him win Miranda back.

He inhaled a lungful of biting air. Scooping snow

stretched his cramped muscles. Better yet, it helped take his mind off last night.

Almost as good as running.

Running had been his way of coping when he'd lived in Boston, but dealing with difficult clients or looming deadlines was nothing compared to his total obsession with Miranda.

He could run or shovel his ass off, but the tight knot in his stomach lingered. She still haunted him.

Somewhere along the way, Miranda and her mossy green eyes had stamped herself on his heart.

Biting the inside of his cheek, Declan picked up his pace.

Stop thinking and shovel. You screwed up. You can't do anything about last night, but you're here now.

When he finally came up for air, he'd not only scooped Cora's walk, but the front of the neighbor's house as well.

Breathing hard, he propped the shovel next to the door. Once inside, he shed his coat and, with numb fingers, unlaced his boots, leaving them next to Cora's on the rubber mat. He stood in his stockinged feet, waiting for his eyes to adjust to the dim interior, his ears tingling in the warmth.

A cat crouched at the foot of the staircase. As soon as Declan met the animal's unblinking stare, the feline zipped up the steps and vanished.

Numerous clocks ticked an uneven cadence from the darkened shop. He turned the other way and padded through open pocket doors toward a welcoming rectangle of light that had to be the kitchen.

Declan paused on the threshold, squinting at the bright yellow walls. His mouth watered at the appetizing aromas of brewed coffee and frying bacon.

"Take a seat." The tall woman's wild, unruly hair had been tamed into a single braid at the nape of her neck. She filled two large pottery mugs with coffee and set them on the round table next to matching plates. Cora served a heaping platter of fried eggs, bacon and golden-brown biscuits.

"Dig in," she said, sliding the dish closer.

Declan shot her a cautious smile. In spite of his edgy stomach he was hungry. She didn't seem mad. After all, she'd cooked him breakfast. It would be better to eat first and talk about Miranda afterward. "Wow. Thanks. You didn't have to go to all this trouble."

She lifted the steaming coffee to her lips. Amusement danced in the brown depths of her eyes. "I like having the company, and you shoveled my walk. Besides, it's well worth the effort to see those dimples of yours."

Heat flushed his face. Declan bent his attention to filling his plate. His dimples were a blessing and a curse. Usually he ignored the comments or changed the subject, but for some bizarre reason, he was flattered.

"You're a handsome rogue. I'll give you that." She buttered a biscuit, adding a generous dollop of honey.

Declan split one of his own and topped each half with a fried egg. He'd had nothing but a large black coffee this morning.

Her watchful gaze never left his face.

Forking a generous bite into his mouth, he chewed slowly and swallowed, feeling like a specimen under a microscope. Raising a shoulder, Declan turned his attention back to his plate. He'd find out what she was thinking soon enough.

Eventually, Cora uttered a sharp sigh and helped herself to the platter of food.

After devouring the eggs, three pieces of crisp bacon and two mugs of coffee, Declan sank back in his chair. His eyes drifted shut. Last night was catching up with him. The long drive, navigating the dark canyon road through blowing snow to the hospital in Denver had been hellish.

He smiled to himself. It had been worth every agonizing

mile when Miranda had walked into the ER, her copper hair pulled back in a cute ponytail. She'd hugged him tightly, whispering his name, her breath hot against his neck.

Now feeling weightless, he floated somewhere halfway between wakefulness and sleep. His breathing slowed. He heard the distant hum of the fridge, the stirring sound of a spoon and...

Something warm and heavy landed on his balls. Declan yelped and jerked awake. A multi-colored cat meowed, its claws penetrating the denim fabric of his jeans.

"You're better off sitting still, Mr. Elliot." Cora's voice was laced with laughter. "Agnes is just trying to hold on."

"It hurts like f-ing hell." Declan glared from the cat to Cora. He eased his butt back on the chair and struggled to relax.

Eventually the cat retracted its claws, and settling on his lap, stretched out one of its front paws.

"Agnes wants you to pet her. She likes you for some odd reason. She doesn't take to many strangers, especially not to men."

Declan massaged the animal behind the ears. The cat closed its eyes to mere slits. "I haven't had much experience with cats. We always had dogs when I was growing up."

He rubbed his hand down along the cat's jaw. "It sounds like a little buzz saw."

"Its name is Agnes and she's purring. Keep petting her and she'll be happy." Cora sipped her coffee and shook her head. "Damn if you haven't charmed my cat too."

Declan smiled and gently stroked his index finger under the cat's chin. "Agnes, you sure as hell have a funny way of introducing yourself."

"So, Mr. Elliot, what did you come to talk to me about?" Cora rested her arms on the table, her expression intent.

He continued to pet the cat absently. So many questions

about Miranda spun in his head. He wanted to know everything about her, as much as Cora had the time and inclination to tell. He opened his mouth, not sure what he wanted to say.

She leaned closer and pressed her thin lips together. "I saw how the two of you looked at each other at the ball."

Declan stared down at the faded linoleum floor. Here it comes.

"Why did you leave? Mandy was worried sick. She was looking all over for you. What's between the two of you is none of my business, but deliberately hurting her is my business."

His hand stilled and he clenched his jaw. He hadn't meant to hurt Miranda, but she'd known the truth about Tom's past and she hadn't warned him. Maybe he wouldn't have been able to do anything about his partner's scam, but he wouldn't have been blindsided either.

"Not only were you her guest, you were her escort. Common decency dictated that you remain with her and see her home. After her grandfather was taken to the hospital, instead of standing by her side while she filled in as his hostess, you left without excusing yourself. You deserted Mandy when she needed you the most. I wanted to kick your butt clear across town." Cora's voice shook with repressed fury.

The disturbing image of Miranda, desolate in her superhero costume filled his mind. He remembered his last glimpse of her leaving the ER.

Head bowed, shoulders sagging, she'd waved without a backward glance. Before the door closed completely, she'd collapsed against the wall, hand clamped to her mouth.

He'd let her down twice.

Guilt burned in the pit of his stomach.

"Mandy deserves better. She has her faults, we all do, but

her strengths outweigh her weaknesses. The girl doesn't have a selfish bone in her body."

He knew that. Miranda had already gone out of her way to rescue him twice. That night in his bed she'd trusted him with her body and her fears.

Cora rose and stacked Declan's plate on hers. "If anything, she's too responsible, probably because she's always had to be and wants to prove to herself that she's nothing like her mother—or Nikki."

The older woman packed up the leftovers, stowing them away in a vintage refrigerator, similar to the one his nana had kept down in the basement at her old house.

He pictured Miranda as a freckle-faced little girl, eager to please.

Agnes thrust her head under his hand. Declan resumed petting, stroking the cat's spine to the tip of her tail. She lifted her haunches and purred louder.

Cora cleared her throat and scooped coffee out of a brown bag labeled *Rocky Mountain Bookstore*. "Mandy's grandmother, Marguerite, was a spiteful woman, who left her lasting mark on her children and grandchildren. Jakob Spencer married the money he needed to build his empire, but he paid a high price."

Cora turned and cast Declan a wry smile. "However, without Marguerite, we wouldn't have our Mandy, would we?"

Our Mandy.

Agnes rose without warning and jumped off his lap. She wandered over to a white mat stamped with paw-prints and lapped water from one of her bowls.

Declan brushed off his jeans and picked up the plastic bear filled with honey. He turned the sticky container over in his hands. "No, we wouldn't."

His smile faded. *Jesus.* His throat constricted and he felt as though he were free-falling out of a plane without a chute. Declan bit his lip. He looked up and met the older woman's gaze. "Do you think she'll ever forgive me?"

He held his breath, heart pounding in his ears. It was the same childhood anxiety he'd felt when he was ten, lying in bed on Christmas Eve, fearful that he hadn't been good enough and the red bike he'd asked Santa for wouldn't be under the tree.

Cora squeezed his shoulder. "I'd say that depends on you, Mr. Elliot, if you're honest about how you feel. You have to be willing to be patient."

Declan doubled down. "Do you think she'll ever let me call her Mandy?"

The older woman laughed. "Here, give me that. You're squeezing the poor thing to death."

She firmly pried the plastic bear from his grasp. After wiping it clean, she set it down on the table. Grabbing his wrist, she just as capably applied the warm, wet dishcloth to his palm and fingers, as though he was a toddler. "Patience, young man. Remember?"

Mouth open, he stared dumbly from his clean, damp hand back to her.

Aunt Cora rolled her eyes. "You aren't sticky anymore are you?"

Declan shook his head. "No. I was just surprised."

"Yeah, I do that to people." She ran water from the tap and squeezed dish detergent into the sink. "I can't speak for Mandy, Declan. I'm afraid you'll have to leave that decision up to her."

Cora turned off the water. Putting the dirty dishes into the suds-filled sink, she cast him a sympathetic glance. "Mandy needs to trust you. I'd say your chances are good if you're willing to work at earning her trust."

Declan grinned up at her, gauging her expression. "Really?"

An instant later, he sighed and ran a hand through his hair. "Shit."

"Shit?" Cora chuckled. Drying her hands on a towel, she sat back down across from him. "I wondered what brought you here with that down-in-the-dumps look."

Declan relayed what had happened at the hospital the night before.

"So, I drove my sorry ass over to Mom and Dad's and spent the rest of the night kicking myself."

He scrubbed his hand down his face. "She won't answer my calls or texts. I don't know what else to do."

Cora nodded. She reached across the table and patted his hand. "As difficult as it may be for you right now, you need to back off and give Mandy time."

She arched a brow in his direction. "I may be a silly old woman, but what the two of you have is rare. Trust me, you don't want to jeopardize that kind of love."

She lapsed into silence and her eyes took on a remote, wounded expression. "When you lose someone you love, someone you've shared your soul with…" she said, tightening her pale, thin lips. "It's like losing a part of yourself."

Declan covered the woman's arthritic fingers with his, his own pain momentarily forgotten in the face of her obvious grief. He rose from the table and, grabbing the coffee pot, refilled both their mugs. "That happen to you?"

She clutched his wrist in a hold so fierce, Declan was forced to set the pot down on the table.

"Yes." Cora's voice was a bare whisper. She turned her head, hiding her expression.

He remained still, his arm anchored in her vise-like grip. He wanted her to know he cared. After all, she'd listened to him.

Cora sniffed, withdrew a white handkerchief from the pocket of her apron and wiped her nose. Releasing his wrist, she glanced up at him with a trembling, bemused smile. "I never expected that I'd be talking to you about David."

She shook her head. "Somehow, I've always known I'd have to tell my secret to a stranger, but you, young man, are no longer a stranger."

She gave a dismissive wave. "And after talking to Jakob the other day, it seems that David had confided in his older brother after all."

Disbelief edged her voice. "Jakob had known all these years and had never bothered to tell me. If it wasn't for Willa, he probably would've gone to his grave letting me think that he was partly to blame for his father's wrongdoing."

Declan replaced the coffee pot and sat back down at the table. He wanted to hear more about Miranda's grandfather.

Cora folded her hands, revealing irregular brown spots and thin skin, a striking contrast to the youthful glow that lit her face and spilled from the depths of her eyes.

"His name was David Owen Spencer." Momentarily dropping her gaze, she gave a deep sigh and absently stroked the fingers of her left hand. "I was in Jakob's class, but since we all attended the same one-room schoolhouse, we were all thrown together. David was eighteen months younger, but he was big and sturdy for his age."

Bright spots of color highlighted her angular cheekbones. She cast a winsome smile at Declan. "Like the biblical David, he was ruddy and handsome, with dark curly hair and laughing eyes the color of muted gold—and a spirit incapable of deceit or cruelty."

Miranda's expressive green gaze came immediately to mind. Declan folded his arms and shifted his weight. "I thought all the Spencers had green eyes."

Cora's smile faded and her eyes clouded over. Pain laced

her voice, and the etched lines of sorrow around her mouth deepened. "David and Jakob were so different from one another.

"Back then, Jakob was ambitious, bent on making a name for himself and the Spencer family. To his credit, he loved David, but as the oldest, Jakob lived under his father's thumb and played by Thomas Spencer's rules."

Cora fisted the crumpled handkerchief. "Mr. Spencer did not approve of me. I had nothing to bring to the table, no social position and certainly no money."

She snorted and tightened her lips. "Needless to say, my radical stand regarding the Vietnam War and women's lib did nothing to enhance my suitability. His father tried feeding David false information about my activities, about the people I associated with and the demonstrations I attended. The contemptible man dug up as much dirt on me as he could."

She swallowed. Clenching her fingers, she inhaled deeply. "I'm afraid I blamed Jakob for taking his father's side." She bowed her head. "It turns out I was mistaken. I should have known that Jakob had no influence with that rigid, sanctimonious jackass. Once Thomas Spencer believed he was right, there was no convincing him otherwise. It's all water under the bridge now anyway. Bad-mouthing the dead does no good and can't undo the past."

Declan nodded. Behind Cora, the muted gleam of wintry sunlight filtered through the window.

A wan smile played on her lips. "Anyway, in spite of Mr. Spencer's meddling and my hard-headed political views, David and I grew closer."

Cora shook her head and clucked her tongue. "People these days are too impatient to find love. It's so important to first develop a kinship, to wait for that seed to grow and mature with time. Our friendship deepened and…" Pressing trembling fingertips to her throat, she toyed with the silver necklace she wore. "His love softened my sharp edges."

Her liquid gaze met Declan's and she bit her lower lip. "David said my love challenged him, made his life exciting and lit him on fire."

She dabbed again at her nose and eyes. "We'd kept our relationship a secret through high school. When my parents relocated to Denver after graduation, I didn't want to leave Spencer, so I moved into this house with my grandmother and worked in the shop."

Cora waved her handkerchief and laughed. "How I do run on. I always seem to have to go around the block to walk across the street."

Declan shook his head and grinned. "No worries, I've got plenty of time."

"Well, to make a long story short, I'd planned to go to Boulder and major in journalism, but my dad got sick." Cora twisted her hands and stared down at the table. "Everything happened that summer David graduated. He used to drive down with me to Denver and we'd sit outside on the back patio. Talk and hold hands for hours."

She smiled to herself. "I remember how happy and relieved I was when David told me his father had stopped hounding him about us."

The corners of her mouth turned down and her voice faded to a mere whisper. "I imagine Mr. Spencer was thinking that once David went off to college, he'd forget all about me."

She shook her head. Tears trailed down her cheeks, tears Cora didn't seem to notice. "But David, David was such a romantic." Clearing her throat, she swiped at her nose. "He surprised me the Friday after the Fourth of July weekend.

"We hadn't seen each over the holiday because we'd both had to work. It's one of Spencer's busiest days of the year.

"David didn't say much on the way down to Denver. He acted the same as always." It was as though she'd forgotten Declan was in the room. "I'll remember that summer night until the day I die. David blindfolded me first and led me outside on the patio. The heat of the day still hung in the air and the crickets were chirping their heads off. He had me hold my hands out with my fingers like this."

Smiling at the recollection, Cora held out both slightly trembling hands towards Declan, her fingers spread apart. "He kissed me. It was the longest, sweetest kiss of my life. The clean smell of his freshly shaved skin made me forget all about the heat and the crickets.

"When we finally came up for air, he slipped a ring on my finger and took off the blindfold." Her thin lips parted and the gaunt contours of her face softened. "I remember his eyes shining in the moonlight. He dropped down on one knee and said, 'Cora Fleming, please say you'll marry me.'"

The dreamy expression on her face afforded Declan a glimpse of the girl she'd once been. He smiled and absently tugged on his ear, reluctant to say anything and interrupt her story.

Reaching inside the bodice of her shapeless knit shirt, she withdrew the long silver chain around her neck and lifted a thin, delicate circle of gold into view. A red multi-faceted gem glinted under the kitchen light. "David slipped this on my finger."

Cora reverently cradled the ruby ring in the palm of her hand, transfixed. As though punctuating the moment, a multitude of clocks chimed, striking the hour.

"And," Declan prompted, once it was quiet again.

Cora started and raised her stunned gaze to his. "Oh. That's when I saw the dozen red roses and the champagne. It wasn't the cheap stuff either."

Declan leaned forward. "Did you say yes?"

She looked at him as though he had three heads. "Of course, I said yes. I said yes and started bawling like a baby. David held me in his arms and I buried my face against his chest." Cora closed her eyes. "I felt the rise and fall of his breath and his beating heart beneath my cheek." She brought the ring up to her lips. "I wanted to stay in his arms forever."

She smiled to herself. "Back then, I wore my hair down. I'll always remember the touch of his hands stroking my hair. David led me back into the house, down the hall to my father's sick room. Holding my hand, he asked my parents for their blessing." Cora shrugged. "Those were his words, even though he knew damn well I was a self-professed agnostic."

She beamed at Declan. "I was too caught up in the moment to even get pissed.

"Dad was overjoyed. He thought David was a taming influence on me. Mother started crying." Cora lapsed into silence and stared down at the ring, warring emotions visible on her face.

Declan wanted to assure her that she didn't have to tell him anything else. Yet, he sensed that she needed to get this story off her chest. He was oddly touched that she'd chosen him.

The compressor on the ancient refrigerator clicked on and hummed.

Cora's knuckles whitened. Her bony frame trembled and her chest rose and fell.

Closing her eyes, she drew another deep breath. "Being the impulsive girl that I was, I wanted to get married imme-diately." A pained smile crossed her lips and her brow furrowed. "David wanted to wait until after both of us finished college. He wanted to be a teacher and he believed education was crucial."

Licking her lips, she slid the ring back and forth along the links of the chain. "Five years seemed an eternity at that time. So much could happen." She gave a mirthless laugh. "I was worried he'd fall in love with another girl, one younger and more attractive."

Fresh tears seeped from beneath her closed lids. "It was a week before school started. I was working here that afternoon." She wiped her nose, her voice thick with emotion. "David was an excellent swimmer, Red Cross certified, in fact. Those stupid city boys had no business being out on the lake when a thunderstorm was brewing." Cora pressed the heels of her hands to her eyes.

"David was working at the lodge when someone came running into the lobby, screaming that two boys were out in the middle of the lake in a canoe. That's all David had to hear. Witnesses said he bolted out the door and commandeered a golf cart before anyone could stop him. He had his own boat with an outboard motor."

She shook her head. "I suppose he intended to tow them back to shore before the storm hit. Damn him, he knew how fast the weather could change up here."

Abruptly, she stopped and sank back against the chair, looking old and sad.

Declan wanted to give her a comforting hug, but he wasn't sure how she'd respond.

She raised her arms in a helpless gesture and let them fall into her lap. "David had no way of knowing that the boys had managed to paddle to shore on the far side of the lake and were safe.

"They recovered David's body later in the week. The coroner determined he'd been struck by lightning."

She covered her face with her hands, her voice raw with anguish. "I couldn't…I couldn't attend the funeral. The family held a private graveside service. After everyone had left, I laid down next to the fresh turned dirt and cried until there were no more tears left. I took his ring off my finger and put it on this chain. I've worn it around my neck next to my heart ever since."

Declan reached across the table and covered the woman's clasped hands with his. "Does Miranda know?"

Cora shook her head. "I thought nobody else knew until the other day when Jakob dropped by to return his costume. The old fart confessed that David had confided in him after all. He also gave me their grandmother's ring, the ring David had asked for and Thomas Spencer had refused to give him."

She offered Declan a bleak smile. "I should have known he'd told Jakob. Along with his generous heart, my David was scrupulously honest." She sighed with a resigned expression. "And he loved his big brother.

"Excuse me." Wiping her pink nose, she rose from the table and left the kitchen.

A door closed. Declan sighed and rubbed his gritty eyes. Cora's secret had connected him with her in an odd way. He heard the muffled sound of the tap turned on, then off, accompanied by the shuddering groan of ancient plumbing.

Cora emerged, wiping her hands down her apron. Her braid was neatly coiled around her head, and the ring was once more hidden beneath her shirt. "When you walked into my shop to rent a costume, I suspected you were special. That's why I suggested the magician's costume. Nobody's rented it since David some fifty years ago."

The hairs lifted on the back of his neck. There was the connection. Declan rose from the table, took their mugs over to the sink, and put them to soak with the plates in the soapy dishwater.

"I'll get those later. With today's weather, I'll have plenty of time on my hands." Cora's voice was once more composed. She moved about the kitchen in a brisk, efficient manner.

Declan wandered over to the refrigerator. Folding his arms, he studied the photos, cards and magnets that obliterated the rounded white surface.

A scalloped-edged card caught his attention. The greeting beneath the photograph read, "Family, the reason for the season. Wishing you a Merry Christmas from our family to yours. Love, Scott, Miranda and Jeremy."

Miranda, the man, and the little boy all wore identical red-and-white sweaters with matching Santa hats. It was the same cute little boy that he'd seen pictured in the magnet on Miranda's fridge.

Miranda's ex looked arrogant, like a true asshole. Miranda's stiff smile didn't quite reach the depths of her eyes. What drama had transpired behind the scenes?

Declan imagined the jerk pressing his fist hard into the small of her back. It was evident by the photograph that Miranda was trying her damnedest to hold her family together.

Tapping down his anger with effort, Declan shifted his gaze to the card beside it. He immediately recognized Matt Chandler's rugged face. The striking woman with raven hair, sitting on the porch step beside him, must be Miranda's deceased cousin, Nikki. She didn't look like she was going to kill herself, but then nobody ever did, did they?

His focus returned to Miranda and the small boy sitting in her lap. One mystery hopefully solved. He picked up the card. "Who's Jeremy?"

Cora was at the sink rinsing a plate. She put it in the drainer without looking up. "Jeremy is Scott's little boy from a previous marriage. When that self-centered bastard walked out on Mandy, he took Jeremy and left her with nothing. No partial custody, no visitation. The adoption wasn't final, so Mandy has no legal recourse.

"Mandy loves that little boy like he's hers. She refuses to

talk about him at all, even to me. I think the loss still hurts too much. It's as though she's put Jeremy in the same deep part of her heart she's put Nikki."

Cora glanced over at Declan. "Mandy and Nikki were so close, they shared so many things. Mandy blames herself for Nikki's death. In some warped way, she also feels responsible for Matt and the boys.

"I've already tried telling her that she isn't and suggested she needs to move on with her own life, regardless of what she thinks Nikki would want. Mandy agrees with me, but... it's like deep down, she can't hardly let her guilt go. That guilt is eating her up from the inside out."

Declan examined the card in his hand and then the card still stuck on the fridge. No wonder Miranda had been so emotional the night she'd told him about her cousin's suicide.

"Declan, are you a patient man?

"I've always thought so."

"I hope you are, because what Mandy needs most right now is a friend. Do you understand what I mean by a friend?"

Declan's throat tightened and he nodded.

"She needs someone who is simply there just for her. No expectations, no demands, no promises and no lies. Mandy needs loving arms to hold her and give her hope. She needs love, acceptance and time for her wounded heart to heal. Most of all, she needs to believe and trust in someone again."

Declan was reminded of the night they'd spent in his bed. Miranda's poignant wish had been that she'd had parents like his.

He'd glimpsed the skinny, red-headed girl with large green eyes and freckles sprinkled across her heart-shaped face. He'd recalled how his physical need had suddenly been replaced with a fierce tenderness and desire to protect her.

A chill draft swept the back of his neck. Declan turned,

looking for an open door or window and met Cora's knowing brown eyes. He rubbed the tingling skin at the base of his skull. "Did you feel that?"

Without any hesitation, Cora shook her head. "No, but I believe you did. If it's cold you felt, that would most likely be Nikki. I imagine she's not happy. You're spoiling her plans for Matt and Mandy."

Declan stared back at the woman in disbelief. "You can't be serious?"

"Oh, but I am." Cora hung a dish towel on the rack attached to the inner door of her lower cupboard. "Nikki quit this life in a sudden, violent manner. In spite of all the blessings she had, she was never happy."

Cora sighed. "Nikki often told me how much she hated Spencer and its confining, small-town atmosphere. She insisted her life and Mandy's should've been reversed, because Mandy belonged here in Spencer with a husband and family to care for. Nikki wanted to have Miranda's life and her freedom, as she imagined it."

Declan frowned and folded his arms over his chest. "So, you're saying that Nikki was so unhappy she killed herself. And that her ghost," he pronounced the word with obvious sarcasm, "communicates her pleasure and displeasure to certain people in her life?"

Cora leaned back against the sink, her unblinking gaze direct. "That's it in a nutshell, as incredible as it sounds."

"You really believe that?" Declan shook his head and snorted. How much of her secret story she'd just told him was really true?

"That so-called draft, as you called it, was real enough, wasn't it? Ask Mandy if you don't believe me."

Declan looked down at Miranda's holiday card and gently drew his thumb across the image of her face. He couldn't deny he'd felt the eerie blast of air, but the rational part of his mind had trouble making sense of it. However, his mind and his heart were united and decisive when it came to Miranda.

He looked up from the Christmas photograph into the older woman's watchful eyes. "So, Cora Fleming, just how should I propose marriage to Miranda. It's going to take more than a puny blast of cold air to scare me off."

CHAPTER 19

*M*iranda wheeled Deirdre in front of the large picture window. "Look at the view, Mother. It will be beautiful when the sun comes out."

A wall of windows in the spacious room provided a magnificent vista of snow-capped peaks. Though the afternoon sky was drab and dismal, Miranda visualized how it would look on one of the bright, spectacular days Spencer was famous for.

Deirdre grunted and scrawled TOO COLD in large, uneven letters.

Miranda bit back a tart retort. Her patience had already worn thin. She didn't know how long she could keep this up. A never-ending calendar of daily visits stretched in front of her. She steeled herself to remain civil to the woman who, for most of Miranda's life, had been her mother in name only.

On the other hand, if she abandoned the fragile woman slumped in the wheelchair in front of her, who else would advocate for Deirdre, visit her and convince her that she had a reason to try and get better?

Sal, Deirdre's current live-in, had assured Miranda he'd come when he could, but he lived in Denver and worked all week.

Hunter lived in Chicago. Heath was preoccupied with his tech and personal security business based in D.C. Miranda wouldn't ask her brothers to interrupt their busy lives and travel all that distance to help when she was already here in Spencer. *Put on your big girl panties and deal with it, Miranda. You've taken care of Deirdre before.*

The bleak winter landscape reflected the state of her life at the moment. It had been less than a week since she'd walked out on Declan in the ER.

He'd had good intentions. He'd driven down from Spencer and apologized for cutting out on her. However, in the next breath he reproached her for not warning him about Nagle's scheme. She hardly needed to be reminded of her omission, she already felt bad enough, but when he accused her and Grandpa of interfering, frazzled and stressed, she'd snapped.

The more she thought about Declan's outburst, could she blame him? He was still reeling from losing his business and his so-called friend's con job. She had to admit Grandpa had meddled in Declan's life, and though she'd only meant to be helpful, so had she.

The dull headache she'd awakened with pounded on one side of her head. After five days rooming with Deirdre, she needed to go home. Home to her own space, where she could sleep in her own bed and insulate herself from the pressing demands of the outside world and get some space between her and her mother.

No, she corrected, she was dying to drive to Declan's, throw herself against his chest and remain there in the security of his strong embrace.

If only she could take a long, hot shower in his tiny,

cramped bathroom, step over the discarded clothing piled beside his bed and crawl under soft sheets that combined his woodsy scent with the tantalizing heat of his body.

Deirdre pounded the arm of the wheelchair, brandishing the white board that now had BED scrawled on it.

Miranda stooped to look into her mother's slack features and shook her head. "Soon, Mother, but not right now. After Mrs. Kelly comes, remember?"

Deirdre's blank expression dissolved. She shook her head vehemently, like a rebellious child. The white board clattered to the floor.

Miranda repressed the urge to scream. She retrieved the board and clutched it to her chest until her fingers ached. She pitched her voice low and even to say, "Mother, Mrs. Kelly should be here any minute to welcome you and answer the questions we've already talked about. I know you're tired, but Mrs. Kelly shouldn't be too long."

Miranda prayed the administrator would hurry so she could get Deirdre settled and leave.

Deirdre hung her head, her rounded shoulders heaving.

Miranda's throat constricted. "Mom." She sank down on the firm mattress to face her mother and cradled both of the woman's cold, thin hands between hers. Tears of exhaustion and helplessness welled up in her eyes and she swallowed. Her voice quavered. "Mom, please don't cry or I'll start crying, and I don't think I'll be able to stop."

Plucking tissues from a nearby box, Miranda gently dabbed Deirdre's cheeks, then her own. "Shhh," she soothed, lapsing into the even tone she'd been using the past five days. "Everything's going to be okay, all right?"

She forced a reassuring smile and kissed her mother's pallid cheek. "You're going to get better, and you'll be back home before you know it."

Deirdre shook her head and sobbed louder. "No, no, Sa."

She shook her head harder, her sagging features a mask of despair.

"Mom, I talked to Sal. He told me he loves you. Hasn't he come up to the hospital every day after work to see you? He brought you flowers and chocolate and those balloons over there." Miranda heard her pleading tone. Closing her eyes, she imagined she was talking to a frightened child.

"I spoke with Sal this morning before you woke up and he'll be up Friday after work. He said he'll stay until Sunday. He's going to call and talk to you again tonight, like he's been doing."

Sal was another gem of a man. As long as Miranda could remember, her mother had attracted devoted men, men who declared their love and would do anything for her.

Yet, Deirdre had taken all of them for granted, exhausting their love with her ceaseless demands and her insatiable need for constant reassurance. Coupled with her emotional highs and lows, her self-absorption was more than anyone could handle.

They left, most stealing quietly out of the house in the middle of the night. Miranda remembered Dennis, the cowboy, in particular. He'd been one of her favorites.

On his way out, he'd spotted her standing at the top of the stairs in her nightgown. Putting a finger to his lips, he'd pulled out his wallet and crept back up the stairs to press a twenty-dollar bill in her small palm.

"Sorry, sweetheart," he'd whispered, "but your mommy just plain wore me down."

He'd planted a tender kiss on her forehead. "Take care of yourself and those two hellion little brothers of yours."

Miranda used another tissue to gently pinch Deirdre's nose. She could only hope Sal was a keeper. Her mother had first introduced him to Miranda as Salvatore, her passionate Italian Stallion.

Sal cooked and cleaned for Deirdre, waited on her in the manner which she was accustomed. The way Deirdre's face still lit up when he came into the room was promising.

The fact that Sal was a widower without the complication of children and that Deirdre and Sal had been together five years were very encouraging signs.

Deirdre's good hand brushed Miranda's arm. Her uneven smile offered Miranda affection. She attempted to speak, but all she made was a weak, smacking noise.

Miranda smiled back. "I love you too, Mom."

A knock on the door sounded, and a pleasant-faced woman stepped over the threshold. She wore her short white hair in a stylish cut. Her white blouse and tailored slacks were impeccable. She advanced with an outstretched hand. "My name is Rachel Kelly. Welcome to Spencer Peak Wellness Center."

Thirty minutes later Miranda walked out of the building into the frigid windswept parking lot and checked her phone.

Nothing.

She was tempted to drive out to Declan's under the pretext of thanking him and apologize for her rudeness. Sighing, she set her phone down in the cup holder.

Face facts, Miranda, you're done, emotionally and physically.

A hot shower and a good long nap in her own bed was less desirable than spooning with Declan in his bed, but the smarter solution. After she woke up refreshed, she'd see things with a better perspective.

❦

Declan stared at the blueprint on his computer monitor. Had he been serious when he'd asked Cora how he should propose to Miranda?

He'd meant it when he'd stated his intention in the older woman's kitchen four days ago, and he hadn't changed his mind.

What gnawed at his gut were his countless unanswered questions. Questions regarding Miranda's family. Jakob Spencer, in particular, and concerns about how much the old man would try to meddle in their lives.

He'd get a pretty good idea at today's meeting at the Lodge. In spite of no job, other than the equine project, he would politely refuse any handouts the man offered him.

On the other hand, after hearing Cora's tragic story regarding Jakob's younger brother, Jakob reconciling with Cora and giving her the ring David had intended to give her, Declan didn't know what to think.

His biggest quandary was in asking Miranda to marry him. How in the hell was he going to go about that? She'd most likely tell him to go straight to the devil.

He forced his attention back to work. Cora had advised him to give Miranda time and, as hard as it was, he would. But, how much time, how long should he wait? Could he wait?

Leaning back in his chair, Declan grabbed both wrists, stretched his arms over his head and stared at the ceiling. "As long as it takes," he said out loud, the determination in his voice bolstering his flagging spirits.

Smiling at the capricious universe, he straightened his shoulders and trained his gaze back on the blueprint. His questions would be answered in time. They always were.

❧

As Declan was ushered into Jakob Spencer's spacious office that afternoon, he resolved to keep his mind open for Miranda's sake. He owed it to her to hear what the old man had to say.

Edgar, the bear rug Miranda had told him about, lay before the stone hearth. Spencer rose from behind the massive mahogany desk and extended his hand. "Mr. Elliot."

Declan gripped Jakob's hand firmly and maintained contact with the man's glittering green eyes, eyes like Miranda's. Her presence was evident everywhere, from the family resemblance down to the framed photographs on the credenza against the back wall.

Following the direction of Declan's gaze, Jakob walked across the room. Retrieving one of the photos, he handed it to Declan. "Those two little girls were inseparable growing up. Both chock-full of Spencer spirit, gumption and grit."

The older man shook his head, his expression sad. "Unfortunately, Nikki was her own undoing."

Declan examined the image of two fresh-faced adolescent girls, arms wrapped around each other, dressed alike in Levis and boots, down to their identical braids.

He only had eyes for the red-haired, freckle-faced girl with the sweet smile.

"Mandy could always calm Nikki down and had a knack for reasoning with the girl when the rest of us could get nowhere. When Mandy's mother shipped her off to school back east, it was hard on both the girls, but Nikki became a lost soul."

Jakob replaced the photograph on the table. Shoulders slumped, he continued to stare at the picture. "As soon as she was old enough, Nicole married Matt Chandler and had the two boys all within the next four years." He glanced at Declan with a perceptive smile. "You're wondering what in the hell all this has to do with the project I want to talk to you about, aren't you?"

Declan shrugged. Not what he'd expected, but fascinating. A veteran of board and committee meetings, he maintained professional protocol. "The thought did cross my mind, Mr. Spencer."

Jakob stuck his hands in the pockets of his slacks and tipped his head to one side. "Have a seat," he said, indicating one of the two wingback chairs.

Declan sat and hunched forward. He wanted Spencer to know he was relaxed and interested in what the other man had to say.

Jakob settled back in the other chair, and the corners of his mouth lifted, another uncanny reminder of Miranda. He cleared his throat and narrowed his gaze slightly. "As you've probably guessed by now, this project involves Miranda."

Declan tugged his ear and frowned. It had to be the schoolhouse project. Realizing what he was doing, Declan dropped his arm and clasped his hands together. Let the man finish, he reminded himself. He'd hear Jakob out because he loved Miranda and because Miranda loved her grandpa.

"Now, I'm aware that the two of you have butted heads in the past, and I've been told that I've had a hand in the conflict. I was so damn happy and excited the night of the ball that I monopolized Mandy and excluded you.

"That being said, I took a dim view of what happened after I was rushed off to the hospital."

He shot Declan a stern glance. Without a word, you walked out on my little girl, leaving her to deal with my guests, along with a security breach and a child's kidnapping. I heard that she did a magnificent job. Many of my guests were unaware of my medical emergency or the kidnapping until the next morning."

Declan nodded, a hollow feeling in the pit of his stomach. He'd been reprimanded by both Aunt Cora and Jakob Spencer, the two people Miranda loved and trusted the most.

He recalled the last time he'd seen her. The wounded

expression on her beautiful, heart-shaped face that night at the hospital was etched in his memory. If only he could have that one night to live over again.

Declan looked the older man in the eye. "There's no excuse for what I did. I've already apologized. Miranda was gracious, even under the stress of her mother's medical condition." He gave a rueful laugh. "Of course, it didn't take me long to screw that up. I said some things I shouldn't have."

Jakob chuckled and slapped his thigh. "Trust me, son, I know the feeling. I've made my share of mistakes with women. I've apologized only to step right back into it again. You're not the first and you won't be the last."

The old man leaned forward his expression earnest. "Declan, I'm known as a hard man. I'm also known for being honest and for speaking my mind."

"Yes, sir." Everything Declan had heard about Jakob Spencer supported what the man had just stated. Like the hallmark green eyes, frankness ran deep and wide in the Spencer family. Miranda's grandfather appeared sincere, but just how transparent was he? After Nagle's double-cross, Declan's confidence in his own judgment had been shaken.

Could he trust any man's word again?

Miranda's ecstatic smile and her freshly scrubbed face stole into his memory and overrode his doubts, reminding him of his love for her and his future intention.

"I want you to know that along with Tom Nagle and Snow Peak Properties, I investigated you."

Declan clenched his jaw so hard it ached. It took all the self-restraint he possessed to keep from leaping out of his chair. "You knew all along that the company was going to go under." He couldn't resist adding, "And you told Miranda, but nobody thought to let me know. I was just collateral damage, was that it?"

Jakob sat back and clasping his hands over his stomach, regarded Declan for a moment before speaking. "Based on your misguided opinion of me, I was fairly sure that initially, you would have questioned my motives, along with the results of the report itself.

"The man might have hung around longer, possibly defrauding you and other prospective investors of more money. Not a comforting thought is it?"

Jakob glanced at the small round table between them and frowned. He rose slowly to his feet. "All this talking makes my throat dry. You want a drink? He chuckled. "By drink, I mean water. I used to enjoy a shot of brandy in the afternoon, but Doc wants me to lay off the alcohol because of those damn pills I have to take."

He waved his arm in dismissal. "Stay where you are. I'm no invalid just yet."

"Water would be great, thanks." Declan watched Jakob fill two squat highball glasses with water from the crystal decanter nearby. The man looked hale and hearty. Hard to believe he'd recently had a heart attack.

Jakob handed Declan a glass and settled back down in his chair. He took a swallow. "Anyway, getting back to what I was saying, I was damn impressed with the fact that you weren't born with a silver spoon in your mouth, yet you paid your way through an Ivy League school and landed a plum position at a top Boston firm."

The facts were accurate, and the old man's compliment sounded sincere. Declan nodded and sipped his water.

Jakob lifted a shaggy brow. "Contrary to what you may believe, I wasn't born wealthy either." Remorse tinged his voice. "I took the easy way in by marrying money, compromising my family and the woman I really loved."

He shook his head. "Don't get me wrong. Looking back, I don't regret all of it. I screwed up with my daughters and my son, but I was given another chance to make it right with my grandchildren, and most of all with the love of my life, my Willa."

Jakob wagged a gnarled finger at Declan and looked him sternly in the eye. "Don't take the woman you love for granted. Don't let time—or—pride, build a wall between you. Life's too short and too precious to waste a single day."

Jakob drained his glass. He sighed and stared over at the hearth. His glance fell on the bear rug, and his lined features lifted in a reminiscent smile.

Declan thought of Miranda. She was in the middle of her mother's health crisis, dealing with the suicide of her cousin, her broken marriage and losing the child she loved and wanted to adopt.

His appalling behavior at the ball, his selfish pride and his intolerance of her wealthy family had only further complicated her life and added to her load.

He'd been swindled out of his life savings, but he still had his parents, who'd always loved him and been there for him.

He could always earn more money, and as he'd observed in Boston and here in Spencer, money didn't always guarantee happiness, especially at the sacrifice of those you loved.

"Regarding the schoolhouse restoration. I know you're not looking for a handout, and I wouldn't insult you by offering you one."

Jakob's voice startled Declan back to the present and the meeting's focus.

The man's keen gaze probed his. "I'm impressed that you're already working with Ryder and Jack on converting the old Michaels ranch. I've seen those designs and I like them. According to Jack and Mandy, you've got an innovative vision for renewable energy and construction."

Declan shrugged, oddly flattered by Jakob's comment. "I don't have a formal contract with the historical society. My services are predicated on revenue from grants and donations. I've got a hunch that's why you wanted to speak to me."

Jakob smiled. "Your position is secure and a legal contract will be drawn up pending your acceptance. Allow me to catch you up on the financial status of that project. Again, I want to assure you my proposal is not a handout and, by the way," the old man arched his brow, "Mandy has never in the past or present asked me to bail her out of any difficult financial situation.

"Thanks to her, the schoolhouse project has recently received two substantial grants, which she wrote, and a sizable donation from the David Spencer Charitable Foundation.

"I have to give Cora Fleming a lot of credit for offering Miranda a position and a cause to hold on to when the girl needed it most. In spite of Mandy's efforts, more funds are needed and because time is of the essence, I've proposed to Mandy and Cora that I offset some of the other costs. I've agreed to fund moving the building to its permanent site in Olde Town, in addition to paying the salaries or consulting fees to those persons providing the labor, such as contractors, painters and…" he narrowed his eyes at Declan, "Architects."

Jakob withdrew a cigar from his breast pocket and slid it beneath his aristocratic nose, followed by a benign smile. "So, Mr. Elliot, will you accept my financial offer, which has nothing to do with Mandy being my granddaughter and everything to do with your professional qualifications?"

Declan flushed. He had to admit a grudging respect for Jakob Spencer based on today's discussion. "You're sure Miranda still wants to work with me?"

Jakob's hearty laugh filled the enormous room. "Mandy informed me that you wouldn't accept my offer because for some reason, you resent rich people—and me. I believe those were her words."

Declan half rose out of his chair and opened his mouth to object before he realized that what she'd said rang pretty damn true. He drained his glass and set it on the table.

Rifling through the briefcase at his feet, he withdrew a sheaf of printed blueprints and, with a shamefaced grin, passed them to Jakob. "Take a look at these. See what you think and if you still want to pay me, then I'll accept your offer."

Jakob nodded, the unlit cigar hanging from the corner of his mouth, his green eyes twinkling. He sat back and leafed through the designs while Declan waited.

Wind whistled outside the windows, and the mantel clock ticked off the seconds. Edgar's glassy eyes stared blankly. Declan's concern about the man's interference in their lives in the future had been put to rest. At least for now.

Jakob rattled the papers and passed them back to Declan. The older man's ruddy face split in an ear-to-ear grin and his startling green eyes nearly disappeared as he roared with laughter. "How do you like your crow served, Mr. Elliot?"

CHAPTER 20

*D*éjà vu.

Miranda parked and strode across the hard surface of the Wild Card's lot. She'd finally gotten a hold of Matt. He'd apologized for not calling, but he and the boys would be spending Thanksgiving with his folks. He thanked her for inviting them and suggested meeting for a beer to mend fences.

She'd agreed. She was so done with stewing over the way they'd parted. If only she could do the same with Declan.

Many times she'd started to call or text him. She missed him terribly. Memories and images of the night they'd spent together blurred and merged with the night of the ball and the night at the hospital.

Beneath her parka, Miranda wore jeans and a flannel shirt. She had left her hair down with a wide knitted headband to keep it out of her face.

She passed from the chilly, starlit night into the restaurant's warm interior.

Ace stood behind the bar washing glasses. He grinned and shook his head. "Back again?"

Miranda gave him a helpless shrug and scanned the room. Maybe Matt was running late.

"Your buddy is in the last booth." Ace rolled his eyes. "You're turnin' my place into a helluva reality show. Will it be the cowboy or the city slicker?"

"You're such a comedian." Miranda grinned and headed in the direction Ace had indicated. It really had never been a contest. She'd chosen the city slicker, hands down.

It was early and the Wild Card was deserted, save a party of older couples sitting at a far table. They were busy studying the menu and conversing.

"You know I was just teasing," Ace called after her.

Miranda turned and stuck out her tongue.

Ace laughed and tossed a bar towel over his shoulder.

Teasing or not, if Ace took notice of all her comings and goings, how many others were speculating behind her back? Besides, he did have a point. Lately she'd felt her life had taken on the surreal drama of a reality show.

Matt must have overheard the exchange. Before she could greet him, he slid out of the booth and stood, a welcoming smile on his face. "Hey."

"Hey, yourself." Impulsively, she closed the distance between them and hugged him tight. His friendship was too precious to squander, and Nikki lived on in both his boys.

He gave her a gentle squeeze and sighed. "Mandy, I'm sorry for hassling you about the pills and the picking up strangers crack."

Miranda smiled and patted his back. "It's okay, Matthew. 'It's because you're my friend and you care about me.'"

Releasing her, he flashed a wry grin. "Sounds familiar. Let's eat. How about a beer and Ace's deep-fried dills?"

"I was thinking the same thing." She laughed and slipped out of her parka, compressing its bulky, down-filled fullness on the seat beside her.

"Dawn's off today." Matt poured each of them a glass of amber brew from the pitcher and shot Miranda a self-conscious smile. "We're going out tonight. Nothing serious." He shrugged and took a swallow from his glass. "Gotta start somewhere."

Miranda raised her glass and followed suit, taking solace in the cold, flavorful ale with its hoppy bite. "Yeah, I hear you."

Matt was moving on with his life and she was going nowhere, both feet planted in the present, caring for her mother and writing grants, no one with whom to share her sorrows or her victories.

The night she'd spent in Declan's arms felt as distant a memory as the long ago, secret kiss she'd shared with Matt at the shack. Miranda sipped her beer and reached for another pickle. Time to change the subject.

"How are the boys doing?"

Matt nodded. "They're doin' good. Both of them. Last week when Jack was out to see one of the horses, he was telling me how he and Ryder are fixing up the Michaels ranch. He suggested I talk to Ryder about enrolling Zach in the therapy program when the camp opens."

The server arrived and set a red plastic basket heaped with breaded pickle slices on the table. "Anything else?"

Plucking a pickle off the pile and tossing it into his mouth, Matt pointed his thumb at Miranda. "She'd like a big dish of ranch dressing." He licked his lips and glanced her way. "Am I right?"

"Damn straight!" Miranda popped a fried tidbit into her mouth and raised her glass mug. "Thanks," she called after the retreating server.

"I'm not sure she heard you." Teasing lights danced in Matt's gaze.

"Very funny." She sighed and washed down another pickle. "It's been a long day."

And it'll be an even longer night.

God, she missed Declan. She missed his voice, his laugh, his damn dimples. She wanted to rest her head against his broad chest, her ear pressed against his heart and whisper her hopes, her fears and all her dreams for the future.

"Knock, knock. Anybody home?" Matt lightly tapped her forehead with his knuckles, a sympathetic expression beneath his playful grin.

Miranda flushed and forced a bright smile. "You're full of it tonight, Matthew. So, did you talk to Ryder, like Jack suggested?"

The server returned with the ranch. Matt methodically dipped a breaded pickle in the dressing, chewed and swigged his beer. "I talked to Zach first and he was actually interested. So, I'm signing him up."

Matt sounded hopeful and she was glad Zach wanted to go. "That's great. I've heard equine therapy has been very effective in treating emotional stress."

Matt poured himself another glass, his expression relaxed. "I've been taking Zach with me on weekend trail rides. He's been helping me out." He chuckled. "Don't get me wrong. Zach still has his moments, but even his therapist has noticed the boy is opening up more."

He wiped the heel of his hand over the beaded ring of moisture that the pitcher left on the table. "Both Zach and Stevie have been asking about you. They're bummed about Thanksgiving."

Miranda's throat swelled and tears pooled in her eyes. She laughed and swiped her cheeks with her fingertips. "God, I love those two little boys." She sniffed and gazed at Matt. "You tell Zach and Stevie since they can't come on Thanksgiving, you're all invited for dinner at my house. Let's

say the Sunday after? They can pick the menu, as long as chocolate milk is included."

"Sure. They'll like that." He exhaled a long breath and cleared his throat. "Mandy, I have a confession to make." Frowning, he raised his index finger. "Just listen. This is hard enough." He gazed down at his clenched hands. "When Nikki killed herself, it was like the rug was pulled out from under me. Life got crazier than it already was. Since then, I've been so busy taking care of the boys and my business I haven't taken time to sort out my own feelings."

He rubbed his bearded jaw and glanced up at Miranda with grief-stricken eyes. "Nikki left me a note. She wanted the two of us to get together and raise the boys." Polishing off the last dregs of his beer, he set his glass down and shrugged. "Between her note and all the good times we had growing up, and that kiss—when you moved back to Spencer I thought." He smiled down at the tabletop. "I got confused and thought it meant more than it did."

He shrugged and raised his bleak gaze to hers. His nostrils flared. "God help me, Mandy, but I loved Nikki. As high strung and difficult as she was, I loved her. I always loved her." He cleared his throat and swallowed. "I loved the wild, spirited part of her that couldn't be tamed."

Miranda nodded and gripped his large rough hands. "Oh, Matt," she whispered, the pressure behind her eyes building. "You'll always hold a special place in my heart, but I—."

He gave her hands a hard squeeze before letting go. "I know. I watched the two of you at the ball. Hit me right between the eyes when you and Elliot were dancing."

"I do have strong feelings for Declan."

Just saying his name made her heart beat faster. How could she explain her feelings to Matt, or to herself for that matter?

She inhaled deeply. "I've decided I need to do some

thinking about my life and in what direction I want to go. I think it's important to give myself time and not rush into another relationship."

That would be the most sensible course of action, but her heart argued otherwise.

Matt searched her face, his expression guarded. "Are you going to stay in Spencer?"

Miranda had been so occupied lately she hadn't even thought that far ahead. It was too soon. A lot depended on Deirdre's rehab, the schoolhouse project and Declan.

But, hadn't she felt as though she was home running the half-marathon beneath the brilliant blue Colorado sky?

Hadn't she felt at home, jammed in a booth with her boisterous cousins at Pearl's or sitting in Aunt Cora's kitchen eating iced lemon cookies?

Yes. She'd instinctively made her decision. Just as she'd chosen the city slicker over the cowboy, she already realized her future lay here, tucked among the lofty Rockies in Spencer, Colorado.

A heavy weight lifted from her chest. "Yes," she stated emphatically, startling Matt. "Yes, I'm staying."

Matt grinned. "I'm glad, Mandy. Zach and Stevie will be over the moon."

A muted buzz sounded. Miranda glanced down at her phone's dark screen and her stomach sank. "Not mine."

Matt slipped his phone out of his shirt pocket. "It's probably Zach. I told him to text me from Mom and Dad's."

Miranda ate the last, soggy pickle and drained the warm beer in her glass. She combed her fingers through her hair and watched Matt deftly thumb a reply.

What was Declan doing tonight?

According to Aunt Cora, he'd met with Gary from the historical society earlier this afternoon for an update on the schoolhouse.

"Hey Mandy, I've got to get going. You should head home, too. I just got a text from Dawn. There's a weather alert, predicting high winds and blizzard conditions tonight through tomorrow morning."

Miranda stood and fumbled for her purse. "Here, let me pay for half."

Matt frowned, put his hat on and snagged his jacket. "Put your money away. Go home and call Elliot." He yanked his zipper up and moving Miranda aside, fished her parka out of the booth.

She clutched the wad of cash in her hand. "What?"

"In that order." He shook her coat open. "Don't argue. You're obviously pining away for the dude and, according to Ryder, Elliot's been talking about you nonstop. He wants to call, he wants to text. Hell, he wants to send you flowers and say he's sorry, but Ryder said that Aunt Cora told him to wait. Something about giving you time."

Bewildered, Miranda stood while Matt helped her into her coat.

Declan was giving her time?

Her pulse pounded in her ears. She followed Matt to the door. She wasn't going to wait until she got home. She'd call Declan as soon as she got to her car.

"Get home safe. Blizzard's coming," Ace called after them.

Matt waved his arm. "Headin' home now."

The biting wind stung Miranda's face. She pulled her hood up and drew it tight. "Wow, the temperature's dropped."

Matt squinted up at the sky. "The storm's coming in fast. I'll walk you to your car."

She tightened her fingers around her phone buried in her pocket. "That's okay. I can see it from here."

A strong gust slammed her back a step. She gasped and ducked her head.

He pulled her against him in a brief hug. "Text me when you get home," he said, his voice pitched above the wind roaring through the trees.

She backed away and cupped one hand beside her mouth. "I don't live that far."

Matt lurched forward, extending his arm. "Then I'll follow you."

"No. Good grief, Matthew, I'll text you." Keeping her head down, Miranda sprinted to her vehicle.

❦

Declan uncapped his second bottle of beer and padded back to the couch. A glance at his mounted flat-screen confirmed that the Lexus commercial was still playing. He picked a few errant popcorn kernels off the cushion and ate them before dropping despondently to sit.

A weather alert ran beneath the picture. Yellow text warned of high winds, frigid temperatures and blizzard conditions tonight.

Good thing he'd moved up the meeting with the historical society to this afternoon instead of waiting until tomorrow.

He raised a leg and swept a pile of empty wrappers and microwave dinner cartons off the cluttered coffee table to make room for his stockinged feet. This place was a pit. Tomorrow was definitely cleaning day.

Meeting with Gary and going over the plan for moving the schoolhouse had reminded him of Miranda. Hell, everything reminded him of her. Declan had hung on Gary's every word, hoping the short, stout middle-aged lawyer would mention her.

Instead, Gary had peppered Declan with ruthless questions about cost, logistics and timelines. It was obvious

Miranda had hand-picked the little gnome as her replacement.

The game came back on. Declan sighed and tipped the bottle to his lips. The Patriots took the ball and moved it down to the red zone. On fourth and goal, they scored. The point after was good.

He was going out of his mind waiting to contact Miranda as Cora had suggested. Every cell in his body screamed for him to do something.

His obsession was spilling over to the job. Yesterday at his onsite consult with Ryder, when Declan had asked how Miranda was, Ryder had snapped. "Screw Aunt Cora. Screw waiting. Call Mandy and find out for yourself."

Declan stared at his phone perched on the armrest and willed the device to do something. After several seconds his gaze wandered back to the screen. More damned commercials.

He tapped out a text addressed to Miranda.

Please inform historical society and J Spencer that either Gary goes or I quit.

He threw his head back and closed his eyes with a grim smile. Petty, childish, but satisfying.

Declan's satisfaction was short-lived. The Patriots fumbled and the Jets recovered. "Shit."

Glancing from his phone to the game, he deleted the text. Clenching his jaw, Declan palmed the phone and sat on the couch through half time, alternately chugging from his beer and glaring at his phone. The panel of retired football players and coaches analyzed each team's scores and turnovers.

The Patriots were blowing a crucial division game, and

he'd blow his chance with Miranda if he wasn't careful. He sat up, planted his feet on the floor and set his empty bottle on the table. Tugging his ear, he texted.

I'm sorry, Miranda. Please give me a second chance. I love you.

Scanning his message a third time, he shut his eyes, took a deep breath and pressed send.

The wind howled outside and the loose gutter he'd meant to fix on the front porch banged against the side of the house.

The Patriots received the opening kickoff and ran it back to the Jets' forty-yard line. Declan jumped to his feet and pumped his fist into the air. "Yeah."

Sending Miranda that text had broken something loose inside him. He'd waited as long as he could. He'd spoken from his heart. Now it was up to her.

"Touchdown." Declan whooped and toasted his team with the empty beer bottle. The kick was good and it was time for another slew of advertising.

He jogged into the kitchen and peered into the fridge. Well, shit. He was out of beer. There were still two hotdogs and half a roasted chicken from the supermarket that still smelled okay.

Hotdogs sounded good. He'd nuke those. The bag of chips was still over on the table. Had he left the buns there too?

The doorbell chimed, chimed again and again. Rapid fire. Someone pounded on the door. "What the hell?" Declan crept to the closest window and peered outside.

Miranda's car.

Heart pounding, he slid back the deadbolt and yanked the door open.

"Declan."

He glimpsed a flash of her hooded, heart-shaped face and her enormous green eyes before she tackled him. Her weight and the momentum of her body knocked him off balance. He staggered backward and barely managed to stay on his feet. While snowflakes swirled around them, Declan cradled her, icy coat and all, on the threshold of his wide open door.

CHAPTER 21

*T*he dazzling sun sparkled on last night's fresh snowfall. Miranda squinted out the windshield of her car even though she wore shades.

Declan had called again the night before. It was snowing. Would she like to come over and keep him company like the last three times?

Miranda's breathless response had assured him that she was more than willing, but she'd already promised to meet Deirdre and Sal for dinner at the Lodge.

"We're celebrating Mom's move back to Denver. I would've invited you, but I thought you'd be down at your mom and dad's."

He'd blasted an exaggerated sigh in her ear. "I thought I told you. They flew south for a couple of weeks. Some tropical island where there's no snow and Dad can walk around in his khaki shorts and black socks."

"I'm sorry."

"It's okay, my love." He gave a low, suggestive chuckle. "I like it when you're sorry, because you always make amends, such sweet, sexy amends."

She'd closed her eyes and pitched her voice low and sensuous. "Oh, and I will. I'll knock on your door, wearing my parka, but everything else I'll be wearing will be a surprise. After you give me one of your hot, delicious kisses, I'll let you unzip the parka and slowly slip it off my shoulders."

"Stop. Stop immediately." His tone had sounded desperate and aroused. "Okay. Okay. Plan B. Meet me down at the schoolhouse tomorrow morning."

"But tomorrow's Sunday."

"That's too f-ing bad. I have something. I have a rare historical object that I was going to show you tonight and I can't wait past tomorrow, dammit."

❦

Spencer's empty streets glittered like a carpet of diamonds and the only audible sound was the crunching of her tires. Miranda sighed and frowned.

"This better be good Declan," she said out loud, her breath a frosty cloud in her car. At this speed the heat wouldn't kick in until she'd reached her destination.

She'd have to enlighten the man. Obviously, he didn't realize that Sundays were sacred, her designated morning to sleep in, stay in her pj's all day and finally have time to pore over all her magazines.

Cruising past the building housing the *Spencer Herald*, reminded her of Grandpa's phone call last week. He'd embarked on another new project.

He'd bought the paper, building and all from Hartwood and he needed a good solid managing editor to turn it around. She was just the woman to do it. Spencer's Katherine Graham.

Miranda had requested forty-eight hours to think about

it and had accepted. She'd consulted Declan, who'd first congratulated her, thought she'd be fabulous, and was glad that the paper would be saved from being a sensational rag.

He reminded her that her grandfather wouldn't have asked her if he hadn't thought she was capable. Then he reminded her that regardless of her grandfather's enthusiasm, it was her life, her decision to make, nobody else's.

The stretch of Olde Town was just as deserted, except for Declan's black truck parked at an angle in front of the schoolhouse.

Miranda's heart swelled with pride and all traces of grumpiness vanished. The derelict building stood on its new foundation, still an ugly duckling, but scheduled to be transformed into a swan by next summer.

She closed her eyes and envisioned Declan's 3-D model, the fresh coat of white paint, the gleaming bell hanging in the tower, and a row of new windows on both sides.

Had it been less than a year since she'd moved back to Spencer and jumped into her new life with both feet? In that time she'd put so much pain and sorrow behind her.

Occasionally, her inner skeptic still tormented her. Life was going so well, she sometimes worried about the other shoe falling.

She still missed little Jeremy, and her heart still ached for Nikki, but she'd moved forward and healed in many other areas of her life.

Mom for example. Miranda smiled. She'd never have thought the day would come when she'd refer to Deirdre as Mom, but forgiveness and understanding had gone a long way to forging their new relationship.

Thanksgiving dinner had worked miracles. Both Heath and Hunter had attended. They'd remained cynical, but Mom's heartfelt apology, and her longest stretch of sobriety yet, had softened them up.

Miranda's gaze drifted to the schoolhouse's temporary construction door, and her heart quickened. Declan's enthusiasm for this project was contagious.

He lifted her sagging spirits and reassured her that whatever crisis they faced was just a temporary setback and there was a perfect solution just around the corner.

He encouraged not only her, but the historical society as well, communicating with them in addition to being on site, constantly monitoring the contractors.

Funny, at first she'd been the one to come to Declan's rescue, but in the end he'd been the one to take her by the hand and teach her that she was loveable and there was strength in forgiveness. He'd saved her in more ways than he knew.

She anticipated wrapping her arms around his strong, solid body, the minty gust of his breath on her face and the warm pliable contact of his mouth against hers.

He'd shoveled the walk and swept the steps clean.

The door opened before she could even reach out to grasp the paint-caked knob.

"I thought you'd fallen asleep out there." Declan unceremoniously grabbed her by the arm and hauled her inside.

He tipped her face up to his and kissed her, his mouth every bit as delicious as she'd just imagined.

Miranda tightened her arms around his neck and parted her lips. "Ummm. You taste good. You smell good. Which is a good thing, because I could be home in my jammies and robe with a mug of coffee and my *Runner's World*."

Declan laughed and grazed his thumb along her jaw, sending a shiver of pleasure surging through her.

"These will only get in the way." He slipped the mittens off her hands, and one by one, they sailed across the room.

"Declan." Miranda gave an astonished laugh.

"I've never liked this thing." His expression intent, he

unsnapped her fleece hood, sending it the way of her mittens.

"It's warm," she feebly protested, her face heating nicely on its own.

With long fingers, he deftly unbuttoned her jacket. Sliding it off her shoulders, he whirled it over his head. With a playful smile, he dropped it in a heap next to his own. "Don't want to knock anything over. What's this? More fleece." He tugged on the hem of her shirt, lifted it and peered underneath. "More clothing." He grinned up at her. "You're like peeling an onion."

Robbed of her breath and rooted to the floor, Miranda's pulse roared in her ears. The space heater glowed orange. "I dressed for the weather. So, where is this rare and historical object you're dying to show me."

High color flushed Declan's shadowed cheeks and his grin faded into a contrite smile. "I'm just teasing you. I don't have Runner's World, but I do have coffee.

"But first," he said, releasing her and snagging a colorful, printed scarf lying on a makeshift counter supported by three sawhorses. "I need to blindfold you."

His engaging smile, his equally engaging dimples, the dancing light in his blue eyes—eyes she could drown in, hypnotized her. "It's a good thing you're not a sociopath. Did anybody ever tell you you'd be dangerous?"

His dimples deepened. "Just you. Now please turn around."

He gently knotted a silk scarf over her eyes, his hot breath gusting against the back of her head. She leaned into him, her heart hammering.

"Okay," he coaxed, his low voice soft as velvet. "Please hold your hands straight out in front of you with your fingers flexed."

"What?" Miranda laughed nervously, biting her lower lip. "Why?"

"No questions allowed." He swept the mass of her hair off her neck and dropped a fleeting kiss against her nape.

Miranda shivered and tightly curled her fingers. The idea of the blindfold was growing on her.

"Can you see anything? You can't see anything, right?"

"No," she whispered, raising her hands to her temples.

"Give me your hands, sweetheart, please. Fingers spread."

Above the beating of her heart, she heard a muted snap. Her throat constricted and tears stung behind her closed eyelids. She attempted to smile. "Where's the piñata?"

Declan silenced her with a tender kiss.

She could kiss him forever. Deprived of her sight, Miranda's remaining senses were heightened. Beneath her layers of clothing, her skin tingled pleasantly and she ached to have him peel them off, layer by layer, until there were no barriers between her flesh and his.

Declan groaned and tore his mouth from hers. "Dammit!" His fingers tightened on her shoulders and he took a few calming breaths. "I should have brought duct tape for that sweet mouth of yours." He gave a breathless chuckle.

"Okay. No more talking, Miranda, my darling and no more kisses." His lips brushed her ear. "Please, this won't take long. Just be quiet for once and listen." He wrapped one arm around her and anchored her closer. "Now, don't move," he whispered.

Eyes still closed beneath the blindfold, she nodded. If her heart beat any faster, she would faint.

If he was going to do what she thought he was going to do. She stood still, engulfed in his woodsy scent, immersed in an intriguing pool of pleasurable anticipation.

Outside, an icicle cracked off the eave and plopped into the snow punctuating the silence.

He grasped her hand. With a surprising, swift move he slipped something onto the ring finger of her left hand.

Her throat constricted.

"Marry me, Miranda Buffet. I'll share my life with you and love you with my body, my soul, my heart, my words and my actions as long as I live."

Oh my God. He was proposing. Not so soon.

"The blindfold," she whispered in an emotion-choked voice.

He muttered a soft curse and gently tugged the silk scarf down to rest loosely looped around her neck.

Miranda blinked at the florescent lighting. Amid the dark spots floating in her field of vision, Declan stood rigid, his lips pressed together, his hands clasped behind his head. A muscle beneath his jaw twitched.

Instinctively, she understood. Just as she'd realized her home was here in Spencer among her family and friends, her future was inextricably bound to this courageous loving man. Declan steadied her, strengthened her, sealed the cracked-and-chipped parts of her.

Her gaze drifted to her hand and the delicate gold band. She lifted her curled fingers higher and examined the multi-colored precious stones in the light. "It's beautiful. It looks old-fashioned. This must be the rare historical object."

Gazing from her to the ring, Declan nodded with a weak smile that faltered. "Aunt Cora insisted I take it. It's a long story."

❦

Declan couldn't stand the suspense.

Miranda lifted her hand and stared at the ring, then transferred her expression of delighted surprise to him. Her eyes darkened, her lips parted and pink colored her cheeks.

He swallowed, remembering the time he'd asked his dad how he'd know when he'd found the right girl to marry.

Dad had nodded sagely. "You'll know son, because she'll be so beautiful in your eyes it will take your breath away and you won't be able to live without her."

Now, here he was and Dad had been right.

"Declan?"

He blinked and drew a shallow breath. "What? You are going to say yes, aren't you? If you don't, Cora told me to slap you silly for the fool you'd be—and those were her exact words. I wouldn't do it, of course."

Tilting her head, Miranda folded her arms. "Yes. I'll marry you—on one condition."

Declan frowned. "Don't tease me, woman. Not today."

Reaching up, she cupped his jaw, her expression tender. Tears sparkled in her mossy-green eyes. "Call me Mandy."

His throat tightened.

"Mandy," he whispered, tracing her pale brow with his index finger, nuzzling her silky, copper tresses, inhaling her enthralling, flowery scent. He rained slow, gentle kisses on her temple, her cheek, the tip of her freckled nose.

Clasping her chin, he tilted her face to his. "I love you, Mandy. I promise you won't be sorry."

Gracing him with her dazzling smile, she swept her thumbs beneath his eyes. "I love you, too."

Declan claimed Mandy's soft, full lips and cradled her against his chest. Come what may, he'd cherish her, protect her and love her all the days of his life.

Once upon a time a group of writer friends—helping a member with a particularly difficult thread in a continuity series contrived by her editors—got the grandiose idea to create a continuity series of their own.

Yes, this was us, and we threw ourselves wholeheartedly into developing characters, fashioning families, family dynamics, and a setting, which evolved from one member's love of all things Colorado. We created family trees, character profiles, detailed maps, brainstormed titles and themes. We collected photos and researched and even started the stories. We proposed our idea to a few publishers and got no traction. So, after a time the contracted books came first, two members dropped out of the group, a couple new ones came and went. But the core group remained.

In a tragic turn of events we lost a beloved friend and co-writer. Grief took the remaining wind from our sails. We recovered slowly, welcomed a new friend to our critique group. Then came a day when we got together and said, "We're going to get serious and do this!" Energy built, and the series took on new life. A previous co-creator joined us again. Now, here we are, years after the initial idea, sharing the finished stories with you and hoping you will feel the same intensity and appreciation for this project as we do. We have many more stories to share, and the ideas keep coming. Look for more books to follow in Aspen Gold: The Series.

So, come along. We welcome you to Spencer, Colorado, to have a look inside the families, to laugh in their good times and cry in their sad times, to follow them as they solve mysteries, expose secrets, recover from their pasts, reach for their goals, and most importantly—as they fall in love.

❧

The Aspen Gold Books
   Dancing In The Dark Cheryl St.John
   He had everything a man could want--except her forgiveness...
   <u>**Call Me Mandy Debra Hines**</u>
   The last man Miranda loved took everything from her...
   Ryder's Heart *lizzie starr
   Ryder discovers an intriguing woman in his bed...
   For Keeps Barbara Gwen & *lizzie starr
   Hiding the truth is like denying the sun...
   Second Chances Donna Kaye
   She tried the fairy tale and the fairy tale didn't work...
   Sleepin' Alone Bernadette Jones
   Hunter Lawe...riding the line between enforcing the law and breaking it...

Also *Coming soon* a new tale from M.A. Jewell

❧

To learn more about the Aspen Gold Series, the books and authors, visit our website and sign up for the <u>Rocky Mountain Rumors newsletter!</u>

We love to hear from our readers. Contact the Aspen Gold authors at mailto:rumors@aspengoldseries.com

ABOUT THE AUTHOR

Colorado native, Debra Hines and her husband have lived everywhere from California to Oregon and now call Iowa/Nebraska home. She's a world traveler, with stickers from England, Ireland, Scotland, Italy and Sicily on her passport and tickets to New Zealand/Australia in her carry-on. Somehow on her whirlwind planes, ships and automobiles tour, she still manages to spend most Friday evenings with her critique group and is invested in writing tales about the fictional residents of Spencer, Colorado. Debra is a long-time member of Romance Writers of America and its local chapter Romance Authors of the Heartland, of which she has been vice-president, program director and is currently treasurer. She's a devoted mom to three, grandmother to four, and will follow Hugh Jackman anywhere.

Find Deb on Facebook: https://www.facebook.com/debahines19/
    Email Deb at debraia94@gmail.com